I0734828

TAMING HER TIGER

TIGER SHIFTERS 9

KAT SIMONS

TAMING HER TIGER

Copyright © 2017 by Katrina Tipton
All rights reserved.

Published 2017 by T&D Publishing
Cover art design © 2017 and 2019 The Killion Group
Interior book design © 2019 T&D Publishing
ISBN-13: 978-1-944600-20-4 (Trade Paperback Edition)

This book is licensed for your personal enjoyment only. All rights reserved.
No part of this book may be reproduced, scanned, or distributed in any
print or electronic form without written permission from the author,
excepting brief quotes used in the context of a review.

This is a work of fiction. All of the characters, places, organizations, and
events portrayed are either products of the author's imagination or are used
fictitiously. Any resemblance to actual persons, living or dead, business
establishments, events, or locales is entirely coincidental.

First printing: May 2019
For information, contact T&D Publishing www.TandDPublishing.com

Amy Donovan hurried up the wooden stairs to the fifth floor of the Brooklyn art studio, out of breath and trying not to panic about being late. Damned weekend subways. She cleared the huge, rolling steel doors and stepped into the brightly lit, high-ceilinged loft, winter sun pouring in from the wall of windows opposite her. The gray sunlight was augmented by the overhead lights, reflecting off the scuffed pale wood floors and bright white walls.

She sighed in relief when she saw the open session hadn't started yet.

The familiar smells of the art studio—paint, solvent, charcoal, paper, and canvas—filled Amy with that sense of belonging, settling into her bones. The familiarity helped slow her racing, panicky heartbeat as she made her way across the room to a free space. Easels, chairs, and tables were already arranged in a rough semi-circle around a central model platform, the piles of pillows in the middle of the platform were draped in neutral, tan sheets. A dozen artists, the monitor, and the model coordinator all hovered around the room. A few people stood in small groups, chatting and drinking take-away cups of coffee and tea. Others were already at chairs or easels, setting out their materials or flicking through their sketch books.

She waved at acquaintances and other studio members as she wove past a section of seats to her easel. This was the final long-pose session of a four-week cycle, her last opportunity to have the figure model in front of her while she finished her oil painting.

Thoughts of said model scattered her focus and she nearly tripped over someone's bag. Apologizing, she hurried to her spot, pushing the momentary lapse aside. She was a professional; this was a professional setting. She refused to entertain the strong feelings and longings she'd experienced when Ethan Gupta had first taken the dais three weeks ago.

It hadn't exactly been a sexual reaction, though that was part of it. She'd done so many life drawing sessions over the years, she didn't really view the nude models that way —she saw lines, shadows, proportion, perspective, angles, and light contrasts. Or at least she had before Ethan.

But her reaction to him had been a lot more than just the sexual punch of seeing a man as beautifully masculine and perfect as Ethan was in real life. It was more stunned shock, a realization that she was staring at an actual muse. Her brain had exploded with images, colors, a longing to capture…something. *Him.*

She didn't believe in muses, exactly. Not in the mythical sense of the word. She knew a good figure model could inspire and energize her and her art. She'd had the experience on numerous occasions. But with Ethan, everything was different. More instant, more overwhelming, more…vivid.

That first time, she'd even sensed him before he'd come into the room, as if he projected an aura of creative inspiration she could feel along the length of her spine without having to look at him. The fact that she could sense him now, even though she couldn't see him, even though she knew the feeling was just a figment of her imagination, left her edgy and anxious.

After that first three-hour session, she found herself counting the days until the next one, and the one after that. Yet a part of her also dreaded each session, dreaded that sense of being overwhelmed and awed. The sense that her skills would never be good enough to capture the purity of the inspiration he offered.

Settling into the area she'd used for the last three sessions, she focused on putting out her supplies, collecting her canvas from one of the storage lockers provided to regular members, organizing her brushes, setting up her palette, studying her progress on her painting, determining where she needed to make adjustments and what she'd need to do to get the work done today…

One of her dearest friends, Reese Jordan, sat down next to her in a place already set up and ready for the session to start. Reese was a superbly talented sketch artist, oil painter, and sometimes sculptor. He was also the person who'd originally directed Amy to this studio and encouraged her to become a member. They'd known each other since Amy had come back to the art world two years earlier, and now she couldn't imagine her life without him. At forty-three, Reese tended to treat her like a little sister, and he'd become the big brother as well as the art mentor Amy had never had.

He kissed her cheek. "I thought you were going to miss the class."

"Subways," she growled, making him grin.

On her other side, Devine, artist, gallery manager, and another of Amy's good friends, settled into her station, rubbing Amy's arm by way of hello. Despite being in her mid-thirties, Devine was ageless, with flawless, smooth skin, hair that changed colors and cut frequently—that week it was a beautiful pale lavender shaped to imitate a 1950s flip—and blue eyes she accented with perfectly penciled black liner drawn to make her eyes look tilted and cat-like. She'd confided to Amy once that her ever-changing look was designed to appeal to her clients because they expected artists to be eccentric and "artsy." Devine ran a gallery in Soho that catered to art collectors of the rich-but-not-very-knowledgeable type. She could sell sand in the desert and ice in the arctic.

And for reasons Amy had never figured out, Devine kept encouraging Amy to take her art more seriously, turn it into an actual career. Despite Amy's insistence that it wouldn't happen anytime soon. Her refusal to accept the possibility of art as a career had never deterred Devine from nagging her about it.

Before Amy could say more than hello, the shuffling,

shifting sounds of people settling into their seats distracted her. She looked past Devine…in time to see Ethan step out of the bathroom at the rear of the studio, near the storage lockers and slop sinks. He'd changed out of his street clothes and into his simple dark blue robe, a color that did fantastic things to his wavy dark hair and eyes. He paused at the back of the room to chat with the coordinator and monitor, smiling and relaxed.

Amy caught herself staring, her gaze drawn to the perfect shape of his mouth, the solid line of his jaw, the way his hair curled around his ear. She blinked a few times, trying in vain to look away. She felt like such a fool, such a cliché, becoming obsessed with a model. But once he came into the room, she had trouble concentrating on anything else. To her embarrassment, he glanced up and caught her staring. His soft smile and nod of greeting only humiliated her more. She nodded back and turned to face her canvas, heat crawling along her skin and making her scalp prickle. He wasn't on the dais yet. He wasn't hers to study. He was a skilled human being who deserved her respect and admiration—not her obsessive ogling.

"He's magnetic, isn't he?" Reese leaned closer and said. "I can't stop watching him either."

His voice was quiet, but Amy still looked around to see who might overhear them.

"He's just so damned good at holding these long poses and still being…present, isn't he?" Devine said. "It's like watching performance art every time he hits the platform."

"I keep forgetting I'm supposed to draw and not just

stare," Reese said, chuckling. "If I don't sell this piece, the world has no taste whatsoever."

Amy smiled at that. Reese's oil paintings and charcoal sketches were displayed in galleries across Manhattan and Brooklyn. He was one of the most gifted artists she'd ever encountered, and his work sold regularly even in the competitive New York market.

"The world doesn't have taste, darling," Devine said. "That's why I have a job."

Reese snorted. "And we're all very grateful for the job you do."

Devine nodded at Amy's unfinished painting. "That'll be worthy of sale, too, when you're done."

Amy stared at the canvas, at the way Ethan occupied the scene she'd built around him, the long, muscled lines of his body draped across the pillows like an ancient god. "Maybe," she said noncommittally. More than her resistance to considering art as a profession, the thought of parting with this particular painting actually caused something tight and painful to collect in her chest.

The final shuffling and noise of preparation settled and silence descended around the room as Ethan stepped up to the platform and dropped his robe.

E than settled onto the pillows, using the tape set down by the moderator after the last session to resume the exact position he'd held for the last month. The pose was comfortable, his upper body resting against the piled pillows, one knee bent and one arm resting on that knee.

He could recline like this for the thirty-minute period without it hurting too much and without drifting off to sleep.

He concentrated on his own body, putting himself in exactly the same angles as the weeks before. Keeping his mind off the beautiful artist just to his right.

Amy Donovan.

She caused him more difficulty than he'd ever had during a life drawing class. Usually, he let his mind drift into a zone that embodied the pose, managing to remain present without focusing on any of the artists around him. But an *awareness* of Amy kept him on edge the entire time. He'd been hyper attuned to her for the last four weeks, and it was all he could do to keep his body from showing just how much he wanted her.

After seeing her, catching her scent at the first session, he'd very nearly backed out of this job. It wouldn't have done his reputation in the art world any good, but for the sake of self-preservation, he'd almost made the sacrifice. Only a keen sense of wanting to finish what he'd started kept him coming back. That and sheer, stubborn pride.

By the end of the first session, he'd managed to convince himself that his reaction was just because Amy bore a resemblance to a woman Ethan didn't want to remember. The thick dark hair, the blue eyes, the pale skin were superficially the same as Siya's. Amy's hair was curly where Siya's had been straight. Amy was a little taller and curvier than Siya. But the similarities in appearance were hard to ignore. And they made a great excuse for dismissing his reaction to Amy. Nothing he had to worry about. He'd be over that superficial attraction by the time he saw her again.

Unfortunately, when he'd shown up for the second session, he'd had to admit he wasn't just struck by Amy's beauty. She *drew* him the way a magnet pulled metal. He found himself overly focused on her, aware of where she was even when he couldn't see her, conscious of the subtle shifts in her scent—honeysuckle and art studio and woman. A combination that set his blood on fire.

He'd had a very similar reaction to Siya. And that was the real danger.

He hadn't had that kind of reaction to any other woman before or since—until Amy. It felt a little like obsession, impossible to control, overwhelming and consuming. Like being around Amy was as necessary as his next breath. He hated that feeling more than just about anything he'd ever experienced before. The same kind of preoccupation with Siya had almost gotten him killed. He could *not* do that again. He'd come to New York to escape the memory of Siya and what she'd done to him. He'd refused to have anything to do with the tiger shifter world, outside of his immediate family, after that.

Amy was human, which should have made her safe. But she called to his tiger so strongly it reminded him of being around a tigress. Which meant he should avoid Amy Donovan at all costs.

And yet, he couldn't bring himself to cancel the remaining two sessions. He was a professional, it was just once a week for a few hours, and for the most part, Amy seemed intent on avoiding him. He assured himself all of that would make it easier, and he wouldn't have to sacrifice his reputation just to avoid a human woman who didn't seem particularly interested in interacting with him anyway.

Unfortunately, his keen sense of smell picked up her attraction, the spice of desire in her scent, the way it enhanced the womanly musk that was part of her essence. He wanted to disregard that flavor, to pretend he didn't know she wanted him, too. She never showed any signs of acting on the chemistry and lust. He didn't have to act on those feelings either.

But his tiger saw her resistance to her own desire as a challenge—a challenge that was impossible to ignore. So hard he'd found himself walking past her during each break at the third session, making excuses to exchange small talk with her, to pass a comment on the progress of her painting. Despite his efforts to resist, he still pulled in her scent, holding his breath to keep the flavors on his tongue as long as possible, savoring the complexity. And more often than he cared to admit, his mind wandered to more erotic thoughts, musings that had been invading his dreams during the intervening week. What her skin might taste like, feel like, what she'd look like stripped out of the loose jeans and t-shirt she always wore to the studio, what she'd look like in the throes of orgasm…

Those thoughts during a nude session were *not* good. The entire room would notice his erection, which wasn't exactly the look he was going for with this pose. It happened to male models sometimes, and artists generally ignored it. But as a tiger shifter, Ethan rarely noticed being nude and never had trouble controlling his body while he was. He'd spent his life taking his clothes off in front of other shifters so he could let his tiger out. Unlike most humans, Ethan was as comfortable without clothes as he was with them.

Except with Amy Donovan in the room.

Even now, during what was thankfully the last session of the four-week cycle, it took a concerted effort on his part not to let his awareness of Amy show. The room was mostly silent except for the sounds of brushes lapping over canvas and pencils scraping across paper, or the occasional groan of a seat as someone adjusted their position. His pose kept his focus on a point in the room where the steel frame around one window butted up against the white wall, so he only caught glimpses of Amy from the corner of his eye. If he didn't focus on it, her scent blended in with all the other smells in the large, open space, just one more part of the complex essence of an art studio.

But even without trying, he still ended up parsing her scent out from the more complicated background. And her lust was there, tamped down by her concentration but still there, heady and rich...and tempting.

If it wasn't so quiet in the room, he might have groaned out loud.

This was the last session, he reminded himself. After this, he wouldn't see her again, and he'd go back to living his life without this preoccupation. He couldn't afford to lose his heart and soul to a woman again. In fact, he wasn't sure how much he had left to lose after the damage Siya had done. Amy called to that part of him, and he just couldn't give in to the desire and risk any more pain. So lust or no lust, Amy Donovan was off limits.

At the first break, he donned his robe and made a circuit of the room, stretching and loosening muscles that had gotten stiff over the last half hour. Some of the artists stopped him to make small talk. One or two gave him their cards, offering the possibility of future work. He managed to keep his distance from Amy, but only barely. His tiger kept urging him to walk past her, test her reaction to him, see if he could make her desire overcome her focus on her painting…

His focus on keeping Amy at a distance while still being utterly aware of her was his excuse for missing the feel of another tiger shifter nearby.

He frowned and glanced at the huge windows. What the hell was another tiger doing in this area?

Settling back onto the dais, Ethan opened his senses to that other shifter, trying to get a sense of who it was.

There were two other males in the city. When Ethan had moved here, they'd met to set up territorial boundaries which would allow them to remain neighbors without conflict. Of necessity, they did occasionally have to move through each other's territories, but those incursions were overlooked if they didn't last long or happen too frequently. Ethan specifically chose modelling jobs that avoided the other males' territories—usually in places that were neutral. His freelance work as a tax accountant rarely brought him into contact with the others either.

He'd never sensed one of the other New York males nearby during his previous sessions here, but he supposed it wasn't out of the question for one to have come into Brooklyn for personal reasons. This was neutral ground, so there was no reason for one of the other males to avoid the area. And being New York, tiger shifters from other places did make their way into and through the city on business, travel, or just as tourists. But this area of Brooklyn wasn't on the typical tourist routes, and it was a Sunday afternoon, so there shouldn't be a lot of reason for a tiger to be here for business.

Despite his senses being fully open, the other shifter remained just at the edges of his awareness, too far to give Ethan much information. He couldn't even be sure if the tiger was male or female. He kept his attention on the shifter throughout the next half-hour period, and the tiger remained in the same place the entire time—maybe eating at a local restaurant?

When the break was called, Ethan blinked in surprise. He hadn't even noticed his wrist on his bent knee falling asleep. He rose, slipped into his robe, and wandered close to the big windows in his circuit to stretch his muscles. Glancing outside in hopes of catching sight of the other tiger didn't help. Whoever it was, they weren't in plain sight from the studio.

With his mind on the mysterious shifter, Ethan didn't realize he'd wandered close to Amy until her scent hit him hard. He fought off a scowl when he noticed he'd stopped just behind her. She didn't glance back at him, but she did sit a little straighter on her chair.

Cursing his unconscious pull to her, he made an effort

to look at her painting so he could pass a comment as an excuse for why he was just standing there.

For a long moment, he stared at the painting, unable to actually form a coherent word. When he could speak, he said, very quietly, "That's magnificent. You're amazing."

Pleasure and surprise filled her honeysuckle scent with citrus and a touch of vanilla. He edged closer, unable to resist her, wishing there weren't so many people in the room watching this exchange.

Wishing he could back away before he lost his mind completely.

"Thank you," she murmured. She glanced over her shoulder, smiling shyly at him, her blue eyes sparking with pleasure through the fringe of her long lashes.

The sexy look combined with the husky sound of her voice hit him hard, right in the gut and lower. His blood pounded, his breathing sped. In that moment, he was extremely glad to have his robe on because his body reacted instantly. He took a half step closer to her when she faced her painting again, raising a hand to test the texture of her hair before he realized what he was doing. He snatched his hand back and with a grunt, he spun away from her and stalked to the farthest end of the studio.

Damn but she was dangerous. Without even trying. Even the puzzle of a strange tiger in the area couldn't fully distract him.

If he wasn't careful, he was going to give in to this lust, and to hell with the consequences.

He sighed when his tiger growled in his head—in approval.

CHAPTER TWO

Amy returned to concentrating on her painting after Ethan walked away, but it took a great deal of effort. She was so overwhelmed by the muse that was their model, even the brief exchanges they shared were enough to leave her tongue tied and churning with lust she was embarrassed to feel. And that voice of his… It seemed entirely unfair that the physical muse also had such a deep, resonant voice to accompany his stunning male perfection.

When the session finished and Ethan donned his robe for the last time, Amy leaned back and looked at the completed composition. She blinked a few times and breathed out a stunned sigh.

She was typically very critical of her own work, never fully satisfied, always striving to get better and better with each piece. But this time, with this painting…it was as if someone else had created it. She was looking at something that should be hanging in a museum.

Reese stepped up behind her, and she braced for his always helpful critique. Nothing came. She glanced back at him. He looked as awed as she felt.

"Baby," he murmured, "you've made art."

She snorted. "I don't really know how this happened."

He smiled crookedly. "Looks like you found your muse."

"Stop," she warned under her breath.

"Can't argue with a masterpiece," he said, giving her shoulders a gentle squeeze. "Coffee this week?"

"Text me. I don't have my work schedule settled past tomorrow yet." She did temp work because it was flexible enough to fit around her college classes, but she had fallen into regular work as an assistant to a business lawyer. The lawyer worked around her schedule and other commitments, but her hours dependent on the tasks that needed to get done and so her schedule wasn't fixed from week to week.

"Fair enough." Reese kissed her on the top of the head, looked at the canvas again with an appreciative sigh, and moved off to chat with a few of the other artists.

Amy stared at her painting for a bit longer, lost in it for long enough that she forgot the time. From the corner of her eyes, she sensed the room getting emptier. She blinked out of her trance, remembering she needed to pack up. They had to clear the space in a timely fashion since the studio loft closed early on Sunday. The private booths for members on the two floors beneath stayed open for another few hours, but everyone still had to clear out of the loft after the open session ended.

She hurried to clean and re-pack her supplies into her large, wooden case. Because this was the last session for this particular piece, she wanted to bring the canvas home to finish drying, which meant lugging her large plein air painting case from Queens to Brooklyn. The case wasn't all that heavy, given its size, but it was awkward on the subway, so she only brought it to the studio when she needed the sliding storage area that kept wet canvases protected. By the time she finished, she was the last artist in the room. The monitor was waiting by the steel doors for her, not nagging Amy to hurry but still checking her watch.

Ethan had left already, along with everyone else. That was something of a relief. Amy ignored the nagging inner voice that wondered if she should have at least said goodbye to him. After all, thanks to him, she'd just created the most stunning thing she'd ever painted. But she was always afraid if she talked to him too much, she'd reveal her nerves—and her inappropriate lust.

She walked out of the building with the monitor, then pulled her coat tighter around her shoulders and headed out into the late February New York evening, the air chilly from the dampness of a recent rain.

She made a beeline for the R train station. It was going to take the better part of an hour and a half to get from Brooklyn back up to her apartment in Queens on the R on a Sunday evening, but it was too cold and her supply box too awkward to consider the long walk to another more direct train. At least she'd be able to sit and read on the ride home. She still had to cover two and a half city blocks to reach the train, though.

Hauling up her case, she hurried across a busy intersection and down a quieter side road, taking the route she used all the time. She'd never once, in the almost two years she'd been going to the studio, felt unsafe in this area, even late at night. She was a city girl, so she was careful and watched her surroundings, but she'd always felt comfortable here.

The fact that her nerves were jumping for some reason tonight was more than a little irritating. Was it because she'd finally finished the sessions with Ethan and wouldn't see him again? She'd barely given herself time to even contemplate that, and it was…bothersome in a way she wasn't prepared to delve into. In fact, she was actively trying to ignore her preoccupation with Ethan. But her edginess didn't seem tied to that.

She glanced over her shoulder. Typical traffic for a Sunday evening, with plenty of people around. No one seemed to be paying any particular attention to her. No one looked to be following her. Nothing out of the ordinary.

So why did she feel so…hunted?

Scowling, she adjusted the strap of her box over her shoulder and stomped on, affecting her don't-fuck-with-me New Yorker attitude—the one she infused into her every step whenever she felt a little nervous about the area she was walking through. She'd never had to do that here before, though, and it was annoying.

Turning a corner, the brighter lights of a commercial street greeted her, the subway entrance in sight at the opposite end of the block. Pedestrian and street traffic were heavy enough to give her a sense of security. She glanced over her shoulder again. Still nothing suspicious that she could detect.

She cursed under her breath, ignoring the frown she got from a passing woman, and berated herself for being silly. What had gotten into her? She was used to having a detailed and expansive imagination, but scaring herself unnecessarily was a new one. Her sister would laugh when she heard.

A chill shivered down Amy's spine, an awareness that made her steps falter. The man walking too close behind her nearly collided with her. They apologized at the same time, and Amy chuckled awkwardly as the man moved on. The strange awareness didn't. She stepped to the side of the walk, putting her back to the window of an indie bookstore, and scanned the area.

What the hell was bothering her so much?

The sense of being hunted was overwhelming, but she couldn't pinpoint anything obvious. The feeling crawling along her nerves reminded her a little of that awareness she had of Ethan, but a lot less pleasant and welcome. She *liked* the way Ethan felt when she knew he was around. This was…dark. Scary.

She hated being scared. It pissed her off. And brought up bad memories.

Worse yet, she could swear she *also* felt Ethan somewhere. Now that was just weird. He'd left the studio well before her. He was long gone from the neighborhood.

Mad at herself and her instincts—which she could usually trust—she decided she needed the cover of more people and a moment to calm down. Her pulse was actually pounding with adrenaline and her knees trembled with fear, even though she had no obvious reason to be afraid. She edged closer to the entrance of the coffee shop next to the bookstore, feeling silly for acting so paranoid, and then turned into the door as someone else opened it to leave.

The scents of coffee and pastry washed over her in a relaxing wave of deliciousness. The sense of being hunted eased enough to give her some breathing room. Her nerves continued to dance, but the edge of panic dimmed. She hefted her case and made her way to the counter, scanning the back of the café for an available seat. She had to get home and walk Spike, but she could afford to wait out the panic for a few minutes. Maybe if she sat here, sipping coffee, surrounded by disinterested New Yorkers, she'd come to her senses and stop feeling so jumpy.

She was in line, waiting to be served, when another wave of awareness moved down her spine—the pleasant version of awareness. Frowning, she glanced around.

And spotted Ethan. Looking right at her.

Amy blinked, so surprised she forgot not to stare. Ethan was sitting alone at a two-person table near the front window, and when she met his gaze, his smile widened and he lifted his cup to her in greeting. She returned the gesture with a jerk of her head, then looked away fast, her cheeks heating.

The line moved forward. She went with it, trying to focus on her order—an ordinary coffee because she didn't want to waste money on something fancy tonight. She paid and made an effort to look casual as she scanned the crowded tables for a free seat. When she felt a tap on her shoulder, she didn't even have to turn to know who it was. Closing her eyes briefly, she forced a smile and turned to face him.

Ethan *felt* taller standing in front of her this way. At 5'8", she wasn't a tiny person by any means, and she'd known that Ethan was tall because he'd walked past her at the studio. But she couldn't remember standing face to face with him before, not this close. His masculinity was as powerful outside of the studio as it was in. And for some strange reason, he was even more stunningly handsome fully dressed—his casual jeans and t-shirt hugged his muscles too nicely. He even smelled good. Like soap and male with just a hint of the art studio.

"Amy, right?"

She nodded, too overwhelmed to speak.

"If you're staying," he said, "I have a free seat." He motioned back to the table by the window where his ski jacket hung on the back of his chair.

"I wouldn't want to intrude," she muttered. *Especially because I'm so ridiculously attracted to you I'm not sure I can speak without sounding like an idiot.*

He smiled a little wider, and she had a brief and horrifying moment of fear that she'd said that last part out loud.

"I'd love to have you join me," he said.

"Thanks." She forced herself to look pleased instead of panicked. Her stomach tightened and tumbled in crazy summersaults. She felt unbearably awkward now. And even more ridiculous for the fear that had driven her into the café to begin with.

He motioned her ahead of him, following her to his

table. She tucked her case close to the window and sat, cradling her coffee so he wouldn't see her hands shaking, hoping he assumed the flush heating her cheeks was because of the cold outside and not her embarrassment.

As he settled across from her, he tilted his head, studying her. God, how could she hide anything from those amazing eyes?

"Does it bother you, talking with one of the models outside of the studio? I know it can be…awkward for some of the artists. I can always leave…"

"No," she said too fast and too harshly. "Sorry. No, you don't have to leave. It's not that. I'm happy to talk with the life models I meet outside of the studio." Usually.

"Good." He sipped his coffee. "You normally go right home after the sessions." He nodded to the window. "I need a coffee after the long poses. I see you pass on your way to the subway."

She forced a laugh, which sounded high and breathy. She winced inwardly. "Yeah. I have to get home and walk my dog. But finishing a big project leaves me a little drained, so I thought I'd treat myself."

She did *not* want to admit she'd come into the coffee shop to escape…she wasn't even sure what. Her own imagination? Any sense of being stalked and hunted had vanished and now she just felt stupid.

"What kind of dog?" Ethan asked.

"Miniature poodle. Spike."

"Your poodle's name is Spike?"

She let out a more genuine chuckle this time. "The

name seemed to suit her. You don't want to mess with her when she's in a bad mood."

"I'll keep that in mind."

Thinking about her funny little dog helped ease some of her awkwardness, and she settled into the familiar pattern of small talk with a virtual stranger. "So what do you do, Ethan? Is modeling your main job?"

"No. I model for the love of it, not for the money. I'm a tax accountant."

She blinked. Twice. "You're an accountant."

"Yes. Why is that surprising?"

"Ah... I don't know. You don't look like an accountant."

She took in his loose, dark hair with its slight wave, his arresting dark eyes, his heavy eyebrows, his perfectly shaped mouth, the strong lines of his jaw. He looked like a supermodel. He looked like a hero out of some mythological story. He looked like a god. He did *not* look like he'd do something as...normal as accountancy.

"What do accountant's look like?" he asked.

She shrugged and gave in to it. "No idea."

Of course he was an accountant. Because this was the real world, and in the real world there was no such thing as mythical muses or gods. In the real world, people went out and made money doing ordinary things like figuring out other people's taxes, or selling useful stuff, or answering phones and typing up legal documents. Her mother had always been right about that.

"Do you make your living with your art?" he asked.

She shook her head, as much to answer to his question

as to clear out the sound of her mother's very practical voice reminding her that art was a hobby, not a career. "I'm finishing up a business degree. And I do temp work to make ends meet. Art's just a hobby."

"You're very talented. You could do more with it if you wanted to."

Oh, the temptation of that idea… She smiled wanly. "I don't have the time to put into pursuing an art career. I have a younger sister to take care of."

His eyes narrowed and she knew he'd ask more. But this wasn't a topic she wanted to discuss with someone she barely knew.

"So, what got you into modeling?" she asked to change the subject. "If it's not your main job."

He stared at her for a moment before saying, "I model because I love art and artists. And I couldn't draw a straight line if someone held a gun to my head."

She smiled at that. "Everyone who doesn't draw says that. It just takes a little practice."

"Maybe. I don't seem to have the motivation to work on the skills. I'm better at modeling."

"That's a pretty rare talent, though. Holding a pose for so long? Dropping your robe in front of a room full of strangers? A lot more people can draw a bowl of fruit than can do what you do."

She meant every word. Earnestly. The people willing to life model were such a vital part of an artist's growth and training. They were as valuable as the right brushes and paints, as indispensable as pencils and paper. It was almost impossible to study art without studying the human form in all its variations, but asking someone to get naked in front of a crowd was a big deal in most societies. That anyone did it always filled Amy with a great deal of gratitude.

Ethan seemed to realize how much she meant the compliment because he didn't brush it off. "Thank you. It's nice to know I can contribute to what you do."

"Oh, you do. Very much."

"I loved the painting you produced. I know I said this already but it really was…amazing."

She felt her cheeks heating again. And just when she was starting to feel less awkward… "Thanks. You were an inspiring subject." Did that sound weird?

"I have to admit, looking at your painting was one of the very few times I've looked at a picture of myself without seeing myself in it. And yet…it was me. That doesn't make sense. I'm not sure how to explain it. It was like looking at something hanging in a museum. I've never seen myself in a painting in a museum before, so it was kind of a…disconnect. Surreal?"

He frowned, the line between his brows way more adorable than it should have been.

"I'm not being very clear, am I?" he asked.

She grinned. "I understand. I think. It can be hard to put the ephemeral nature of art into words sometimes."

"And what you did was art."

She glanced down at her coffee cup. "Thank you."

"Are you doing a showing any time soon? I'd love to see more of your work."

"Oh. Oh, no." She tried to dial back the slight panic in

her voice. "I don't… I'm not ready for a show or anything. I'm just a hobbyist."

"You're a talented artist. I'm sure the studio's gallery would include you in a showing. Or your friend Devine…I bet she'd display your work in her gallery."

Since Devine had been trying to talk her into just that, Amy narrowed her eyes. It wouldn't be beyond Devine to bribe Ethan into pushing Amy in that direction. "I'm not ready," she said, a little more firmly. "I'm too busy at the moment to put a whole show together."

She could tell he had more questions, that he wanted to push further. And she didn't want to answer those questions. "Thanks for the seat." She rose. "I need to get home. Spike will leave me a *present* if I don't walk her soon."

Ethan stood with her. "It was good talking with you." He hesitated, his dark eyes narrowing. "Would it be…too forward to ask for your number?"

She froze. Every part of her just froze up…including her brain. Ethan was asking for her phone number? Ethan Gupta the god-muse who'd been occupying her every waking thought for a month. The man she was so overwhelmed by, she reverted to teenage awkwardness around him. Wanted her number.

That was not something that happened in the real world. At least not her real world.

She must have frozen up for a lot longer than she'd realized—even if it did feel like forever inside, she would have sworn only a moment passed—because he let out a breath and eased back a little.

"That was too forward, wasn't it? Sorry. But maybe I'll see you around?"

"No. I mean… No. Wait. I'm…" She closed her eyes, pulled in a steadying breath, ignored the heat crawling across her neck and cheeks, and forced a smile when she looked up at him again. "I'm not saying what I mean to say. I'm just surprised you'd want to see me. Outside of the studio, I mean."

"Why?"

Well, how the hell was she supposed to answer that? *Because you're a gorgeous god and I'm a struggling twenty-six-year-old just trying to make ends meet while getting my younger sister through college?*

"I…" She couldn't answer without sounding even more ridiculous than she already did. But she didn't want him to think she was offended either. "I don't really date much," she said. "It's not personal. I just don't have time."

"It's okay. I understand."

"No. I don't…" She gave in and admitted the truth. Because really this couldn't get any worse. "I think you're gorgeous and I'd love to see you outside the studio, but I really don't have more than a spare minute in my life and every single second I get outside of school, work, and my sister goes into my art. I really really am a boring homebody who doesn't date. Like, ever. And I wouldn't want to…to disappoint you. Because I'm as awkward and weird as I'm coming off right now, at least when I'm around gorgeous men, and I'm quite sure that you'd feel the need to run away after one date and you're such a nice man, I don't want to put you through that, so I thank you very much for the compliment of asking for my number but I'm going to save you a world of awkwardness and say no, but not because I wouldn't enjoy seeing you again." She sucked in a deep breath, so far past embarrassment now, she couldn't even feel it anymore. "So. Yeah. That's me."

He stared at her, his expression impossible to read, his perfect lips pressed together in a straight line she couldn't interpret.

After a too-long silence, he said, "You have a poodle named Spike. I could never regret spending time with a woman who named her poodle Spike."

She frowned, looked away from him, then back at him from the corner of her eye. "Is there something wrong with you? Cause most men would have run away from me by now."

"I'd be disappointed not to see you again," he said, his deep voice even deeper than usual.

The sound tingled along her skin like a caress. Her stomach tightened, dancing with nerves that had more to do with lust than embarrassment now. Heat suffused her, a hot flush that made her overly aware of her body, the texture of her clothing, the press of her breasts against her bra. The look in his eyes captivated her. Intense and waiting, almost like a predator's stare. But she wasn't afraid of him. In fact, holding his dark gaze left her knees wobbling and her pulse throbbing. He was standing so close now, his scent surrounded her, wrapping her in a deliciously sexy cocoon. The longer she remained transfixed by him, the more her breathing sped, the harder her heart beat.

She bit the inside of her cheek to break the spell, then opened her mouth to say something… Nothing came out.

She pulled a pencil stub out of her coat pocket—no wonder she was so warm; it had to be because she still had her coat on, right?—and snatched a napkin off the table. She scribbled down her cellphone number and handed it to him. With a fleeting glance, a powerful moment of eye contact that she broke quickly, she nodded goodbye, hefted up her case, and left the coffee shop before he could say anything else to disarm her.

She was waiting for her train on the subway platform before she remembered why she'd gone into the coffee shop in the first place.

Damn but her imagination had gotten her into serious trouble this time.

E than watched Amy go down the steps into the subway, waiting until he was sure she was safe, before leaving the café. He couldn't sense the other tiger shifter anymore, but that didn't relax his jumping nerves.

After the session, he'd left the studio, intent on finding the tiger, or at least the tiger's scent signature so he could assure himself nothing was wrong. He'd been edgy, his instincts warning of danger throughout his final pose. And not just the danger Amy posed to his peace of mind. Something about this other tiger so close to the studio bothered him. If he could at least identify the shifter, he'd be able to discover the source of his anxiety.

By the time Ethan hit the street, though, he couldn't

find any signs of the tiger. He took a circuitous route to the coffee shop, hunting for a telling scent, but any evidence that one of his people had been in the area was lost to the rain and the pervasive aroma of New York.

He'd headed into the café for his pick-me-up shot of caffeine, half convinced he'd been worried about nothing. The other shifter was probably just a tourist or here for a meal. They'd finished their business and left the area. Whoever it was had no doubt sensed Ethan and didn't want to risk a territorial discussion.

But as he'd sat with his dark roast coffee, pretending not to be waiting for Amy to pass on the way to the subway, he'd sensed the other tiger again. This time along the side road he knew Amy used to get from the studio to her train.

It had to be a coincidence. Just a fluke. A lot of people walked around on the same streets. No reason to think the tiger being near Amy was deliberate

Or so he'd thought before Amy had ducked into the café. And the other tiger had lingered at the corner just out of sight…waiting.

Ethan checked the street around him, then headed in the general direction he'd last felt the other tiger, letting his sense of smell absorb all the various flavors around him— the cold air, the undercurrent of cement and tarmac, the cacophony of foods from the different restaurants, pubs and cafes along the street, the chemical smell of the dry cleaners on the corner, the food cart with roasted nuts, the lingering scent of tiger shifter…

He reached the intersection where Amy moved from the

side street onto the main road, the corner where the shifter had paused to watch her. Ethan hovered near the brick building just as the other shifter had, pulling in a deep breath. A male, but he didn't recognize the scent. So not someone he'd met before. And not a relative of someone he knew.

He glanced back toward the coffee shop. From this angle, he could see people coming and going from the café without being seen himself. And he had a clear view of the subway entrance.

He'd been telling Amy the truth about needing coffee after long poses. He hadn't admitted he went to the window seat every time, just to make sure she got to the subway safely. The first week had been a fluke. He'd been minding his own business when he'd seen her walk past the café and go down the R train stairs. He couldn't use the same excuse for the second week. Or the third. Or today. His tiger just kept insisting he had to make sure she reached her train safely, and he'd given up arguing with his animal side by the third week. At least about where he sat at the café.

Today, he hadn't been the only one watching Amy get to her train.

He growled quietly, a subsonic sound most humans wouldn't have heard. It was entirely possible the male had just seen a pretty girl and followed her, hoping for an opening to meet her. But Ethan's instincts insisted it wasn't that simple. He scanned his surroundings again. The main street moved with heavy foot and vehicle traffic. A double length bus coasted through a yellow light to the bus stop across the road, partially blocking traffic. A few horns sounded. Then the cars simply drove around the obstruction. Streetlights and storefronts cast enough light that his excellent eyesight picked up every detail.

Not even a hint of the strange tiger anymore.

But whoever he was, he had definitely been following Amy. Not just coincidentally in the same area. Not an accident. The tiger—who could sense Ethan as easily as Ethan could sense him—had made an effort to remain hidden. If his intensions were harmless, why so blatantly avoid Ethan? And why the hell had he been following Amy?

Frowning, he glanced back down the side street where she'd come from. The tiger hadn't returned that way. The scent wasn't strong enough. He'd obviously moved deeper into the human traffic, a very good way to mask his direction. Despite Ethan's best efforts, he couldn't seem to pick up the man's trail—at least not without making it obvious. This might be New York, where people tended to ignore strange behavior, but putting his nose near the ground to track the other tiger would still get looks. He didn't want to take the risk of calling *that* much attention to himself.

He faced the subway entrance again.

Amy was already on a train by now, he was sure. He wouldn't be able to follow her. He *shouldn't* follow her. That would be too much like stalking her. And he'd been skirting close to that line already, making sure she reached the subway safely after each session. But he couldn't shake the feeling that the strange male was a danger to her, and his tiger kept pushing him to guard and protect her from the threat—despite the fact that Ethan had no idea what the threat was.

It was his excuse for impulsively asking for her number. Not because he wanted to see her again. Not because he *needed* to. He just wanted to…ensure she was safe. That was the only reason. Nothing to do with the beautiful blush that had risen up her throat and into her cheeks when she'd explained how awkward she was. Nothing to do with his magnetic draw to her. Definitely nothing to do with the way her scent seemed to fill him up every time he was near her, or the way his fingers itched to tangle in her hair, or the way his attention kept dropping to her lush mouth. He certainly wasn't planning on asking her out because he wanted to start dating her. He was just doing a good deed and keeping a nice human woman out of harm's way. The date would just be to verify she was okay. He wasn't really using the other tiger's presence as an excuse to see her again.

He snarled at the litany of justifications, knowing he was full of shit. A passing group of school girls looked at him with wide eyes and hurried across the road, against the light. He sighed, berating himself for scaring the poor kids.

Pushing away from the building at his back, he moved through the foot traffic opposite Amy's subway station. His own subway was a bit of a walk from here, but he needed the stretch and movement. In fact, he might just walk all the way home. At human speeds it would take him an hour or so, which might be just enough time to ease the tension in his gut.

And clear Amy Donovan from his head.

CHAPTER THREE

Amy pushed into her two-bedroom apartment, grinning at the yippy, bouncing fluff ball that greeted her. "Hey, Spike." She frowned a little. "I see Cat's been working on your style again." The normally white poodle had a dark streak of purple across her back now, each soft ear had been colored blue, and her puffy tail was a matching shade of blue. Amy considered the look, and nodded. "It suits you. Good symmetry. Wanna go for a walk?"

The poodle bounced off Amy's leg, ran in a tight circle, and then sat down, her mouth open and tongue hanging out as she waited for Amy to get the leash.

Amy chuckled, set her art case to one side in the entry-way, and reached into the hall closet for Spike's collar, leash, and a spare plastic bag for the clean-up. Her sister Cat had gotten Spike an actual spiked collar not long after they named her, but neither of them liked leaving the thing on her when they weren't around. So it only got added to Spike's look when they went for a walk.

"Did you have a good afternoon?" she asked the dog as they headed out the door, to the elevator.

Spike's happy bark echoed in the hallway.

Outside, Amy let Spike lead the way, pausing at sidewalk trees to sniff and do her business, her newly blue puffball tail wagging happily in the cold air. Amy pulled in a cleansing breath, letting the night and familiarity of walking her dog relax her fully.

She'd had trouble focusing on her book on the subway ride home, anticipation at the thought of Ethan calling her, of seeing him again blowing her concentration. The giddiness made her feel foolish. If he did call, she'd probably be too tongue-tied to say anything coherent. If he didn't call…

She rolled her eyes. She'd be hurt, damn it. It would hurt her feelings and that just sucked. That was why she didn't date. Men were a distraction. She had too many things to do, too many responsibilities. Too much she *wanted* to do. Dealing with all these girly musings were just annoying.

She wondered if that was why she'd had that weird moment of thinking she was being followed earlier? Was her distraction with Ethan sending her imagination into new directions, seeing danger where there wasn't any? If so, she really shouldn't have given him her number. She didn't have the time or tolerance for jumping at shadows. The real world presented more than enough dangers without her having to make them up.

Rounding the corner as she and Spike made their circuit

of the block, she spotted her sister walking down the hill from the subway. She waved and headed up toward her, Spike pulling hard at the leash, yipping loudly as she tried to reach Cat.

"Hey, sis," Cat said, jogging the last few yards and squatting down to hug the bouncing poodle. "Hey, Spike." She looked up. "What do you think of her new hairstyle? Nice, huh?"

"Beautiful color choices. You did use the good stuff, right? Nothing that will hurt her?"

"Duh." Cat let Spike lick her chin and cheeks, then set her back on the ground and stood. "How was the final session?"

"Great. Great." Amy almost groaned at the forced cheerfulness in her tone. Cat knew her better than that.

Which Cat proved by narrowing her eyes at Amy. "Did you finish your painting?"

"I did. It turned out really well. I'll show you when we get home."

"And…?"

"And what?"

"And that gorgeous model. Did you get his number? Are you going to see him again? Did you find out where he's posing next?"

Amy shook her head. "Cat, I don't make a habit of asking life models for their phone numbers. It isn't professional."

Cat snorted and adjusted her oversized carrier bag across her chest. "I can tell you see more in this man than an ordinary life model."

"Not true." Liar liar, she scolded herself silently.

Cat gave her a deadpan look that spoke volumes. "Your loss. You'll be the old maid with a dozen pets underfoot if you keep this up."

"Keep what up?"

"The celibacy thing. You're too young to be so old."

"Stop already. I don't need dating lectures from my baby sister. How was the study session?"

Cat switched moods in a blink, from scolding to enthusiasm. "Brilliant! I'm gonna ace this mid-term. Watch."

"You always ace science exams."

Catalina Donovan was a genius. Not just really smart, but an authentic Mensa-qualifying-IQ genius, with a particular talent for theoretical physics. She was already in graduate-level physics classes, and was only still an undergrad because she had trouble passing some of the more basic requirements for her degree. She got bored and lost interest and then failed the classes she wasn't obsessed with. If it had to do with subatomic particles or cosmology, her sister flew through the class with straight As. If it didn't, she had trouble just passing.

"How's the essay for your English class going?" Amy asked pointedly. This was the fourth time Cat had taken this same class. She had to pass it or she'd have to delay getting her bachelor's degree again. She had a graduate school scholarship waiting for her. And each failed class cost money. Cat needed to pass English lit this time around or Amy was going to threaten a semester of *only* English and history classes as punishment.

Cat let out a dramatic sigh and her shoulders slumped. "You always know how to hurt a girl, don't you?"

"Do you need help?"

"No, no. I can do it. It's just so boring. If the prof would let me write about something interesting, I'd ace this, too."

"He wouldn't understand what you found interesting. That's why he won't let you write about it."

Cat stuck her tongue out at that and blew a raspberry.

Amy pushed open the glass door leading into the foyer of their apartment building, holding it for Spike and Cat, and let Cat unlock the inside door. As she waited for Cat to get her key into the finicky lock and open the heavy inner glass door, Amy felt a strange tingling along her spine, another weird burst of *awareness*.

Her stomach tightened with that hated fear. She flexed her hands around the leash. A burst of panic started to pulse in her blood as her adrenaline surged. Every self-preservation instinct she had jumped to the fore.

She scowled, searching the sections of sidewalk and street she could see from where she stood inside the foyer. This neighborhood in Forests Hills was really quiet most of the time, except when the local high school let out for the afternoon and hordes of teenagers clomped by. There had been people out when she'd been walking Spike, but as she studied the area outside the building, Amy couldn't see anyone at all. Not even a passing neighbor or someone else out walking their dog.

She had to be imagining things. There wasn't any reason at all that she could see to be scared. But she still tapped her foot impatiently waiting for Cat to get the door open. Spike, picking up on her nerves, growled quietly. Feeling both silly and irritated that she'd upset Spike, Amy soothed the poodle with a few murmured words. She made an attempt not to show she was hurrying inside when Cat finally got the lock to cooperate.

Once they were inside the elevator, the weird tingling on her spine went away and Amy berated herself again for the sudden paranoia. Something really must be wrong with her. Seven years of stress and effort coming back to haunt her, maybe?

At least she'd gotten Cat off the subject of Ethan. Her sister could be very tenacious when she wanted to be, but was fortunately almost as easy to distract as a little kid. Just give her a more interesting topic, or a more contentious one, and Cat's quick mind moved fast into the new subject.

Unfortunately, because Amy had left her art case in the entryway instead of tucking it into her room, Cat remembered their earlier conversation well before Amy was ready to discuss it again.

"Can I see the final painting now?" Cat asked as she set her carrier bag onto the wooden table they used for mail and shrugged out of her coat, hanging it on the wall rack next to the door. She pulled off her wooly hat emblazoned with New York's hockey team logo, releasing a profusion of spiky dark blond hair. "After hearing so much about it, I'm dying of curiosity."

Amy groaned and tossed Spike's leash to her sister before she shrugged out of her own coat. "Take the collar off. Give me a sec to get the canvas out. It's still wet so no touching."

Cat held her hands up, the leash looped around her fingers, her palms facing Amy in a gesture of surrender. "I know the rules."

Amy left her to settle Spike and carried her case into her bedroom farther down the hallway. She hefted the large box up onto her double bed, clicked it open, and pushed the lid up, then hesitated. She was almost afraid to look at the painting again, afraid the awe and satisfaction she'd felt finishing it would morph into a critique of all the things she'd done wrong on the piece.

She was still waffling when her cellphone rang just as Cat ambled into her room. She motioned her sister onto her bed as she answered the call.

"Amy? This is Ethan, Ethan Gupta. Did I catch you at a good time?"

Amy's mouth literally dropped open. Cat's eyes widened and she mouthed a "what" that Amy couldn't begin to answer.

"Hi," she muttered, cleared her throat and tried again. "Hi. Yes, this is a good time. I just got back from walking Spike."

"Did she leave you a present or did you make it home in time?"

The fact that he'd remembered that much of their conversation made Amy's head spin. "I made it back in time." She started to say something else but wasn't sure where to start.

Cat was still staring at her, mouthing things that Amy was too distracted to decipher.

"Good," Ethan said.

His voice was as deep and sexy on the phone as it was in person. That shouldn't be possible, should it?

"So, I was wondering if you're free Saturday?"

Amy had another moment where she just simply froze and couldn't think how to respond because her brain had stopped working. Cat punched her in the arm and Amy stuttered, "I'm free. What did you have in mind?"

"A day at the Met? Lunch and some of the classics? I'll let you pick which area we go to first."

She chuckled at that, surprised she could do anything normal during this incredibly unusual phone call. "I love the Met. It's one of my favorite places in the city. How did you know?"

"You're an artist," he said as if the answer was obvious. "And it's one of my favorite places, too. Say noon?"

"That sounds…very nice. Thank you." She rolled her eyes, sure she sounded stupid and stilted. She was a grown fucking woman. What the hell was with this teenage awkwardness?

"Great. I'll meet you in the main entrance, by the museum store."

"Okay. Fine. Great. I'll see you then, then." She winced.

"See you then."

She heard a smile in his voice as he wished her a good-night. She stared down at the phone for a long minute after disconnecting. Then she looked up at her impatiently waiting sibling.

She blinked a few times to bring the room into focus.

"I... I have a date next Saturday," she said, sounding as disbelieving as she felt."

"You? A date? With who? Who was that? You looked so stunned I was worried at first."

Amy heard the very slight wobble in Cat's voice on that last sentence and she cursed silently. She should have taken a moment to reassure Cat everything was okay. The last thing she wanted to do was worry her sister by reminding her of *that* phone call, the one that had informed them of their parents' sudden death.

"That was Ethan," she said, her tone more soothing now than shocked.

"The model? The god among men who inspired you like a muse? That Ethan?"

Amy nodded, her eyes widening as the full impact of what had just happened fully sank in. He hadn't just asked for her number, then blown her off. He hadn't waited any kind of game-playing time to contact her. He hadn't texted. He'd called immediately and asked her out. On a date. To her favorite place in the city.

Cat punched her in the arm again and laughed before throwing herself backward onto Amy's bed. Amy scowled and rubbed her sore bicep. "Stop punching me," she scolded.

"You have a date with the god-muse!" Cat crowed. "When? Where? What are you going to wear? Can I do your hair? You need to get a wax in case you sleep with him."

Amy's head almost exploded at the thought. She held a hand up and stopped Cat mid-stream. "I'm not sleeping with him on the first date. He's taking me to the Metropolitan Museum during the day on Saturday."

"Is he feeding you?"

"Yes. *Lunch*." She emphasized the word as if that made some sort of a difference to Cat's logic.

"It'll lead to sex eventually then. Men who feed women on a first date are infinitely more likely to get a second date."

"Date does not necessarily equal sex," Amy said firmly.

Cat grinned. "I've seen your sketches, sis. You are so going to sleep with that man."

"No," Amy said, as much to herself as to her sister. "Get your head out of the gutter. It's just a lunch date."

"When did you give him your number?"

"Tonight. After the session."

"Bold!"

"He asked."

"And he called already?"

Amy nodded, still trying to get her own mind around that.

"You are *definitely* sleeping with him."

She threw a pillow at Cat's head.

Amy hovered near a stand of books just inside the Met Store, waiting for Ethan and trying not to let her nerves get to her. The open entrance to the museum was crowded with tourists and locals alike, standing in long lines at each side of the rectangular room or resting on the wooden seats in the center, all waiting to step through any of three entrances into the wings of the giant building. White marble, stone pillars, and some carved accents gave the place an elegant feel, fitting given the museum's contents.

She loved the smell of this place, though she could never quite describe it. There were hints of old parchment, canvas, stone, books, and paint with the freshly scrubbed-clean scent of filtered air over it all. A little like combining a library and an antique store but without any dust. The lighting in this part of the multi-wing building was bright and inviting. And despite the cold outside, it was warm and cozy inside.

She'd debated leaving her large wool coat at the coat check, since carrying it all day would be a pain, but she hated waiting in the line to drop it off and collect it. And if her date with Ethan went monumentally badly, she wanted to be able to escape as quickly as possible. She adjusted her coat over her arm and the strap of her courier bag across her chest as she scanned the entrance again, watching for Ethan to come through the bag check lines at the main doors. With each passing minute, she had to talk herself out of bolting. This was probably why she didn't date much. It wasn't just that she didn't have the time. The entire process of a first date left her so edgy and nervous, it wasn't worth the trouble.

And what if he didn't show? What if, despite his quick call last Sunday, he stood her up?

She made a face and focused on the giant coffee table Renaissance art book in front of her. If he stood her up, she'd go inside, set up somewhere with her sketch book—which was in her bag—and spend a soothing and wonderful afternoon sketching. In fact, the more she thought about it, the more she kind of hoped he didn't show so she could spend the day working on her art.

She rolled her eyes at herself and snorted under her breath. Okay, she'd mind if he didn't turn up. It would be… disappointing. But she'd still enjoy her day. Really, how could she not at the Metropolitan.

A strange sense of awareness crawled along her spine and she glanced at the entrance, expecting to see Ethan. Her heartbeat sped as she studied the people shuffling into the museum. But that sense of excitement and anticipation didn't follow the awareness she felt when Ethan was around. She shivered as adrenaline-fueled panic started to pump through her blood. That weird *hunted* feeling she'd experienced last weekend tugged at her. Again. What the hell?

She hadn't said anything to Cat, but she'd been having weird moments of paranoid edginess all week. Like she was being watched. At the oddest times, too—coming out of a class at college; Tuesday morning when she'd been walking Spike; Thursday night when she'd left her long-running temp job with a Midtown business lawyer; and once even on the subway home from work. Despite studying her surroundings and the people near enough to trigger her instincts, she could never spot anything suspicious.

If she hadn't known better, she'd think she was being stalked. But she never spotted the same person at any of these places, and she wasn't social enough outside of art circles to have picked up a stalker who would be able to pinpoint her schedule. Because of classes and temping, she didn't actually have the same schedule day-in and day-out. While her work for the lawyer was ongoing, the days and times she worked for her changed depending on Amy's schedule and when she was needed at the office. She did have regularly scheduled classes, of course. Someone could have spotted her on campus and followed her around enough to figure out her schedule. But Amy wasn't feeling this weird sense of being watched all the time, and it hadn't been going on long enough for a stranger to have learned her erratic schedule.

The feeling was disturbing, not the least because it was so similar to the feeling she got when Ethan was around. That same shiver of awareness down her spine, the same sense of…something being nearby.

She huffed an irritated breath and moved deeper into the shop, trying to pinpoint the source of her unease. If someone was following her, she wanted to know who the hell it was. Then she was going to the cops. And maybe getting a new canister of pepper spray.

But despite her not-so-subtle search, she couldn't locate whatever was giving her the willies. Almost as soon as she started moving, the sense of being watched, the dancing of nerves along her spine, went away and she had nothing to follow. Damn it. This was getting really weird.

Maybe she should talk to Cat about it. She really hated to worry her sister. She'd spent years working hard to protect Cat as best she could after their parents were killed. She didn't want to admit there might be a problem.

And there was still a part of her that kept thinking this was all her imagination. That she was worried over nothing, just stressed because of college and work and everything. Maybe if she just got a little more sleep, she'd feel better?

She moved from the book section of the Museum Store into the area filled with delicate collectables and the central glass-covered cases of jewelry. To distract herself, she studied the various antiquities-inspired pieces. She loved Met jewelry. She couldn't really afford any of it, not without sacrificing food and a few bills, but she was saving so she could treat herself when she graduated with her own bachelor's degree next year.

Occupied with one particularly lovely gold and red necklace, she didn't notice the awareness along her spine immediately. When the sensation registered, a bolt of panic shot through her and she looked up…

And found herself staring at Ethan.

"Oh," she said, both flustered and embarrassed. "Hi."

"You look surprised to see me," he said with an expression between a frown and a smile. "We do have a date, right?"

"Yes. Yes. Sorry. Just…got distracted." She shrugged. She'd warned him she was awkward. Might as well let him see just how much from the start.

The crease between his brows eased and he smiled fully. The expression robbed her of sense for another few minutes. How was it possible that a man could be so handsome and exist in the real world? And be nice? And smell *so* good?

She caught herself leaning toward him and made an effort to straighten away.

"Are you ready to go in?" Ethan asked. "I don't know about you, but I'm starving."

As if on cue, her stomach rumbled. "It has been a while since breakfast," she mumbled.

They went to the payment desk at the center of the entry hall. Ethan paid the full price for both their entrance fees—the Met was a pay-what-you-can museum, and Amy could usually only afford about five dollars—then handed her the little round metal tag to clip over her shirt. Today, the tag was a pretty red color. She loved these tags. Even though you could drop them in a recycle box when leaving the museum, Amy kept hers and had a little collection going at home.

"Where to first?" she asked.

He motioned around a large central staircase to the hall-ways that led to the back of the museum's first floor into the medieval section. They strolled together down the brightly lit corridors, walking close without touching. Amy was overly aware of him next to her, the heat and aura of him, but she made an effort not to plaster herself against him since this was only their first date.

Stepping out into a larger area, they faced the iconic choir screen from the Cathedral of Valladolid, behind and framing a statue of Mary and the baby Jesus. The choir screen's wrought iron struts and elegant gold detailing dominated the room.

"I love this area," Ethan said. "The history always gives me perspective."

"It's the best when they have the big Christmas tree up here at the holidays."

"Beautiful time of year. Have you ever sketched it?"

She laughed. "There's always too many people around to get a sketch in. But I study it and then draw it when I sit down for a drink."

"I'd love to see those sketches," he said.

"As in 'you want to come up and see my sketches'?" she joked, wagging her eyebrows, before catching herself. Her cheeks warmed. Again. Flirting was really not her strong suit.

Ethan just chuckled. "Something like that. Where do you want to eat?"

"American Wing Café? I love the light in that part of the museum."

"Perfect. That's one of my favorite rooms."

"Which part, the Tiffany glass, the statues, the atrium…?"

"The armory room with all the swords."

She snorted. "Of course." But if she were honest, she loved that area, too. The intricacy and details of the various weapons and armor was astonishing—metal work as beautiful as any stone sculpture.

The American Café sat at the rear of the open and airy American Wing atrium. One wall and most of the roof were glass, making the area beautifully bright on that sunny winter day, the sunshine almost summer-like. The central part of the atrium was a statue garden with some of Amy's favorite pieces. A black stone fountain at one side of the atrium gave the room just the faint scent of water and chlorine, mixing with the scent of coffee and pastry from the café behind it. On the opposite side of the central area, artificial plants filled stone boxes and looked so real she could almost smell the greenery.

Groups of tourists hovered around their tour guides at the edges of the room, in front of the awesome Tiffany glass windows or by the huge marble and stone medieval fireplaces at the back wall. Smaller groups of visitors, families, and individuals wandered amid the statues. Artists sat in their portable seats around the atrium, sketching statues or the elaborate stairway and pulpit.

By the time she and Ethan wove their way through the crowds to the café at the back of the room near the floor-to-ceiling walls of windows, Amy was starting to relax. This was just about her favorite room in the entire museum. The familiar feel of it settled her still-jumping nerves so that casual conversation with Ethan didn't feel so awkward. A hearty tomato and mozzarella sandwich and a rich roast coffee went even further.

She wasn't sure why, but she was surprised at how easy it was to talk with Ethan once she got out of her own way. He steered the conversation toward her favorite subject, art, and from there it was easy. It helped that he was as passionate as she was about the art world. For most of the meal, she forgot to be overwhelmed by him. She still got an obscene amount of joy just looking at him. And she caught herself staring at his mouth on more than once occasion. But just as the nerves and awkwardness were about to get the best of her, he'd say something that completely distracted her.

When he threw away the remains of their meal as she gathered up her coat and bag, she realized this was probably the best date of her life. And a part of her kind of wanted it to end right then so she didn't ruin it. She strolled beyond the seating area to the grotto of statues, hovering at one in particular that always caught her attention. It was a white marble carving called *Struggle of the Two Natures in Man* by George Grey Barnard—one large male figure lay on his side on the ground while a twin version of that male seemed to be coming out of the reclining figure, parts of their two bodies blending into one.

Ethan came up behind her and read the plaque over her shoulder. "I've never fully understood this one," he said.

"I think of it as the dual nature of man. The inner self breaking free of the outer."

"Looks painful," he said.

She laughed.

"And what's with the bat?"

There was a strange little bat-like figure resting on the reclining man's left arm where his arm and the standing man's foot seemed to fuse.

"It's cute," Amy said. "All statues should have a bat on them somewhere."

"You're the artist. I'll take your word for it."

The flirty exchange left her stomach dancing. And she knew she wasn't really ready for the date to end.

They made an ambitious plan that took them through the armory—for him—then on to the wing with the

Masters' paintings. They debated all the way through the tall corridors, past priceless statues and the glitz of Renaissance furnishings, about what to do after that—if they'd even have time before the museum closed.

"How can you come all the way to the Met and *not* go to the Egyptian pyramid?" he asked.

"First, not a pyramid."

"Yeah, yeah. I know. It's a temple. But it's the closest thing to a pyramid in the museum."

She rolled her eyes, knowing full well he was goading her, and more than a little pleased with his efforts. "Second," she said, "I haven't seen the Greek and Roman section in a couple of years. They've done up a lot of that wing."

He groaned and took her hand. "You're making it hard to argue with you."

"Why?" Her entire arm tingled from the contact of having his big hand wrapped around hers, and the dancing in her stomach tightened into something a lot needier than mere flirtation.

"Because this is our first date, and I want to make you happy by doing your bidding so you'll go out with me again."

She stumbled and would have fallen if he hadn't been holding her hand. "Doing my bidding?" She was torn between humor and a sudden image of him…doing her bidding in bed. The thought made her mind explode.

His expression turned knowing, as if he could tell where her imagination had gone, and he approved.

She swallowed, tried to talk, had to swallow again, and

then didn't know what to say. The feel of his skin against hers was warm and firm and she felt very faint calluses on his fingertips which struck her as strange from a life model/accountant. How did he get calluses? And what would those roughened fingertips feel like on her body? She nearly tripped over her own feet. Again.

"Tell you what," he said, tugging her toward the entrance to the modern and contemporary art area. "We'll go poke around the Roman hall today. But next time, we go through Egypt."

"Sounds fair," she managed.

She was still trying to recover from images of a naked Ethan "doing her bidding." And he went and destroyed her ability to think all over again by saying he wanted to see her after this. Another date. Another museum visit.

Another chance to feel like this.

She glanced at him out of the corner of her eye, wondering how much she was risking with this…flirtation. Because it had only taken one afternoon to confirm that Ethan was as fun and easy to talk with as he was stunning to look at. She was starting to feel like that character from the Greek myth, the one that flew too close to the sun and burned up his wings. If she let this go on, she was going to get singed, maybe worse.

She looked at the painting he stopped in front of—a Georgia O'Keeffe flower that looked suspiciously like a vagina—and almost laughed. For some reason the fact that he'd stopped in front of the vagina flowers amused her. And she realized, whether she liked it or not, she was all in now. She wanted to spend more time with him. She wanted to get to know him.

And as she watched him wander to another painting, she realized she wanted to find out just what he might do when "doing her bidding" in bed. That would be an experience worth the price of getting burned. She faced O'Keeffe's flower and released a low breath, blowing wisps of hair off her forehead where the curls had escaped her high bun. Life was short. That lesson had been driven home hard to her at the tender age of nineteen when her parents had been killed. Her awkwardness, her busy schedule didn't mean much in the face of that reality. If life could go so wrong so fast, she really should enjoy the good stuff now, like Cat kept telling her to.

Amy glanced back at Ethan. He caught her eye and smiled in that sexy way of his before moving on. She sighed.

He was definitely the good stuff she wanted to enjoy.

CHAPTER FOUR

While Amy sat cross-legged on a black marble bench and sketched one of the statues in the Roman section of the museum, Ethan roamed the statue grotto, trying to look absorbed in the art around him. Distraction kept him on edge, but he didn't want to admit it to Amy.

He'd spent the week attempting to find out the identity of the strange tiger who'd been following her. If he knew who the male was, he'd be able to assure himself (and his persistent tiger half) that she was okay, that the other tiger hadn't meant any harm, and Ethan didn't need to act as her bodyguard. But no one seemed to know who the tiger was, the other two males who claimed territories in New York hadn't encountered the mysterious stranger, and despite some quiet questions passed through the buffer of his brother-in-law, Nick Chernikov—the grandson of one of the most powerful of the elders—there wasn't any suspicious reasons for a male to be here. That anyone knew of, at any rate.

The closer Saturday got, the more he convinced himself there really hadn't been anything suspicious about the strange male, that he'd just invented a problem so he could see Amy again. Last night, when he still hadn't encountered the other tiger or discovered who he was, Ethan had picked up his phone to cancel the date.

He couldn't make himself do it though. And again, he talked himself into believing this would just be one date to make sure that Amy was safe, *then* he could walk away without anyone getting hurt.

He'd believed that lie right up until the point when he'd walked into the museum and sensed the other tiger. Near the Museum Shop where Amy was supposed to be waiting for Ethan.

Before he'd gone in to find her, he'd searched the immediate area, but the minute Ethan started toward the shop, the other male had left. Ethan had followed the male's scent through the bookstore, growling when he realized Amy's scent was in the same areas—the bastard had been close to her—to a back door, but then the scent seemed to vanish into a stench of a bleach-based cleaning product.

Scowling, Ethan had returned to the main part of the store to find Amy, though he wondered if he shouldn't try to hunt down the other male. The minute he saw her standing over the jewelry case, his debate vanished. He had to go to her. That damned magnetic pull was impossible to resist.

He'd stood behind her a second too long, trying to control the urge to brush the back of her bare neck with his fingers, to tease the little curls at her nape that had escaped her bun. Her honeysuckle scent pulled him in close, too close, close enough to make his body ache. She'd dressed in dark jeans and a fitted, button-front blouse. And despite his best efforts, he couldn't stop imagining slipping apart those buttons, pulling her blouse open, running his hands along her bare skin, testing the weight of her breasts, teasing her until she moaned.

Without conscious thought, he'd leaned into her, and then she'd turned and seen him. She'd looked so confused, he had wondered if she'd even remembered their date.

That had been a very humbling moment. And not one he'd been very pleased with. Because it made him want to ensure she remembered him no matter how distracted she got. It made him want to pull her into his arms, kiss her, imprint himself on her.

The possessiveness of his reaction reminded him sharply of what he'd been through with Siya.

If not for the presence of the other tiger somewhere in the museum, Ethan wasn't entirely sure he wouldn't have begged off lunch at that point. Cowardly as it was, he just couldn't face going through it again. He'd lost sight of himself with Siya, become someone he didn't even like. And he was afraid he'd fall into that same place with Amy. The tangle of emotions he felt for her went beyond simple attraction and lust, in ways he couldn't entirely explain. He'd made that mistake before. He didn't want to make it again.

But knowing one of his people was stalking her overpowered his instinct to distance himself.

As they'd moved deeper into the museum, Ethan hadn't detected the male anymore, and after a while, he'd been able to relax. His tiger kept scanning their surroundings for the encroaching stranger, though. And the question nagged him throughout the day—why was a shifter stalking Amy?

He'd kept the conversation with her light and casual, typical first date stuff. He was afraid he'd scare her off if he pushed too hard for reasons a tiger shifter might have picked her out of the crowd. Instead, he focused on their mutual love of art, provoking her into arguments over whether Picasso was overrated or not—he claimed no, she argued passionately yes; if the Dutch school had produced real art—they agreed yes but he argued no just to play devil's advocate; whether or not Edvard Munch's *The Scream* was creepy or beautiful—she said beautiful, he said creepy.

By the time they'd moved out of the armory toward the modern art wing, he'd forgotten he hadn't meant for this to be a serious date. He was enchanted by her, and keeping his distance was impossible. He loved how her cheeks tinted pink when she was defending her point, and the fire that flashed in her blue eyes heated his blood. He'd made excuses to hold her hand or rest his palm against the small of her back and taken a great deal of pleasure in her little shivers of reaction to his touch. The thread of desire in her scent was so tempting he could barely resist it.

Even now, he found himself hunting the grotto for a quiet corner where he might steal a kiss.

Not exactly what he'd meant to happen that day, and yet he couldn't turn away from her now either. He *liked* her. He savored the way she discussed his favorite topic, the way her hands moved when she talked about lines and shadow in a statue or painting, the way a little crease formed between her brows when she was concentrating.

His tiger had no intention of resisting this attraction to Amy. And his more logical side was having trouble arguing the point anymore.

But the specter of another male stalking her hovered in the back of his mind, keeping him from losing himself in their date entirely.

He glanced at her from the cover of a statue, trying not to crowd her but wanting to return to her the minute she was finished. She was staring at the piece she was sketching, her head tilted to one side, her eyes narrowed. Then she turned back to her sketch pad, her hand moving across the page, the pencil in her fingers dancing.

He could watch her all day.

Because he was studying her and not paying attention to the people around her, he didn't notice the other man until he sat down on a bench next to Amy. He was a human, middle aged and a little paunchy. Ethan's tiger growled when the man scooted close to Amy and nodded at her notebook, saying something Ethan couldn't quite hear over the din of other conversations going on around him.

He moved a few statues closer, and adjusted his acute hearing to focus on the stranger. Amy glanced at the man briefly and flashed a very small, very forced-looking smile, before concentrating on her sketch book again.

"You're very talented," the man said. "Pretty, too. Do you model?"

"No," she said shortly, her tone perfectly neutral.

"You could." He scooted closer, nearly touching her now. Amy shifted positions to put more room between them. The man looked her over, his gaze taking in her fitted button-up shirt and dark jeans, his gaze lingering on her breasts.

Ethan narrowed his eyes and stalked toward them, only a small part of him noticing the way people hurried out of his way.

"I do some sketching, too," the man said, his gaze still on Amy's breasts. "I'd love to have you model for me."

"I don't model." She didn't look at him, just kept her focus on her work.

"Come on. You'd be perfect. A Venus Rising pose would really suit you." The man ran a finger down her arm and Amy shifted farther away, almost to the edge of the bench.

Ethan could smell the man's lust as he neared, and it made Ethan's tiger snarl.

"I'm not a model," she said again, this time through her teeth.

"I'm the model," Ethan said stepping close to her side, opposite the human. He smiled at him, showing his teeth. "If you're hiring, I can give you my card."

The man scowled up at Ethan. Ethan's grin widened. Dangerously.

Amy scooted a little closer to him and glanced up, her eyes full of gratitude. The fact that she needed to thank him for interfering with this asshole's clumsy attempt at hitting on her just angered Ethan more. In his head, he growled, *go away*, to the man. His tiger hissed, *Mine*.

Aloud, he said, "You almost finished, hon? We've got that dinner reservation."

"I'm good. We should go."

She slid her sketchbook and pencil back into the courier bag at her feet, then stood, putting the bag's strap over her shoulder, her coat over one arm, and settling close to Ethan, taking his hand in hers. He squeezed gently.

"Enjoy your evening," Ethan said to the man. He wasn't smiling at the human anymore and his eyes narrowed when the man started to snarl. Ethan let out a low growl, so low it was barely a sound, more like something felt in the bones. Violence rumbled through the sound. The human male's eyes widened. He nodded at them and scurried off, almost tripping in his effort to get off the bench and move away from Ethan.

Amy sighed. "Why do men think it's a compliment to tell you you look like a model?" she asked.

"It's their misguided way of saying they think you're pretty." He tugged her into motion, taking her down the corridor that led to the main entrance, and opposite the stupid ass who'd propositioned her.

"Fine," she said, "but do they have to be so sleazy about it?"

"Only the sleazy ones."

She snorted.

He forced his pulse to slow as they walked, but he was shaken by his reaction, the sharp anger he'd felt for the human just because he'd hit on Amy. Jealousy had gotten Ethan into trouble before—just another reminder that he shouldn't be spending time with Amy. She brought out the part of him he couldn't quite control, the unreasonable part that terrified the hell out of him now.

"That was some intimidating growl you sent him," she said. "He looked like he might pee his pants."

"I hope I didn't scare you."

"Me? No. Frankly, I thought it was funny. That's probably not very nice of me, but what the hell. I'm a New Yorker. I don't have to be nice."

He laughed at that, and the tension and jealousy that had provoked his tiger just moments ago eased.

She bumped against his shoulder, not meeting his gaze when she said, "All that growly protectiveness was kind of sexy, too. I'm probably not supposed to admit that."

His hand tightened on hers as his muscles clenched. He tried not to react outwardly to her approval, to preen under her admission of desire, but his tiger purred in approval.

"I won't tell anyone," he said.

As they passed through a row of columns and back into the museum's main hall, Ethan realized he'd inadvertently brought their date to an end without meaning to. After the confrontation with the human, that was probably for the best. Still, he wasn't ready to say goodbye yet.

As he held her coat for her to slip into, he said, "Obviously, I was lying when I mentioned a dinner reservation, but I am hungry again. Would you like to go to dinner?"

She turned to face him as she buttoned her coat. "I'd

love to, but I have to get home. I need to walk Spike. My sister won't be home in time to prevent disaster."

Disappointment settled in his gut, mitigated only by the fact that he could smell her own regret. He should be grateful to her. The more time they spent together, the harder it was for him to resist her. He was falling down a rabbit hole he'd vowed to avoid. For both their sakes, he should just let things end here. But he couldn't seem to say the words.

Any more than he could keep lying to himself that he was just protecting her from another tiger.

"In that case," he murmured, hoping his inner turmoil didn't show in his voice, "may I walk you to your subway?"

She grinned, and a delightful wash of pink colored her cheeks again. "Sure. Thanks."

He put his own coat on while she donned her hat and gloves. She looked adorable with a wooly hat over her thick, dark curls. For a heartbeat, he stared at the way her hair teased around her cheeks. He reached out to tug gently at a curl, then let his finger slid down her jaw, a brief caress that sent electricity through his nerves. Her faint gasp fired his blood further. This was far from a private corner, with people surging past them in thick waves as the museum neared closing time, but Ethan's ability to resist her crumbled.

He leaned in close, giving her time to pull back if she wanted to. When she didn't, he settled his lips over hers, a gentle brush, a brief taste. A tease that made his world tilt. She tasted like summer, all heat and warmth and flowers, mixed with a hint of honey. That taste combined with her honeysuckle and oil paint scent in a surprisingly perfect harmony. His imagination filled with images of her in a summer field full of wildflowers, a tripod easel in front of her as she brought the colorful scene to life on her canvas, his hands on her shoulders, gently tugging her away from her work to lie with him in the grass and flowers, stripping her naked, tasting her warm skin...

Fisting his hands at his side so he didn't do something rash, he eased away, knowing if he kissed her any longer, he wouldn't be able to stop. The fact that she followed him, holding onto the kiss a moment longer, made his pulse pound.

She straightened away and stared up at him. Her eyes had a slightly dazed look that made him want to pull her into his arms again. She swallowed, her tongue darted out to wet her bottom lip, and he leaned closer, his full attention on her mouth.

The moment broke when a gaggle of foreign tourist plowed past. One overly eager woman bumped into Amy, sending her stumbling into Ethan's ready arms. The woman apologized in broken English before hurrying to catch up with her group.

Amy chuckled softly. He felt the sound reverberating through him, focusing his every nerve ending on where their bodies touched, the way her breasts pressed against his chest even through the barrier of their coats. The scent of her skin surrounded him, tempting him to dip his head and nibble the delicate area beneath her jaw, just so he could breathe her in more deeply.

She glanced up at him, her expression glowing, her embarrassment and desire spicing her scent, the flavors of musk and honeysuckle stronger and deliciously tempting.

"I… I'd better get going."

"Right." He could probably use a hit from the cold air outside anyway.

Taking her hand, they wove through the crowds and out into the winter twilight. He kept her hand in his as they walked along the cobblestone sidewalk at the edge of Central Park, the noise of 5th Avenue traffic on one side, the earthy freshness of the park on the other. Caricature artists, poster sellers, and New York City souvenir hawkers lined the low stone wall separating the park from the sidewalk. A cart selling roasting nuts scented the air with cinnamon and sugar, a weird contrast to the pungent animal and dung smells from the Central Park Zoo as they passed. His tiger found both the smell of deer and goats from the zoo and the sweet scent of roasted nuts appetizing.

Huge trees created an intermittent barrier between the traffic and pedestrians, winter-bare branches arching over the sidewalk creating a natural ceiling to contrast the elaborate stonework of the skyscrapers across the road. The streetlights flickered on but didn't do much to cut through the early evening gloom. Ethan loved this area, the contrast between nature and city stark and stunning. He loved it even more with Amy at his side.

So when they reached her subway station at the bottom corner of the park, he was reluctant to let her go. "What's your schedule like tomorrow?" he asked suddenly. "I have to work tomorrow night—an open studio session on the

Upper West Side—but I'd love to take you to lunch if you're free."

He tried to justify a second date with the knowledge that the other tiger was still out there somewhere with unknown intentions. But Ethan knew that wasn't the real reason he wanted to see Amy again, even if he refused to acknowledge the truth to himself.

A little crease formed between her brows as she stared up at him. He wasn't sure whether to take that as a bad sign or not. She looked confused. The emotion filled her scent too, along with the lingering spice of her desire.

"Aren't you supposed to…wait three days and then call to ask me out for next weekend?" she asked.

"Who says?"

"I don't know. All the women's magazines."

He smiled. "I haven't read them all. Maybe I missed that part."

"You really want to see me again? Already. Tomorrow?"

"If you're not free—"

"No, no, I can manage it. I have a test next week, but not until Thursday."

"I wouldn't want to mess up your study plans." He belied his comment by tugging her closer so he could wrap his arms around her. Her courier bag covered her lower back and her ass, forcing him to keep his hands higher than he might have liked, but given they were standing on a public street, that was probably for the best.

"I can study during the week," she said, leaning into him.

He liked how that felt. Too much. "So lunch?"

"Sounds good."

She rose up on her toes as he lowered his head, and he captured those beautiful, full lips of hers in another kiss. He was losing this fight. Every taste drew him deeper, made him want more, and the sound of his inner voice reminding him why he shouldn't get involved with her was growing faint under his need for her.

He swept his tongue into her mouth, savoring her more fully than he had the first time, tasting her sweetness. She sighed, and his arms tightened reflexively, flattening her against his chest. She felt so damned good, her every soft curve a perfect contrast to his hardness. He clenched his fingers into her coat, desperate to strip the thick barrier off so he could feel her better. She pushed closer, grinding into him as she angled her head for an even deeper kiss. The feel of her, so hot and needy, set him on fire. He stroked one hand up her spine to her neck, loving the way she moaned and arched against him when he brushed his bare fingers along the skin at her nape. The scent of her desire seeped into his skin, into his soul, marking him as his world seemed to shift on its axis. Even the dizziness of that tilt wasn't enough to distract him from the way she tasted, the way she felt in his arms, her heat, the heady knowledge that she wanted him as badly as he wanted her.

He blamed that dizziness for not sensing the tiger male sooner.

Amy eased away and frowned a little, glancing over her shoulder toward the park. Ethan followed her gaze, finally realizing they were being watched. Startled he'd taken so long to notice.

So much for his grand excuse of protecting her. He'd been so caught up in their kiss, the damned male could have walked right up to them and Ethan wouldn't have realized the potential danger until too late.

He narrowed his eyes in the direction of the male as the fact that Amy was *looking* toward the other tiger, that she'd seemed to notice his presence *first*, settled into Ethan's awareness. The sudden spike of worry, the hint of fear in her scent, brought his instincts to full alert and made his tiger growl quietly.

"You okay?" he asked.

"Yes. Fine. Just…" She paused, shook her head. "It's nothing. Just got a weird feeling." She shrugged and forced a smile when she looked back up at him. "The hazards of an overactive imagination, I guess."

"Mm hm." He sensed the tiger moving away, deeper into the park, and beyond Ethan's ability to feel him.

"You okay?" Amy asked.

He dropped his gaze back to her. "I'm good. Sorry. I just thought I saw something."

"Something bad?"

"Why would you say that?"

"You're scowling. Worse than you were at that dumbass that hit on me in the museum."

He snorted a half laugh. "I find that hard to believe."

"Why?"

"I doubt I *could* scowl any worse than I did at the dumbass."

She grinned and the tension and worry eased from her shoulders and scent. "This was a really nice day, Ethan. Thank you."

"Thank you for agreeing to lunch tomorrow." Her delectable mouth beckoned for another kiss, but he was too aware of the other tiger now—even if he couldn't sense him anymore. His need to keep Amy safe overrode his need to seduce her, at least in that moment. "Are you good getting home from here? I could ride back with you, make sure you make it to your door?"

She narrowed her eyes. "I'm fine. I wouldn't want to take you out of your way."

He heard the suspicion in her tone and cursed silently for pushing too hard. She probably thought he was angling for an invite back to her bed. Which he wouldn't say no to, but that hadn't been his intent. "If you're sure you'll be safe."

"I'll be fine. Thanks for worrying. That's kind of sweet."

He cupped her cheek in one hand. Despite the cold, his high shifter metabolism meant he didn't need gloves to stay warm, which meant he could caress her skin without any barrier between them. He savored the silky texture for a moment before forcing himself to step back.

"Do me a favor," he said. "Send me a text when you're home, so I know you're safe." His gaze jumped briefly back to the park.

"You're being very protective for a first date."

"Humor me."

She rolled her eyes. "Fine." The pleasure in her scent

belied her begrudging agreement. "What time and where do you want to meet tomorrow?"

"Noon. 71st and Broadway. I'll meet you at the subway station. We can go from there."

"You have somewhere in particular in mind?"

"I do. It's a surprise. You have any food allergies I should know about?"

She grinned. "Nope. I like everything but fish."

"Shame. I love fish. Fortunately, that's not what I had in mind."

"Good," she said with feeling. "My mom spent years trying to get me to eat fish. If she couldn't succeed, no one will."

He chuckled. And because he couldn't resist her anymore, he pulled her close for one last, hard kiss. He ended it as quickly as he'd started it, because if he didn't, he wouldn't stop for hours, and there was still the mysterious tiger out there somewhere. With a gentle nudge, he got her moving toward the subway stairs. She glanced back once, waving goodbye, and he took a mental picture of how she looked in that moment—her small smile, her pink cheeks, the way her hat was crooked now after their kisses.

If only he could draw the way she could...

CHAPTER FIVE

Ethan stayed at the corner of the park, even after Amy had disappeared into the subway system, his senses opened wide so he could feel the other tiger. When he couldn't pinpoint anything, he went around the corner and into the park proper, heading toward the last place he'd felt the male.

At the base of a tree lining one of the many paths through the park, Ethan caught the male's scent. Definitely the same one he'd detected last week and earlier in the museum. He paused at the tree to pull in all the information he could, then followed the male's path through the rolling, rock and grass hills of the park. It was close to full dark now. Lights brightened the main paths and a large number of humans still strolled past. The air grew colder as the last of the sun's light vanished.

Ethan followed the tiger's path to the center of the park, near the Bethesda Fountain, and then he lost the trail. Damn it. Whoever this was, he knew how to hide from other shifters.

That was as worrying as the fact that he was stalking Amy.

Ethan hunted around the area for another fifteen minutes, trying to pick up some sign of the male, but finally had to give up.

Reluctantly, he left the park, making his way toward the nearest subway station on the west side and his train back to Brooklyn. The male couldn't have followed Amy onto the subway—Ethan would have felt that. And once she was on a train moving away from the male, she was safe.

Unless the male had been stalking her long enough to know where she lived.

Fuck. Ethan didn't even know where she lived specifically, just that she was generally in the Forest Hills area of Queens—not a small area to search. He couldn't follow her to Forest Hills and hope to find where she lived by chance or luck, to stand guard all night. And he couldn't ask her where her apartment was without admitting he was worried about someone stalking her.

He had no idea how to explain how he knew about the other male anyway.

Irritated and worried, he decided to stay above ground in case Amy called. He could walk all the way home if he had to, though at human speed it would take a while.

Maybe he should just go out to Forest Hills. He could…

What? Hover around the area all night with no idea where Amy actually was? And even if she did need help, she was more likely to call a friend or the police than him.

They'd had one date—a very good one, but still. A few kisses did not mean she'd turn to him if she felt threatened.

The sense of helplessness made him grumpy enough that he didn't care if he was scaring humans as he stalked past them. This was New York. Scowling and being pissed off in public was acceptable behavior.

One of the many reasons he loved this city.

He'd walked about twenty blocks before he remembered that Amy had reacted to the tiger's presence before he had—or at least she'd seemed aware of something strange. He turned that over in his mind, wondering at it. She couldn't have sensed the other tiger. She was human.

Unless…

No. That wasn't likely. What were the chances he'd just stumbled on one? The elders had been looking for them for a long time now. Elizaveta Chernikova had been on the hunt for humans who could breed with tigers for decades. Since the first hybrid came forward more than a year and a half ago, and then the little girl hybrid who actually could shift was introduced to the community five or six months after that, the search for more hybrids and humans who could mate with tiger shifters was a major priority for the elders.

Tiger shifters were on the verge of extinction thanks to the extremely low birthrates for females. There were so few females left to them, some tigers argued extinction was inevitable. And except for Elizaveta, most of his people had believed matings between humans and tiger shifters were a myth. Then Nila DeLuca's existence was made public. Followed by Zoe Callaghan. Nila was human and couldn't shift, but she *could* have children with a tiger shifter. Zoe was still a child, but she could shift, which meant she could likely have children with a tiger as well. And while Paige Williams was the daughter of a suspected hybrid who may or may not have been able to shift, according to the tests Elizaveta had done, Paige was also able to conceive children with a tiger shifter.

The entire community was now obsessed with the possibility of the hybrids…and not always in a good way. There were a significant number of his people who felt the hybrids would bring about the end of the tigers by diluting their bloodlines and driving them fully to extinction. Others thought the hybrids—and the humans who could mate with tigers to create hybrids—would be the saviors of their species.

Yet, as far as Ethan knew, no more hybrids had been located beyond the three they all knew about.

It was always possible the elders weren't revealing their knowledge of the other hybrids to the community. For the hybrids, protection as much as anything. But still, it didn't seem realistic that news of more hybrids wouldn't leak out. It seemed the hybrids might be even more rare than female tiger shifters. And since it took DNA tests to determine which humans might be able to mate with tigers, that was also a needle-in-a-haystack search.

But the hybrids could sense tiger shifters the way tigers could sense each other. Even Paige Williams, who was a generation removed from being a hybrid, could still sense tigers. If Amy was a hybrid, or the daughter of a hybrid, she might have sensed the other male the same way Ethan had.

He paused at a traffic light, waiting out the rush of cars. The heavy scents of gasoline and hot tarmac mixed with the smells of musty dirt, humans, and the pizza restaurant on the corner next to him. He stuffed his hands into the pockets of his coat, part of him wishing it were colder.

Could he have really stumbled onto a hybrid? Could the human woman he'd been obsessing over for more than a month now be someone he might actually be able to have children with?

And did that explain why he couldn't seem to stop thinking about her? Why his reaction to her felt so much like the one he'd had with Siya?

If Amy *was* a hybrid, he wouldn't just be allowed to date her, any more than he could have just dated Siya. He'd likely have to fight for Amy. She couldn't do a Mate Run, but the elders were intent on finding alternate ways for males to compete for hybrid females. He wouldn't just be allowed to claim her without other males objecting.

Which brought him right back into the world he'd rejected two years ago, a world that had turned him into someone he didn't want to remember and nearly gotten him killed, all for the sake of a tigress he'd thought he loved and the possibility of children of his own. Ethan hadn't allowed himself the hope of children since turning his back on his own species. He'd been determined to date only human women and promised himself he could be content with a less overpowering love and no family of his own.

Most of the males of his species had to accept that kind of future. The numbers just weren't in their favor.

Now even the hint of that old hope irritated him. He'd left the Mate Run behind for a reason. He didn't *want* to compete for a mate again. He wanted what humans had—simple dating that may or may not lead to something long term. Not this obsessive focus on reproduction and winning a mate. Bitterness at the thought rose, choking him, and making him angry for reasons he couldn't quite explain. He didn't want hope. He didn't want to think about children of his own. He didn't want to find himself competing for a mate, becoming so obsessed with a woman that he lost himself again. If Amy turned out to be a hybrid…

No. His imagination was getting away from him. He was looking for excuses to explain his reaction to Amy, explain why he couldn't stay away from her.

More likely she was just one of those humans with good instincts. She had grown up in the city. It probably came with the territory, being able to sense danger. He was making too much of her reaction. Seeing things that weren't there.

It was safer for her to be an ordinary human anyway, given the split amongst his people over the hybrids. The tiger shifter world was dangerous enough for those who could shift. Humans were vulnerable in that world. He didn't want her exposed to that.

The lights changed and he crossed with the other pedestrians, a tingling of instinct jumping along his nerves, a worry that he couldn't quite shake.

If Amy was just an ordinary human…why the hell was a tiger shifter stalking her?

* * *

Zhong moved deeper into the heavily wooded northern part of Central Park after giving the other shifter the slip. In the darkening night, few humans risked this part of the park, giving him the privacy he needed to reach out to his contact. Settling up high on a black oak branch, his back to the tree trunk, he pulled his cellphone out. The rich smell of oak, pine, grass and soil in the immediate area helped clear the odor of city from his nose.

He worked around the world, in cities far denser and dirtier than New York, but he always needed a breath of nature when on assignment in areas like this, to center himself and remove the stench of humanity from his skin. Above the canopy of winter-bare branches, the stars that could be seen despite the light pollution started to wink on.

After a few taps, ensuring the signal from his phone routed to multiple towers at once so he couldn't be traced, he rang his contact.

The man picked up on the second ring. "Have you located her?"

"Located. Tracked. Her schedule is erratic."

"Will that be a problem?"

"No."

"But there is a problem?"

"She's got a boyfriend." He rolled the last word, mocking it. "I'm sending you a picture."

He eased the phone from his cheek to pull up the long-distance photo of the other tiger and sent it through an encrypted message.

"Did you get it?" he asked, watching a barred owl land on a branch of the oak a few feet away. It fluffed its feathers, hooted twice, then settled down to stare at the surroundings, completely unconcerned with the feline predator sitting just a few feet away. Zhong smiled.

"Got it." His contact paused, then cursed. "Inconvenient."

"Gupta?" Zhong knew there were three males in the city, three unfamiliar males—males who would never recognize his scent. He'd been given pictures of them, but he hadn't been able to get close enough to the other male yet to verify his identity. He wasn't supposed to reveal himself to the other tigers if he could avoid it.

"Yes," his contact hissed. "Does he know who she is? What she is?"

"Not sure yet. I've been avoiding him as ordered."

"I'll have to consult with our mutual friend. This is an awkward turn."

Ethan Gupta's sister had married into the Chernikov family, which meant Ethan had a fast line to one of the most powerful elders of the remaining eight. Zhong didn't know the whole situation—and he didn't ask—but it was clear his client wanted to avoid arousing Elizaveta Chernikova's interest in what he was doing.

Zhong wasn't entirely sure what his client was doing, either. That wasn't his job. His job, now at least, was to find things and recover them. He worked for many wealthy clients, finding and retrieving what they wanted him to, by whatever means necessary. His clients paid him very well for his efforts, his efficiency, and his discretion. Most of them were human, but a few of his own people had retained his services over the years. He was the best at what he did.

This was, however, the first time he'd worked for an elder.

"I'll keep watching and following the woman," he said. "Contact me when our mutual friend has decided what he wants to do."

"I will."

Zhong was about to disconnect but the pause on the other end of the line, like a question not yet answered, made him hesitate.

"Have you…," the contact started hesitantly. "Can you tell if she's one of them? For sure?"

"She seems to know when I'm around, a good indication she is. She's nearly spotted me three or four times this week. An ordinary human wouldn't have been able to. I'll switch now to following her as if she were a tiger shifter."

"Good. Good. He'll be pleased. They're so damned hard to find."

"That's why you hired me."

He'd found them four full-fledged hybrids so far—not just the offspring of a hybrid, but individuals with a tiger parent and a human parent—and had been able to bring in three of them. The fourth could shift and was male, so wasn't of use to his client. The other three had been exactly what his client had asked for: female human hybrids who didn't know the tiger shifter world existed. All four of those he'd located were ignorant of the tigers, even the male who could shift—from what Zhong had learned, the man thought he was demon-cursed and lived like an outcast. Zhong's client wanted it kept that way. Their species hardly needed *more* males.

"Speaking of why you hired me," Zhong said. "There's a payment due."

"Yes, yes. It will be in your account within the hour. Absolutely. Our mutual friend is very grateful for the job you're doing."

Zhong didn't respond to that. He didn't really care so long as he was paid.

"Has Gupta slept with the woman yet?" his contact asked.

"Doesn't look like it. His scent isn't anywhere around her apartment building or neighborhood, and they didn't go home together tonight."

"Well, that's something. If she gets pregnant…"

Zhong knew without the man having to say it that if Gupta got her pregnant, he'd realize she was a hybrid. "Would it really matter if she was pregnant? I can take care of Gupta before he makes the connection or tells anyone else about it."

The man hummed under his breath. "That might become necessary, but we'll have to make it look like an accident." There was another pointed pause before he said, "And perhaps having a fetus to work with would be beneficial."

Something in the man's tone made Zhong's tiger growl, and Zhong lifted his lip in an unconscious snarl. The owl flapped its wings and screeched. Zhong made an effort to rein in his instinctive disgust, pulling in his predatory aura. The owl settled down again.

"Let me know when our friend decides what to do about the woman," Zhong said, keeping his tone neutral. "And Gupta."

He disconnected before the man could say more. While he didn't know what his client was doing with the hybrids, the thought of them harming an unborn fetus brought up memories Zhong didn't want to revisit.

He angled his head back a little to stare up at the dark sky. The glow from the city colored the horizon faintly orange but directly overhead was blackness and a few pinholes of starlight. Quiet night sounds of rustling wildlife and leaves moving gently in the winter breeze mixed with the more distant rumble of traffic, the faint but irritating whine of an ambulance. The air was colder now, fresh and damp against his face.

Zhong considered his current job. His client thought Zhong was able to find these hybrids where Elizaveta couldn't. The other elder assumed Elizaveta had been unable to locate any because she hadn't brought them forward. Zhong had long suspected this to be a false assumption. Recently, he'd confirmed his suspicions. Elizaveta was tracking down hybrids almost as fast as he was— since they were using similar methods.

The DNA of a human-tiger offspring was unique, with a handful of markers that could identify them if one knew what to look for. But discovering a hybrid that way required locating blood samples from the hybrid. He'd only managed to find one directly. The other three, including Amy Donovan, he'd discovered by looking for potential parents. Humans who could mate with tigers also had DNA markers that could be tracked. If a woman with that marker had a child whose father's origins were a mystery, Zhong went looking for that child.

The process required months of research, his favorite part of the job, and had taken him on a number of false trails—sometimes the potential hybrid was just an ordinary human. But he'd still managed to find as many hybrids as Elizaveta's entire team of searchers, locating ones she didn't even know about.

Frankly, he was surprised she hadn't contacted him with the job. That was actually a little insulting.

He grunted and the owl hooted in response. He raised his eyebrows at the bird. The bird stared back, unblinking. Zhong chuckled and leapt off the branch, ceding the territory to the owl. He landed in the soft soil with a quiet thud, straightened his black wool coat, and brushed off his black jeans. He checked the thick silver watch on his wrist, then started out of the park as worry over one detail of the current job dogged him. A detail he'd only picked up today.

Amy Donovan's scent.

He'd finally allowed himself close enough to really study her scent at the museum. And what he'd picked up troubled him, on an instinctive level he couldn't entirely explain. Her scent was...familiar somehow. Not as if he knew her, but like he knew one of her relatives. The scent pulled at very old memories, ones he refused to let surface, though they were closer now than he preferred. Probably why his tiger had reacted so strongly to his contact's mention of doing something to an unborn child.

He'd found Amy by tracing her mother. Zhong was pretty sure he'd never met Luciana Vega—though he would confirm that now—so that wasn't likely the reason Amy's scent seemed familiar. He didn't usually bother finding a hybrid's tiger father once he confirmed he'd found a tiger-human offspring.

But in this case, maybe he should make an exception.

CHAPTER SIX

Amy sipped her tall sparking glass of champagne and watched the milling crowd filling Devine's gallery. Behind her, the gallery's wall-to-ceiling tinted windows that fronted the building let in a few dim streetlights. Outside the Soho night crowds sauntered past. Inside, the overhead lighting was set to a comfortable level that gave an intimate feeling in the otherwise huge space. Along the outer brick walls and central cream-colored insert walls, the exhibition pieces hung under curving spotlights designed to look like old-fashioned desk lamps. The artwork was composed mostly of photographs and a few paintings showing close-ups and details of industrial equipment.

While the aesthetic wasn't to Amy's taste, Devine had done such an amazing job with the instillation, and Amy found the stark, brown and gray images almost charming.

She swirled her glass, hovering near the front of the room as she watched Ethan. He was surrounding by a small group of painters and sketch artists, most of whom Amy had met at various open sessions or other gallery shows. They all looked adoringly at Ethan as he smiled politely and talked art. She might have considered being jealous, but it was hard to take their fawning too seriously when Ethan looked amused and just a little uncomfortable. Especially when a woman with huge feathers in her hair slid close enough to plaster her arm against his.

He caught Amy's gaze, his smile never dropping, but his eyes widened slightly in a save-me expression.

She chuckled and glanced around for a waiter to pass her half-empty glass off to so she could rescue Ethan. Not that she needed much of an excuse to return to him. She'd only wandered away from his side to keep from feeling clingy. She was trying to prove to herself that she wasn't just another one of his admirers, that she could date him and not be overwhelmed by him.

It wasn't working. She was still overwhelmed by him most of the time, but at least she was trying.

Reese stepped up to her while she was still searching for a waiter and kissed her cheek in greeting. She took in his beautifully tailored smoke-gray suit and deep green tie admiringly. His salt and pepper hair, usually purposefully shaggy and unkempt looking, had been tamed into a sleek, sophisticated style.

"Very sharp," she said. "And professional."

He held out his hands and swiveled from one side to the other. "Thank you. I'm trying to impress a few wealthy potentials with my seriousness." He eyed her outfit. "You're also looking very lovely. Cobalt suits you."

"Well, thank you." She grinned and tried to ignore her blush. She'd picked out this strappy, silk dress because the specific color of blue brought out her eyes. And she wasn't ashamed to admit, she'd wanted to impress Ethan. It had worked. When he'd helped her out of her thick winter coat and gotten his first view of her, his eyes had widened and his mouth had dropped open just a bit. It had been worth all the trouble of donning a shorter skirt and heels in this weather.

Reese gestured to the man in question. "Your date needs saving."

"I noticed. I was just on my way."

She glanced back at Ethan who had managed to step away from the feathered lady only to have a man in a top hat step into his face, thrusting his drink under Ethan's nose as he made some enthusiastic point that resulted in Top Hat's red wine splashing onto the polished hardwood floors. The wine missed Ethan's shoes only because he took a step to one side. Unfortunately for him, he bumped into the Feather Lady. She spun and plastered herself to his arm again.

"Poor man." Reese sighed sympathetically. He looked at Amy from the corner of his eye. "When did this happen?" he asked, jutting his chin toward Ethan. "And why didn't you tell me sooner?"

"Technically, we only had our first date two weeks ago last Saturday."

"And you're on date number what now?"

"Uhm…" She actually had to count. "About eight technical dates. Unless you count quick meet-ups for coffee between work and classes. Then we've seen each other every day since that first date."

His eyebrows rose high. "Every day for almost three weeks? It must be love."

Amy snorted. "Don't get ahead of yourself. But…yeah, I like him. Once I got past being awed by him." Not that she really had yet…

"Can't blame you for that. Have you slept with him yet?"

"Reese!" She bumped him hard with her hip.

He chuckled. "So that's a 'no' then."

"I don't kiss and tell."

He just smirked at that. "Sure." He glanced back at Ethan. "You two barely talked at the studio. How on earth did you end up on a date?"

She shifted from one foot to the other, giving one leg a little break from the unusual experience of standing in high heels for so long. "I bumped into him just after the last class at a coffee shop. We got to talking."

She wasn't sure whether to mention the reason she'd gone into the coffee shop in the first place. Mostly because that sense of being watched had vanished over the last week. She'd only gotten the spine-tingling awareness of… something two more times during the week after her first date with Ethan. Since then, nothing, and she was starting to wonder if it all really had been in her head.

Except she couldn't forget how Ethan had looked that Saturday evening after their day at the Met, when they'd been hovering outside the subway. The kiss was burned into her memory. But it was those last few moments before she'd headed down into the subway, when she'd thought she'd sensed something in the park, and Ethan had been frowning in the same direction. He was distracted in that moment, as if he sensed something, too. And he'd looked angry.

She shook off the idea. She had to have been imagining things. Probably because she was overwhelmed by the reality of Ethan—and his kisses.

"Your sister is charming," Reese said, pulling her from her thoughts.

She scanned the crowd, spotting Cat holding court near the back of the gallery in front of a huge photographic image of a rusted bolt against battered metal. The people standing with Cat looked a little dazed, which meant she'd probably started using math to explain the symmetry of the image.

"I'm delighted I finally got a chance to meet her after all this time," Reese said. "It's a crime I haven't known her in person before this. She explained to me in great detail why the whorls in Van Gogh's *The Starry Night* are an accurate visual representation of the principle of turbulence."

"You didn't ask her what she meant by turbulence, did you?"

"Better," he said with a laugh. "I asked if she meant the stuff that knocks airplanes around."

Amy groaned and chuckled at the same time. "So you got the full lecture."

"Yes, I did. Math and all. Went completely over my

head. But I loved it. I don't often get to converse with scientific geniuses."

"Careful she doesn't hear you say that. You'll be down the rabbit hole of quantum mechanics for sure then."

He laughed again.

Amy started to make her excuses—Ethan was looking very desperate for rescue now—when Devine slid up to them in a graceful flow of elegance. She was wearing a sleek black pants suit, the trousers wide and flowing, the single-button jacket cinching in at her waist, the lapels opened just enough to reveal a slice of bare skin and the inner curves of her small breasts beneath. Amy glanced down to admire Devine's mile-high spiked heels, silver and sparkling with little winking clear stones. The height of the things made Amy dizzy just looking at them, but they were beautiful.

"The exhibition is stunning," she told the gallery manager, after exchanging cheek kisses.

"I'm so pleased you could make it," Devine said. "And I shall be in your debt forever for bringing the stunning Mr. Gupta." She waved an elegant, manicured hand toward Ethan and his admirers. "I should be upset because he's distracting from the art, but he's managed to sell at least four different pieces just by expressing admiration for them."

"He has?"

"You'd be amazed at what people will buy when a gorgeous man is around. I could have charged anything and Lady Featherhead would have paid it just to purchase the image Ethan said was his favorite."

Amy snorted.

"I might have to hire him for all my shows."

"Don't look now, but I think you're about to claim another commission," Reese said, nodding over Devine's shoulder.

Ethan was staring up at a photograph of what looked like feathers lying across a steel pipe, though the black and white image was mostly just shadow and light contrasts. Amy had to admit it was a lovely composition. The rapt gazes of the handful of men and women standing with Ethan went a little beyond what Amy felt the image warranted.

Devine clapped her hands together, rubbing them like a cartoon villain. "I'll be back, darlings. Enjoy the canape. We paid a fortune for this caterer."

As the woman disappeared back into the crowd in an expensive perfume-scented swirl, Amy faced Reese again. "I'd better go rescue Ethan before he thinks I did this to him on purpose."

Reese nodded, but his expression turned speculative. "Really quick, now that I know you're dating him, I think I should clear something with you."

"What?"

"I've hired him for a few private sessions next month."

"Why do you have to clear that with me?"

"I don't want you to think I'm…encroaching on your territory so to speak."

"Are you planning on seducing him?" Amy asked with all seriousness. Reese was pretty fluid in his sexual tastes, though mostly he preferred women. But given Ethan's sheer masculine perfection, she wouldn't have been the least surprised if Reese had considered hitting on Ethan.

"I wasn't actually," Reese said, serious now. "He's… I'm not sure how to explain, but I find him too inspiring. It would almost make him too real to sleep with him."

I would take that kind of real. But she wasn't quite brave enough to say that out loud. "In that case, I'm not bothered."

"You're serious about him?"

"I don't know yet, honestly. But…" She swallowed and glanced at Ethan again. "But I could be, Reese. I could get serious about him really easily."

"I'd warn you to be careful, but it would be a little disingenuous coming from me."

She smiled and bumped against him with her shoulder. "Thank you."

"For what?"

"For not telling me he's out of my league or discouraging me."

"Never. He's not. Now go pull him out of Lady Feather-head's clutches."

She laughed as she wove her way through the crowd, catching Ethan's gaze as she neared. The spark of heat in the depths nearly made her stumble. Her stomach danced with the now familiar thrill of desire. As he crossed to meet her halfway, her pulse pumped harder. He really was magnificent.

Tonight he wore a simple black suit that fit his muscular body perfectly, the crisp white shirt underneath opened a little at the collar, drawing her gaze to the strong column of his throat. Her imagination filled with thoughts of dragging her lips along his skin, just at the edge of the material. His hair brushed the top of his suit jacket in soft-looking waves she wanted to run her fingers through. He looked both sophisticated and casual, reminding her of one of the male models that graced the gigantic billboards lighting up Times Square.

People in the crowd watched him as he passed, but his focus was entirely on her. She still couldn't quite believe that he kept asking her out, that someone like Ethan *wanted* to be with her. A cynical part of her brain kept wondering *why* and looking for ulterior motives. But when they were together, he made her feel…special, comfortable, sexy, desirable, and like herself all at once. After almost three weeks, she was starting to accept that he really did like her, awkward quirks and all. And the more time she spent with him, the harder it was to imagine life without him.

When he reached her, he settled a protective hand low on her back and leaned in to kiss her cheek. "Thank you," he murmured.

His breath was hot against her skin, making her shiver. She leaned into him without meaning to and pulled in the deliciously male scent of him.

"For what?" she teased.

"For giving me an excuse to escape that woman with the feather in her hair," he said, his voice low as he spoke near her ear. "No one here could possible blame me for wanting to return to my stunning date."

She wanted to say something smart and funny, to deflect the compliment, but nothing came out. She was entirely too focused on the feel of his fingers stroking along her back, barely brushing her bare skin above her dress's neckline. Imagining where those clever fingers might explore if she wasn't wearing the dress.

She was still half convinced Ethan Gupta was out of her league, but she was in too deep now. She wanted Ethan in her life, and in her bed sooner rather than later. Damn the consequences to her heart.

Life was too short anyway.

E than had spent the last twenty minutes looking for an excuse to get back to Amy. He didn't want to crowd her since she was supposed to be circulating and making contacts in the art world, but his tiger didn't particularly like being away from her. The nagging insistence that he return to her had kept him edgy and continually watching for her even as he spoke to other people.

Having the lady with the feather in her hair plastering herself to his arm hadn't helped matters. She'd been wearing a pungent perfume, and that stench lingered on his clothes, nearly overwhelming his sensitive sense of smell. Which was more than a little irritating because now that he was back at Amy's side, he wanted to savor her scent without anything interfering. Amy's delicious honeysuckle flavor had become an addiction for him.

When he'd seen her heading in his direction, he hadn't been able to stay away anymore. The now familiar magnetic pull of her had drawn him across the room without conscious thought. The startled murmurs of the crowd around him only barely penetrated his focus. Every part of him had zeroed in on Amy. Her shapely legs were made even longer by her heels and temptingly displayed beneath the flirty swing of her short skirt. The way her hips swayed as she glided closer made his heart pound. Her dark hair was arranged in a pile on top of her head, with wisps of soft curls framing her cheeks and cascading over her sleek neck. Her lips glistened with the remains of her gloss and a hint of moisture from the champagne she was drinking.

She would taste like the sparkling wine.

As she smiled up at him, her blue eyes bright, he could no longer resist dipping his head to capture her mouth with his. He kissed her softly, lingering over the fullness of her lips, the soft silky texture sending darts of desire through his gut. The kiss wasn't nearly as heated or deep as he wanted to go. But it would do for now.

His tiger purred in approval.

"Well that sent a signal," she said against his mouth before settling back on her heels.

Her shoes put her nearer to his height, and he realized he liked how much closer her lips were this way. He nearly leaned back in for another kiss, just because he could, but that way lay danger.

Instead, he said, "What do you mean?"

"Your admirers look very disappointed now. Especially Lady Featherhead."

"Lady Featherhead?" He knew exactly who she meant without even having to look behind him. The name suited the heavily perfumed woman a little too well.

"That's what Devine called her. Pretty sure she was being facetious."

"Apt, though. Why did you leave me alone so long?"

She grinned. "You looked to be enjoying yourself."

He pretended to growl and reveled in her little shiver, the scent of her spiking desire like the most heady wine he'd ever tasted.

"If you can't even read my save-me expression," he said, letting his voice drop a little deeper, "we're going to have to work out a better system."

"Fair enough." She leaned into him. "Devine says you've been a wonder for sales tonight."

"So, she doesn't mind me crashing the party?"

Amy snorted. "Like anyone would mind you showing up anywhere."

"You'd be surprised." He heard the too-serious note in his voice and cursed silently that those memories still had the power to hurt.

He'd spent the week after his and Amy's first date making excuse after excuse to see her—the mysterious tiger was still around and a possible threat; if she was a hybrid, he needed to find out for his people's sake; if she wasn't, she was vulnerable to the other male, and Ethan was honor-bound to watch out for her; if the other shifter was stalking her, Ethan needed to stay near Amy so he could catch the male.

All of it had been bullshit. The truth was he couldn't stay away, even when he tried—even when her schedule was so full it would have been easier *not* to see her. By the second week, he'd stopped trying to justify every single phone call and date. This week, he'd finally admitted the truth.

He wanted Amy, no matter what, and walking away from the chemistry between them was no longer an option. Self-preservation be damned. If she turned out to be another Siya for him, so be it. Sometime during the last three weeks, his tiger had decided Amy was his mate, and Ethan's logic couldn't deny his instincts anymore.

The thought that he was risking his heart again, when he hadn't thought there was enough of it left to risk, was more than a little terrifying. Especially with so many questions still hanging between them—like why had one of his people been following her?

He hadn't dug too deeply into her past, afraid if he pushed too hard she'd close up on him. But some discrete questions had confirmed she'd grown up with her mother and father. He'd gotten their names and double checked, carefully so he didn't hint to anyone—even his brother-in-law—that he was trying to determine if Amy was a hybrid. But neither of her parents were tiger shifters. Which should have put the hybrid question to rest.

Except that the other male was still in the city somewhere. Ethan hadn't felt him in a few days, but he kept catching hints of the tiger's scent in areas where Amy was —including her neighborhood tonight, when Ethan had picked her and her sister up in a taxi for the gallery show. The scent of the male had been diluted, as if he hadn't been near her building in a few days, but the fact that he'd been there at all had horrified Ethan. And pissed him off because he hadn't been able to discover who this tiger was.

But the other male hadn't actually *done* anything yet. He hadn't even tried to speak to Amy as far as Ethan could tell.

Maybe he was imagining the dangers. His feelings for Amy had him so twisted up, he wouldn't be surprised if he was misreading the entire situation.

He shook off the worry for the moment, determined to enjoy his date. He scanned the gallery as he looped an arm around Amy's waist, pulling her against his side. The double story ground floor was packed with people weaving around the displays, the conversations in the room a not-insignificant hum of noise. These were the kinds of human gatherings most tiger shifters avoided, primarily because the scents and sounds could be so overwhelming. Ethan didn't usually mind. He could dial back his keen senses enough to tolerate it all. But he had to admit, Amy's subtle, natural honeysuckle flavors, with a hint of her soap and the allspice taste of her desire were a lot more pleasant than the cacophony of perfumes and colognes in the room.

"Where's your sister?" he asked, mostly because he wanted to hear Amy's voice again. He couldn't get enough of the smoky sound.

She nodded toward the rear of the gallery. Catalina Donovan stood with a tall man whose back was to Ethan. He wore a black suit and had short black hair, but that was as much as Ethan could see. Cat was smiling up at him, her young face alight with excitement.

"She's got to be talking about physics," Amy said. "She only ever looks that excited when she's found someone who can at least sort of follow her scientific ramblings."

Cat was as tall as Amy, and almost too skinny, with straight blond hair cut short and shaggy—a pixie cut? Something like that. His sister would know. She had wide brown eyes and an animated, pretty face. Superficially, the two women looked nothing alike. In fact, he might not have guessed they were siblings if Amy hadn't introduced Cat as her sister.

But on closer inspection, the family resemblance became clear—especially in their smiles and the way they used their hands when they talked.

"You sure that's science making her smile so much?" he asked when Cat flashed what could only be called a flirty grin at the man in front of her.

Amy laughed. "If they weren't talking science, she wouldn't be attracted enough to flirt."

Because he was so acutely attuned to the woman next to him, he felt her slight shiver and glanced down in time to see her frown.

"What's wrong?"

"I..." She shook her head and looked around. "It's nothing. I guess I got a chill."

The room was incredibly warm thanks to all the people pressed into the space. He narrowed his eyes and let his tiger senses open up a little more. He'd been ignoring most of his shifter awareness, or narrowing it down to take in only his immediate surroundings, so he wouldn't be over- whelmed. He startled when he let his senses spread out again and realized there was another tiger shifter in the gallery.

Ethan turned toward Cat and the man speaking to her

just as the man glanced at Ethan. The male's dark eyes narrowed and he smiled, a very faint lifting of the lips as he held Ethan's gaze.

Ethan had never seen the man before, but his every instinct jumped to alert. Over the other myriad scents, he couldn't catch the shifter's, but he didn't need to. He knew he was looking at the tiger who'd been stalking Amy.

CHAPTER SEVEN

T he man's smile widened, as if he could read Ethan's thoughts. Without hesitation, Ethan started toward the tiger. He wasn't sure what he would do in the crowded room, but he intended to ensure this male wasn't a threat to his mate.

Before Ethan reached him, though, the man excused himself from Cat and disappeared into the crowds. Ethan cursed and pushed his way through the throng, using his sense of the other man to follow him toward the front door. His pulse thumped with adrenaline and anger. Several of the people Ethan had been talking with earlier tried to stop him, stepping into his path to get his attention. Since some of them could potentially give him work in the future, he didn't want to be rude, so he forced himself to get out of the conversations as politely as he could manage.

By the time he squeezed his way to the front of the

gallery, he knew he'd lost his prey. The other shifter was gone. "Fuck."

He stepped outside onto the sidewalk, into a steady but thin flow of people. Glancing in both directions and allowing his sense of smell to go wide, he tried to locate the other shifter again, but without any luck. The stench from a stack of garbage bags set out for morning collection near a gate next to the gallery masked everything else.

The other male was gone.

Hands on his hips, Ethan hung his head and grunted out another curse. He'd been lax, letting the male get that close to Amy's sister. That close to Amy. He should have kept his attention open, just in case. Especially after detecting the bastard's scent signature near her home.

Stupid mistake. Dangerous and stupid.

Hissing out another curse, he spun to return to the gallery. Amy was waiting for him at the door.

"What happened?" Amy asked, stepping out into the cold before he could reach her. "Who was that? Did you know him?" She rubbed her hands up and down her bare arms. Her silk dress was not intended to keep her warm on a frigid March night.

"Let's go back inside," he said, noticing the gesture. "I prefer that blue on your dress rather than your skin."

She huffed out a half laugh she didn't really feel.

Inside the warm gallery, she pulled Ethan to a quiet corner. "Okay, what was all that about? Who was that guy talking to Cat? And should I be scared?"

He narrowed his eyes. "Why scared?"

"You got very serious and growled under your breath. His smile was terrifying. And even at a distance he…bothered me."

He glanced away, his mouth a flat line, his jaw tight. She couldn't read the expression, but it worried her. She waited patiently, a habit she'd developed with her sister, and like Cat, Ethan didn't leave her waiting for long.

"I need to ask your sister more about him, what he said to her. But…" He met her gaze, his expression unreadable. "Can you tell me why he bothered you? It's important."

She shrugged. "Just instincts I guess. Not entirely sure how to explain it. It's that kind of shiver down your spine you get when you know someone is watching you. And you can tell the difference between a friend trying to catch your attention or someone watching in a creepy way."

"He wasn't looking at you."

"Yeah, well he still gave me that shiver down my spine, creepy feeling. I don't know."

Ethan gripped her shoulders, his hands gentle but firm. "Have you ever felt that before?"

For reasons Amy didn't entirely understand, her pulse kicked up, pounding faster the longer she stared at Ethan. And not for the usual he's-too-gorgeous-to-stare-at-too-long reasons. This had nothing to do with sex and everything to do with fear.

She swallowed hard. "Yes, as a matter of fact. Off and on since that Sunday after the last session where you were modeling. Maybe before that, but I noticed it really strongly on that Saturday." She frowned a little. "It's why I came into that coffee shop." She made a face. "This will sound silly. Especially in New York."

"Say it anyway." He wasn't laughing.

"I felt like I was being stalked. Hunted. It was pretty scary actually. I thought some mugger or rapist had my number and was looking for their chance." She shivered again, though not from cold now.

"It happened on Saturday after the museum, too, didn't it?"

"How did you know that? Ethan, what the hell is going on? You're starting to really scare me now."

He looked around again and dropped his hands. "Let's get Cat. I'll take you both home. I need to make some phone calls."

She didn't move. "I can get Cat home on my own. Explain what's happening."

He huffed out a breath and ran a hand through his hair, the gesture ruffling the thick waves. It should have ruined the effects of his gorgeousness. It only made things worse. Now he looked like he was fresh out of bed and all she could think about was getting him back there. He swallowed visibly, the move drawing her gaze to the strong column of his throat, the lines and curves, the strength. She blinked and scowled, irritated she couldn't look at him without seeing his stunning good looks.

"We need to talk about what happened tonight," he started, hesitantly, "but this isn't something I can discuss in public. And I need more information before I can say more. I...I don't want to scare you."

"Too late. What information do you need?"

"I should get it from those phone calls I mentioned. Let's find Cat."

He took her elbow and guided her through the still-teeming throngs until they spotted Cat in the middle of a small group of bemused looking men in suits. She was gesturing wildly, and the men around her probably had no idea what she was talking about, but she spoke with so much enthusiasm it was hard to resist her.

"Cat," Amy eased between the men around her sister, noting their slightly glazed eyes even as they smiled at the younger woman. "Are you ready to leave?"

"Already? It's early yet. I thought you'd want to stay longer. Or I can get myself home." She glanced at Ethan, hovering just beyond the group of Cat's admirers. "If you want some privacy." She winked.

"No. Come on. Please." She held Cat's gaze for a long moment and an unspoken understanding moved through Cat's expression.

"Right." She grinned at the men. "Sorry, boys. Time to leave. I'll continue the lecture another time."

Some of the men professed their sorrow to see her go as Amy pulled her away. Amy noticed with mild amusement that none of them expressed any interest in a return to the "lecture."

When she rejoined Ethan, he said to Cat, "That man you were talking to earlier, the one in the black suit, short black hair?"

Cat nodded. "The hot guy?" She waggled her eyebrows. "What about him?"

"Did he tell you his name?"

"John Lin. Why?"

She glanced back and forth between Ethan and Amy. Amy shrugged, not sure what to tell her sister.

Ethan nodded at the name. "Thank you. Okay, let's get you both home."

Cat frowned at Amy, her brows creased with her confusion. Amy knew the feeling. She was more than a little confused now too.

Ethan followed them to the coat check and helped them put on their coats, but as Amy watched him she noticed the way his gaze kept jumping to the gallery's floor-to-ceiling windows and the city beyond, how he seemed distracted and edgy. She frowned a question at him that he ignored.

Once outside, he flagged a taxi and ushered her and Cat inside. After a brief hesitation, he climbed in with them. "I want to make sure you get home safely," he murmured. "Make sure you get inside okay."

She narrowed her eyes. If he wasn't scowling so fiercely and clearly preoccupied, she'd think he was angling for an invitation into her apartment. But it was obvious he wasn't thinking about sex. He was worried about something. Something to do with that man Cat had been talking to.

Amy spent the entire ride back to Queens wondering just who the hell John Lin was, and what he had to do with Ethan.

· · ·

Ethan kept silent on the drive to Amy's apartment, considering everything he knew. He wanted to ask Amy and her sister questions about their past, their parents, but until he found out more about this John Lin person, he was afraid anything he said would just scare them.

The fact that Lin knew where Amy lived, however, meant Ethan had no intention of leaving her unguarded tonight.

He didn't know the area around her apartment building well, but he'd find someplace to hunker down for the night so he could keep an eye out for Lin. With luck, he'd know what he needed to by morning and he'd be able to give Amy some answers.

He hoped.

The yellow cab pulled up in front of her building. He climbed out to hold the door for her and Cat, then leaned in and asked the driver to wait a moment until the women made it inside. The driver grumbled about the wait until Ethan slipped him an extra twenty.

Standing beside the taxi, he opened his senses, hunting the area for Lin. Nothing. Amy was still frowning at him—the same expression she'd had since they left the gallery. Cat was already moving into the building, giving he and Amy a moment to say goodnight.

"Do you ever intend to tell me what happened tonight?" she asked.

"I will. If I can. It might be nothing," he tried to reassure her.

"If it was nothing, you wouldn't be freaking out. And neither would I."

He cupped her cheek and breathed out a relieved breath when she didn't pull away from his touch. Her skin was warm, but the night was colder now and a sharp wind had picked up, running down the quiet street.

"I'm sorry our night ended this way," he murmured.

She shrugged a little.

"I'll call you in the morning," he said.

"Fine. Not too early. If Spike lets me sleep in, I will."

He smiled a little at that, the first smile he'd managed since seeing Lin. He brushed his thumb over her cheekbone, savoring the silky skin. For a heartbeat, he forgot the world around him, caught in her eyes, wondering what it would take to bring the playful sparkle from earlier back.

He brushed a soft kiss over her lips. She didn't kiss back, but she didn't turn away either. Which was more than he'd expected.

She murmured goodnight and hurried inside, disappearing into the building's lobby after her sister.

Ethan waited until he heard the inner door click closed then climbed back into the taxi and had the driver drop him on the main street in Forest Hills, half a mile away from her apartment. He returned to her building on quiet back streets so he could move at shifter speed—fast enough that he'd look like a blur to any human who might notice him. Though at that time of night, off the main boulevard, there weren't any people to see him anyway. He slowed to human speed a block from her building so he could concentrate on his other senses.

At the corner across the street from her apartment, he hovered in the shadows of another building and studied the area, hunting for signs of Lin. The streetlights cast a soft yellow glow over the area, the wind whipped down the hill off to his right, funneling between the buildings in a cold stream. Thanks to his fast metabolism and higher body temperature, he didn't mind the chill, but he still pulled his coat up tighter around his neck before stuffing his hands into his pockets.

Minutes passed as he watched and waited. He wasn't entirely sure which apartment was hers since she hadn't invited him up yet, but as he watched lights coming on and turning off in the building, he spotted her in one of the upper floors, just a brief glimpse as she passed by an open window.

Something painful tightened in his gut. He didn't want to analyze the pain, was afraid to look at it too closely, but a sense of loss settled on his shoulders. His tiger objected to that loss instantly, but Ethan was running out of ways to deny what he'd suspected about Amy for weeks.

And if she was a hybrid, she truly would be out of his reach.

Not long after he'd seen her in the window, she startled him by appearing at the building's glass front door. He eased deeper into the shadows so she wouldn't seem him, but still remained close enough to reach her if she needed him.

She walked outside with a yippy poodle pulling at a leash. The infamous Spike, he thought, smiling. The mostly white poodle did seem to suit her name with the spiked collar around her neck. Her curly fur had been shaved and cut to that typical, fluffy poodle style, but along her back they'd colored her in blue stripes, her ears and puff tail were both painted purple, and a ring of thick pink like a necklace wound around her chest. He chuckled quietly. Of course Amy's dog would be painted bright colors.

She moved out to the sidewalk, the dog in the lead scrambling to reach the nearest tree. Amy had changed out of the beautiful silk dress—much to Ethan's disappointment—and now wore a loose pair of jeans, Uggs, and her thick wool coat. Her hair was still up, but more tendrils had escaped to frame her face in a soft halo. She smiled at the dog, murmuring a compliment about the pink color around Spike's collar, and Spike barked once in reply.

His heartbeat pounded hard as he watched Amy. She was so damned beautiful, so soft and tempting. Everything about her called to him, and he flexed his hand inside his coat pockets to keep from crossing the street to her.

As Spike nosed around a tree a few yards from the apartment, Amy suddenly looked up, staring right at the spot where Ethan was hiding. Ethan froze, not so much as breathing. She wouldn't be able to see him in the dark where he stood behind the angle of the neighboring building. Yet she frowned and narrowed her eyes, staring hard into the shadows that enveloped him. In the next instant, she turned away from him to scowl up the hill along the street opposite him. She gasped and Spike began to whine at the exact moment Ethan felt the familiar sense of another tiger shifter approaching. He started for Amy even as he followed her gaze…

In time to see a huge white Amur tiger emerging from the shadows.

CHAPTER EIGHT

Amy couldn't believe what she was seeing. She was so stunned, so beyond shocked, she stood like an idiot just blinking.

A tiger. In Queens. On the street. A fucking tiger!

Then in a blur of motion, the tiger charged her. She started to scream, choking on the sound, and had time to take a single step back when a large dark shape materialized in front of her. Ethan? He'd stepped between her and the tiger as if he'd emerged out of thin air.

She didn't have time for that to sink in before she realized he was standing *between* her and a *tiger*. She opened her mouth to say something, to warn him or scream but before she could utter a grunt the tiger was on him. They moved so fast, she didn't even see it happen. One minute Ethan stood between her and danger, the next he wasn't there anymore.

Instincts finally broke through her paralysis. She

scooped up a quivering, growling Spike and charged back up the hill toward her apartment building. She'd left her cellphone upstairs but it was early enough that one of the neighbors would be awake. They'd let her use their phone to call 911. She glanced back toward the sounds of hissing and grunting, but all she could see was a blur, like smudges on the shadows that changed positions so fast she could almost imagine nothing was there.

She shoved inside the glass entry door, her key already in hand. That and Spike's collar were the only vaguely sharp things she had on hand for weapons, and Spike's collar wasn't really sharp. Her pepper spray was in her coat pocket—something she usually didn't carry in this neighborhood, but after the way Ethan had been acting tonight, she'd felt the need for a little extra security on her walk. She wasn't sure if pepper spray would hurt a tiger—especially one that moved so fucking fast—but it might help her get Ethan to safety. Then they could call the cops, and animal control.

First, though, she had to get Spike safe. She cursed as the lock for the door into the lobby refused to give. Wiggling her key, she watched the area just outside the glass door, hunting for those moving smudges. She was so terrified, her fingers slipped on the keys, giving her a thin slice along her first finger. She muttered another curse as she jerked the key and pushed it in again, desperately jiggling the damned thing until the lock finally gave.

Just as the smudged flew into sight.

There was a moment where the smudges stilled, long enough for her to actually see what was happening. To her relief, Ethan was still alive—thank, God! How was that possible?—but the pale tiger was still there, too, it's huge mouth opened to reveal its terrifyingly sharp teeth. The tiger stalked closer to Ethan, slowly now. Ethan held his ground, his stance low, his knees bent as if waiting to take the tiger's attack.

She pushed Spike inside the lobby, over the poodle's yip of protest, pulled the heavy door closed again, leaving her key in the lock so she could open it faster this time around. Then hand in her pocket, she eased outside again. Her heart was pounding so hard she could barely breathe. She could feel her pulse throbbing in her throat and the thick clutch of fear nearly choked her. She'd never experienced this level of fear before. Something close once, the phone call that had brought her to her knees literally. But the panic that followed that call was slow to come, rising only after the initial hit of grief and denial had felled her.

Now panic rode her as hard as fear. She could barely make her legs move, her knees were shaking so hard. Sweat slicked her hands around the canister of pepper spray. She inched toward the tiger and Ethan, who were circling each other slowly enough for her to watch them, hoping she could actually depress the release on the canister without dropping the damned thing.

The wind blew steadily but harder gusts pushed between the buildings, one so strong it nearly dislodged her bun, leaving it hanging off the side of her head. Jesus, what if she used the pepper spray in this and a gust blew it back into her or Ethan's face? She had to take the chance. It was the only weapon she had. But a new surge of adrenaline made her arms quiver. Edging closer to the side of the building, trying to adjust her position so she was downwind, she kept her gaze on the growling, hissing pair.

She blinked. Ethan was hissing and growling too. He sounded just like the damned tiger. What the ever-loving hell?

The thought had barely occurred to her when the two flew together again, another blur of movement creating smudges on the shadows. She cursed and held up her pepper spray in front of her like a shield as she watched for an opening. She couldn't move fast enough, but maybe the element of surprise would help her reach the tiger before it noticed her.

Another break in the fight, when Ethan seemed to leap away from the animal, landing in a crouch a few feet away from it, and the tiger stopped moving, its front body lowered as it prepared to launch. Ethan was a little more downwind now. She might not get a better chance.

Terror made her movements jerky and awkward but she forced herself forward, as close to the tiger as she dared, her spray raised. The tiger turned toward her, its golden eyes glittering almost yellow in the darkness. And she could swear the beast *smiled* at her. The expression froze her like a fucking deer in headlights for a split second. She heard Ethan shout her name, watched the tiger's form into blur as it flashed from its place several yards away to stand right in front of her. The huge creature leaned in as if sniffing her, grunted as it did so, and Amy finally pushed the button on her still-raised pepper spray.

She'd barely released the line of toxic stuff when strong

arms wrapped around her. She blinked and she was standing inside the entryway with Ethan holding her behind his back, his attention outside the glass door and the tiger. The beast had leapt to the opposite side of the street in that same moment, and from her vantage, Amy couldn't tell if the spray had even hit it. The animal swiped one huge front paw across its nose, sneezed hard, and shook its head. Then it stared at her and Ethan, only the thin glass door between it and them. For a weird, detached moment, she had the sense of being the animal in a zoo, behind the glass of a too-small cage, while the tiger watched them from the outside like a zoo patron.

If she hadn't been so utterly terrified, she might have laughed at the image.

The tiger stared a long moment, and Amy was certain now its eyes were glowing yellow. Then she blinked and the beast was gone, vanished as if it hadn't been there.

"Where did it go?" she forced out around her dry throat and thumping pulse. Her body was trembling so hard she could barely hold herself upright.

"He's gone," Ethan said.

His voice was a low grunt, almost guttural. She'd never heard him sound that way before.

"You're sure?" she asked. "How can you tell?"

He finally turned to face her. She gasped at his expression. He looked hard and dangerous, deadly. And there was a very very faint yellow glow in the depths of his dark eyes.

She had to be seeing things, going into shock from the trauma of being attacked by a fucking tiger. She shook her head to dislodge the image and when she looked at him again, his beautiful brown eyes were their usual color, no strange show of yellow light.

"I can't sense him anymore," Ethan said. "Are you okay?" He held her shoulders gently, studying her face, a frown creasing his brows. "Did he hurt you?"

"He didn't have time to. Thanks for…" She paused. "What the hell just happened? How did you move that fast? How did the tiger? What the hell is a fucking tiger doing in Queens?" She straightened her shoulders. "Shit, we need to get inside and call animal control. That thing might hurt someone else."

She reached for the door, but Ethan didn't loosen his hold on her arms. "Animal control can't help with that kind of tiger. And he won't hurt anyone else. He was here for you."

"Huh?" It was the best she could manage. Nothing made sense and her brain was doing that frozen thing again so she couldn't think enough to form a coherent question.

"Let's get inside. Get Spike upstairs and you safe. I'll explain everything then."

"Finally," she managed to grunt.

It only occurred to her in the elevator, with Spike shaking in her arms, the dog staring at Ethan and releasing a steady low growl at him, that maybe inviting Ethan up to her apartment wasn't a great idea. But since he'd just fought a tiger for her, she'd give him the benefit of the doubt. And if anything went wrong…

She still had her pepper spray.

. . .

C at answered the door before Amy could get her key in the lock—she'd dropped them on the marble floor in a clatter of metal while trying. Twice.

Cat looked between Amy, Ethan, and the still growling Spike and her brows snapped down. "What's happening? Are you guys okay? Why is Ethan here?"

Amy motioned her sister out of the way so she and Ethan could step inside, then she closed and locked the door behind her, slipping the security chain into place. Handing Spike off to Cat, who continued to hold her rather than putting her on the ground, Amy took her canister of pepper spray out of her pocket and purposefully kept it in her hand as she took off her coat and hung it up. She looked Ethan over. He stood at a careful distance, perfectly still, watching her and waiting.

"Take your coat off," she said. "We have some things to discuss. Like why I shouldn't go call animal control."

"Animal control?" Cat asked. "What the hell?"

"Long story." She glanced at Ethan from the corner of her eye. "And I suspect an even longer explanation. Could you put Spike in your room? She's a little freaked out and she'll be happier on your bed, away from Ethan."

Cat scowled at Ethan. "Why is she freaking out around Ethan?"

"It's not him." Amy shook her head and waved a hand. "He's just a stranger to her. Just… I'll tell you everything in a minute. Calm her down. I'll put the kettle on for some tea."

Her sister disappeared into her bedroom talking in

soothing tones to Spike while Amy led Ethan down the corridor to the living room. The carpet runner over the hardwood floors muffled their footsteps, Ethan's nearly silent, which surprised her for some reason. He was so large and solid, the fact that he moved so quietly was... disconcerting. And reminded her how fast he'd moved while fighting the tiger.

She nearly tripped at the edge of the carpet with that thought. Ethan had just been fighting a *tiger*. A figgin' tiger, for god's sake. He was supposed to be an accountant and a model. An unnaturally gorgeous one, but still... The part of her logical brain trained by her infinitely practical mother could not get her head around what she'd just witnessed.

Their comforting living room with its splashes of color, haphazardly arranged rugs, cozy cream-colored walls, and open airiness helped Amy regain some of her equilibrium. She pulled in the lingering smell of the scented candle they were using this month—honeysuckle—letting the familiarity settle her further. Her artwork hung in pretty arrangements on the walls, mixed with some of Cat's favorite science posters—the one of Einstein with his tongue sticking out was one of Amy's favorites, too. The bookshelves that framed the couch were stuffed with art and science books around a significant collection of romance, science fiction, and real crime paperbacks. Under the huge window on the opposite side of the living room, Spike's doggy bed sat comfortably near the heater.

The whole room was eclectic, a little messy with some clothes scattered on the floor and dishes still on the oval coffee table, and perfect as far as Amy was concerned. This was her space. She was safe in her space. This was real. She could take whatever Ethan had to say surrounded by the security of this reality.

She gestured to their large, overstuffed couch against the wall facing the open kitchen, and Ethan sat. They still hadn't spoken since they'd come up in the elevator. She stood with her back to the kitchen's raised bar, facing Ethan, her arms crossed. She still had her pepper spray in hand.

The silence stretched, but she didn't rush to fill it as she studied him. The tension between them was palpable. Ethan leaned back against the couch, his body relaxed and non-threatening. Like he was trying to prove he was harmless. Since she'd just seen him take on a supernaturally fast tiger, *harmless* was not the impression of him she had anymore.

"What were you doing out there?" she finally asked, breaking the silence. "You were close when the tiger attacked. Why?"

He adjusted his position on the couch, sighing. "I was watching out for you. Guarding your building."

She continued to stare without reacting to that outwardly. "You thought I was in danger?"

He nodded.

She considered that. "Because of John Lin?"

"Yes."

"What does Lin have to do with the tiger?"

"It's complicated."

"Does that mean you won't answer?"

"No. I'll explain. It's just…complicated."

She was watching closely so she saw his wince. "Are you hurt?"

"Nothing that hasn't healed already."

She straightened a little. "What does that mean?"

"He was an excellent fighter and I took a few hits but I heal really fast."

"How and why and what the fuck are you?"

"Can we wait until your sister is here? This affects her, too."

"No. Explain it to me. Now." She wasn't sure she wanted Cat in the room yet. She needed answers from Ethan before she could decide if she'd allow her sister around him or not.

"Can you tell me a little more about your parents? It's important. I promise."

She scowled. "What about them? What do they have to do with John Lin and that tiger?"

"Humor me."

She rolled her eyes and huffed out a grunt of annoyance. "They were architects, went to college together. Were best friends before getting married."

"Were?"

"They died seven years ago in a train accident in Europe." She swallowed and dropped her gaze to the floor. "They liked to travel."

"I'm sorry for your loss," he murmured.

She waved away the sympathy. She didn't have the energy for it right now. "Back to Lin."

"I need to ask Cat a question about him."

"What?"

"You...felt him, right? You knew he was different. You...sense me, too?"

She nodded, narrowing her eyes.

"Has Cat ever experienced the same thing? That you know of?"

"No idea." She scowled and looked back toward the direction of the bedrooms. "Cat," she called loudly enough for her sister to hear through the closed bedroom door.

Cat jogged into the living room a moment later. "Spike is doing better now," she said.

She hovered just inside the living room, her gaze jumping between Amy and Ethan. She'd changed after they got home, donning yoga pants and an oversized t-shirt with a pithy science pun on it—something about the nerd side having Pi. She'd combed out the gel in her hair so her pixie cut framed her face in soft blond tufts. As she stared at Amy, questions plane in her eyes, she looked both younger and somehow older than her age—a little scared, but also far too familiar with the harsher side of reality.

Amy hated that her sister had had to grow up fast. She hated even more that she was bringing her sister into something Amy didn't even understand herself yet.

"Cat, did that guy you were hitting on tonight, John Lin, did he feel weird to you?" Amy asked.

"Weird how?"

"Like...did you experience a tingling along your spine or an awareness of him before you saw him? Anything like that?"

"No. Why? Should I have?"

They both turned to Ethan. He was frowning at Cat

without actually looking at her, as if he were deep in thought and his gaze just happened to be turned toward Cat.

He blinked and focused on Amy, still seeming unhappy about something. "Was there anything unusual about your parents?" he asked. "Did one of them disappear from time to time or have to take vacations alone?"

"What the hell are you asking?" Amy said. "Are you saying one of them was having an affair?"

"No, not that." He paused. His gaze jumped back and forth between her and Cat, his frown deepening as he studied them. "Are you… You're full siblings?"

Amy's scowl turned fierce. "What the hell does that have to do with anything?"

"Are you?" he pressed.

"No. We're half. Same mother, different fathers. But my biological father has never been part of my life. The only father I've ever known is the one I call…called dad."

She swallowed hard and looked away from Ethan, blinking to hold back emotion. When Cat wrapped her arms around Amy and laid her head on Amy's shoulder, Amy smiled a little. She squeezed her sister's arm and pulled in a deep breath. They'd been a very close family. Seven years wasn't nearly long enough to get over that loss, and her emotions were already churning at the surface thanks to the strange and terrifying night.

When she felt in control enough to finish the conversation, she said, "What does any of this have to do with Lin and the tiger?"

"Tiger?" Cat said, leaning back from Amy to look at the side of her face. "What tiger?"

Amy sighed, knowing Cat would keep at her if she didn't just explain. "While I was out walking Spike, a giant tiger attacked me. Ethan fought it off. And I pepper sprayed it. I think. Damned thing moved so fast I'm not sure. Anyway, it ran off."

Cat dropped her arms and took a step away from Amy, her eyes narrowed, her brows creased with a frown. "Okay, so a tiger… I could come up with some logical excuse for that. It's weird and improbable but not impossible. This is New York. You spraying it with pepper spray is perfectly logical, because what the hell else would you use to fend off a tiger? It running away from the stench I could even believe." She turned and faced Ethan. "You conveniently being there, I can come up with a logical—albeit kind of creepy—explanation for that. But you fighting a tiger… I don't see any kind of weapon on you."

"I don't have one," he murmured.

"So barehanded?"

He nodded.

"And you're not injured?" Cat said, disbelief thick in her tone.

"He was apparently," Amy said, "but he healed."

Cat's frown only deepened. "Healed? Already? From a *tiger* attack?"

Amy faced Ethan too, waiting expectantly. He shifted on the couch a little, adjusting his position, looking distinctly uncomfortable.

"It's…complicated."

"So you've said," Amy pointed out with her last shred of patience.

"Just give me a few more minutes. I promise I will get around to all that. Can you tell me anything about your biological father?" he asked.

Amy huffed out a breath and glanced at Cat. Cat shrugged.

"Fine," Amy said, half snarling in frustration. "My mom ended up pregnant while she was in her senior year of college. When she told the guy, he denied it was possible to get her pregnant." She rolled her eyes. "Mom said he was very nice about it. Not angry, not accusatory. Just said it wasn't physically possible for him to have gotten her pregnant. They weren't a couple or anything, just occasional 'sex buddies.' Mom's words."

Cat made a gagging noise and Amy flashed her sister a half-smile.

"Do you know his name?" Ethan asked, quietly.

"It's probably with his contact information in our safety deposit box."

Ethan straightened, leaning forward a little. "You have his contact information?"

"He told my mom if she ever needed him for anything, or needed help with the baby, to get in touch. He was completely convinced there was no way I could have been his, but he offered to help her if she needed it."

"And she was *sure* he was the father?"

Amy gave him a deadpan stare. "If my mother said he was the father, he was the father."

He raised his hands, palms forward in a surrender gesture. "Did she ever contact him?"

"No. She got pissed off that he denied being my father

since she was in fact pregnant, and he'd been the only man she'd slept with for several months. She was stubborn, so she decided she'd do things on her own. Our dad was her best friend at the time, so he dove right in to help. About a year and a half after I was born, they got married."

"They fell in love," Cat said in a sing-songy voice.

Amy smiled softly at Cat's imitation of their mother.

"So then," Ethan said, "Cat is your father's child?"

"I am," Cat said, giving him a pointed look because he'd addressed the question to Amy instead of her.

"And your father," he said to Amy, "your biological one…you've never met him?"

"Never even asked his name."

"Why not?"

She shrugged. "It felt like an insult to my dad. The man who really stepped up to take care of me. The man who loved my mom. I didn't need the sperm donor's name. I had a dad."

"Damn straight," Cat said with a sharp nod of approval.

Amy made a face. "I suppose if I needed a kidney or something I'd hunt him down." She glanced at Cat from the corner of her eyes. "I actually considered opening the envelope with his information after our parents died."

"You did?" Cat said. "You never told me that."

"I changed my mind. I didn't want him to think I was looking for a father to replace the one I'd lost." She brushed at an invisible wrinkle in her t-shirt. "I couldn't ever do that."

The silence in the room stretched for another long

moment. Then Amy pulled in a deep breath and shook off the sadness. They had other things to talk about right now.

"So now." She met Ethan's troubled gaze again. "Can you finally explain what the hell is going on?"

"Not all of it."

She opened her mouth to argue, but he hurried on.

"I don't know who John Lin is yet," he said, "or why he's here. I need to call someone first."

"Can you explain *anything*?"

"I'm pretty sure I can explain why your biological father didn't believe he got your mother pregnant. I think he was…like me."

She jerked her hands up, exasperated. "What does that mean? Ethan spit it the hell out or get out of my apartment."

"I'm a tiger shifter. And I'm pretty sure your father was, too."

CHAPTER NINE

Ethan held Amy's gaze even as she and Cat stared at him. He wasn't sure what kind of reaction he was expecting from them, so he held his breath and waited.

Cat turned away and headed into the open kitchen. "I'm getting an orange juice if anyone wants something to drink."

"I'm fine," Amy said, her gaze still on Ethan.

"Should we call the cops on him yet," Cat said as she opened the fridge.

"Not yet," Amy said.

He didn't react to the underlying threat. "Look I know this sounds strange and impossible—"

"It is," Cat called from the kitchen. She hopped up onto the counter and stared out at him over the bar, glass of orange juice in hand. "Shapeshifters don't exist in the real world and it's physically impossible for a human being to alter their form."

"I'm not a human being," Ethan said. "And there are other species on the planet that change. Fish that go from female to male when necessary. Caterpillars turn into butterflies."

"Do you spin a cocoon?" Cat asked, completely serious.

"No."

"How does it work then?"

He shrugged. "It's easier if I just shift so you know I'm serious. Otherwise, you aren't going to believe me." He held Amy's gaze. "You need to believe me. That tiger who attacked, he was Lin. I don't know for sure what he wants from you, but I doubt he's just going to go away after weeks of stalking you and coming after you tonight."

Amy held silent, still staring. She'd barely changed positions since he'd announced he was a tiger shifter. She stood leaning against the kitchen bar, her arms crossed, the mace canister still in her hand, her mouth a straight line. Her scent was a chaotic mix of so many emotions he couldn't begin to parse it all out. But the strongly bitter burnt coffee flavor of her disbelief overlay it all.

After a prolonged silence, she finally said, "Why do you think the tiger was Lin?"

"I could sense him as a shifter even before he appeared. We can feel others of our kind when they're around. And his scent confirmed his identity."

"I want to watch him try to shift," Cat said. "Once he fails, we can kick him out and call the cops."

Amy's brows quirked up at that. Ethan pressed his lips together so he wouldn't smile at Cat's comment, afraid they'd both misinterpret the gesture. But Cat's bluntness did cut to the chase and he hoped it would push Amy.

She tilted her head to one side, studying him. "You think you can turn into a tiger here? Right in front of us?"

"I can. It'll be scary to watch since you're not used to it. And I'll have to strip since I don't have a change of clothes here." When she frowned at him, he clarified, "If I shift while I'm dressed, it shreds my clothing."

"They don't just magically vanish and reappear?" she said, sarcasm heavy in her tone.

"Not for tigers." He watched her eyes narrow, letting that hint sink in. The world was a bigger and scarier place than most humans knew. Which was best for everyone. Most of the time. Right now, Amy would be safer if she realized there were things in the world she'd never imagined.

"Fine," she said with a little shrug. "Try to turn into a tiger."

He glanced past her to Cat briefly. "You're okay with me stripping?"

"I've seen enough of Amy's sketches to take a little male nudity," she said wryly.

To Amy, he said, "I can stand in the hall to change so you don't have to watch the shift. You'll still know it's me, but you won't have to see the…messy part."

"I want to watch," Cat said. "I won't trust this unless I see you actually change."

"You heard the scientist," Amy said. "You can change right here in front of us—or try to."

He stood and moved the coffee table aside. "I'll shift as

quickly as I can, but it will still take a few minutes. When I'm in my tiger form, it's still me. I won't attack you or anything. I'll understand you when you speak to me. I'll just be in a different shape."

"Can you talk that way?" Amy asked, still sounding like she didn't believe a word he was saying.

"No. Physically, at that point, I'm a tiger. But I can respond to yes and no questions if you want to ask anything."

"Right."

He shrugged out of his suit jacket and laid it across the back of the couch, then toed out of shoes and stripped off the remainder of his clothing. When he was naked, he faced Amy again. "You're ready?"

She seemed to be making an effort to keep her gaze on his, which might have amused him under different circumstances. Though her expression hadn't changed, there was a faint whiff of her desire wafting through the riot of her other feelings. He pulled in that allspice smell as subtly as he could, savoring it even though he knew it was pointless now.

Amy would have many more options going forward. He tried not to react to that thought. It wasn't the time for jealousy or fear or anger—not from him. But his tiger hissed quietly at the thought that his people would take her away now. That he'd be denied his mate because she wasn't human. He never should have gotten involved with her. He'd know from the beginning this couldn't end well. Her being a hybrid wasn't exactly what he'd been expecting, but the results would be the same. He'd lose her and there was nothing he could do about it.

He forced himself to focus on the current crisis. They'd deal with the future when it happened. But the fact that she still reacted to him, still wanted him even though he was certain she thought he was crazy…that was a pleasure he couldn't deny himself.

Especially now when it was likely all he'd ever get.

At his continued hesitation, she waved a hand and said, "Get on with it. I'm tired. If I have to fill out police forms tonight, I want to get started soon."

He couldn't resist smiling at that. Watching her eyes widen slightly and the allspice flavor in her scent increase made his smile widen.

"Don't say I didn't warn you," he said. Then he let his tiger out.

For long minutes nothing happened and Amy knew she'd have to accept that the man she was so fiercely attracted to was actually crazy. That knowledge didn't prevent her from staring at him, taking in every glorious inch of him, though. He was a stunning male specimen, with muscles in all the right places, proportioned perfectly, the angles and lines like a statue of a god, chiseled and hard and sleek. She made an attempt to view him with her artist's eye, the way she'd managed to in the studio once she got started sketching and painting. But without the barrier of her canvas in front of her, the act of seeing him naked was infinitely more personal and distracting.

She glanced back at Cat, feeling very weird about having her sister here for this part. Cat stared without showing any reaction but for a slight furrow between her brows, her lips pursed just a little. Amy recognized the look. It was her *thinking* look. She was concentrating, her mind caught in thoughts too complex for Amy. This was Cat the scientist, the one who could lose weight just from thinking. Cat was studying Ethan like she might an equation on her whiteboard.

Amy almost laughed at that. She had no idea how her sister could stare at the perfection that was a naked Ethan and think about math, but the fact that she was made the situation just a little less uncomfortable for Amy.

She turned to face him again, in time to see his muscles start to twitch.

It started in his shoulders and biceps, moving along his arms and over his pectorals. Then the twitching moved everywhere. Flashes of what looked like fur ran over his skin, rising and falling only to rise again. He convulsed and folded forward, his body crunching and shivering, things breaking and reforming.

Amy couldn't close her eyes, couldn't look away, couldn't believe what she was seeing.

She watched the rushes of russet and white fur cover his skin as his face reshaped, his nose and mouth elongating into a muzzle, sharp teeth visible. The sounds were almost worse than the visuals, the crunching and breaking, the wetter sounds that made her want to gag. Surprisingly, there wasn't any smell—given the look of it, she would have expected to smell blood and worse, but the pleasant honeysuckle scent of her living room remained a strangely discordant note to the impossible scene before her. From Cat's bedroom, Amy could hear Spike growling and yipping, her bark growing frantic—her guarding-the-house bark. Amy wanted to go comfort the dog, but she was mesmerized, frozen in place.

She couldn't even look away long enough to see her sister's reaction to this, this…scientifically impossible demonstration.

Though she knew, logically, that the process didn't take an eternity, the passage of just a few minutes had never felt so unending. But as excruciatingly long as it felt, it all seemed to end just as fast, over in the blink of an eye.

And a giant cat stood in her living room, shaking out its fur.

Swallowing hard, Amy gripped the bar counter at her back with one hand and held her pepper spray at the ready, coming up just a little on her toes, preparing to run even though she was pretty sure she shouldn't tempt the predator staring at her by bolting.

The tiger settled on its haunches, its thick tail thumping quietly on the floor, and just stared at her with dark golden eyes that were…aware.

Maybe that was the wrong word. Human seemed wrong, too. Because a wild animal was definitely staring at her from those eyes, but there was logic there, too, consciousness that went beyond anything she'd seen in an animal before.

Except, she realized, for the tiger who'd attacked earlier. The whole thing had happened so fast, and she'd been so terrified, she hadn't had time to process everything she'd witnessed. But now, staring at the creature that used to be Ethan, Amy had a sharp memory of the white tiger looking at her through the glass of the front door, staring with eyes that were much more aware than they should have been.

And she realized as she held this animal's gaze that Ethan was there in those golden depths. The part of him that called to her artist's soul, the essence of him that had been so enthralling in the art studio was still there. Just in the shape of a huge tiger.

"Bengal," Cat murmured.

The sound snapped Amy out of her shock. She glanced at Cat, keeping the tiger in her peripheral vision. "You okay?"

Cat nodded, her eyes narrowed, her lips pursed. Amy might have burst out laughing if the situation hadn't been so weird. Cat was studying the tiger, her head tilting back and forth as she took him in.

"Morphological adjustment, probably at cellular level," Cat muttered under her breath. "Visually identical. Eyes different."

Amy let out a sigh, some of the tension in her muscles easing. Cat wasn't even afraid. She was too busy analyzing and trying to figure out how it worked.

Amy looked fully at Ethan again…or the tiger that was also Ethan. "You're in there and can understand us?"

He nodded.

She swallowed. "You were right. Not pretty."

"Fascinating," Cat added.

"Yeah, well. I guess this means we have to believe you about the tiger shifters, doesn't it?"

He grunted, a sort of chuffing sound that was surprisingly easy to interpret.

"Are you dangerous like this?"

A more hesitant nod.

"This is a hard way to carry on a conversation. Can you change back or do you need time to…rest?"

In answer, he stood and the convulsions started again. She raised a hand to stop him, but it was too late. Rather than watch the process in reverse, she hurried into the kitchen. She set her pepper spray canister down for the first time since returning to the apartment and splashed cold water on her face at the sink, ignoring the damage that would do to the makeup she hadn't had a chance to remove yet, then dried with a paper towel. Her stomach heaved a few times, but the urge to barf wasn't as strong as she might have expected. Shock. It must be shock.

For the second time in one night. This wasn't doing her equilibrium much good.

She glanced at Cat who continued to watch Ethan with her brow furrowed, her attention intense. Amy rolled her eyes. Only her sister could see something like this and not react.

"You okay?" Cat asked without facing her.

That surprised Amy into answering. "Better than I'd have expected, given what I just watched. You don't seem bothered."

"Not. Too fascinating. Shouldn't be able to… Wow. Some obvious mass differences. What happens to the additional…" She trailed off, as if she wasn't really aware she'd been speaking aloud.

Amy waited with her back to the living room until Cat sat back with another, "Huh…" before turning to face Ethan again. He was leaning over, pulling on his pants.

To her surprise, she found herself admiring his beautiful form, the movement of his muscles, almost as if what she'd just witnessed hadn't happened. How could she still find him so damned sexy when she'd just watched him do something impossible and very very not pretty?

Silently berating herself for being an idiot, she said, "Does that hurt? Changing?"

"No." He straightened and slipped back into his shirt, buttoning it closed but not tucking it into his pants. He rolled up the sleeves to just below his elbows, displaying his muscled forearms.

Amy sighed when her stomach clenched in excited little ripples. Something felt very wrong about lusting after him now.

"Excuse me. I need to work out some figures," Cat said. She jumped off the counter and hurried back to her room. She poked her head back out of the hallway to say, "Don't leave before I have a chance to ask more questions." Then she was gone.

"Don't let Spike out," Amy called after her. She shook her head at Cat's shouted but distracted agreement. "Now you've done it," Amy said to Ethan. "She'll be up all night trying to work out the physics of shapeshifting."

"Sorry?" Ethan said and asked at the same time. He

moved the coffee table back into place, lifting and settling the heavy piece of furniture easily.

She frowned. "Just how strong are you?"

"Very," he said with a shrug.

Well that explained how he could fight off a tiger bare-handed. "Easy to kill or hard?"

"Hard. But it's possible."

After the attack earlier, she really wanted to know, "How?"

His mouth ticked up in a half-smile. "For me or for Lin?"

"Potentially both," she said in all seriousness. Although, she wasn't nearly as worried about Ethan as she should be. She blamed that on shock as well. It had been a pretty traumatic night so far. "Does it require silver bullets?"

"That's just for werewolves. We can be killed in the usual ways, if enough of the usual ways are inflicted before we heal."

She ignored the werewolf comment. "How fast do you heal?"

"Very."

"How seriously did that other tiger injure you earlier?" She looked over his clothes. They still looked intact, but maybe she'd missed something. He'd been wearing a coat over his suit when he'd fought the tiger. It hadn't occurred to her to check his coat for rips and cuts.

"Not nearly as seriously as he could have. I got the strange sense that he wasn't trying to kill me. Mostly he just gave me bruises and a cracked rib that fully healed just now when I shifted."

"Shifting helps you heal?"

He nodded. "It can complicate more serious injuries, but it helps the basic ones."

That was…terrifying, amazing, weird. Handy. She shook her head and got back to the important part. "You said you can be killed in the usual ways. What *usual* ways?"

"Decapitation is a sure-fire option. Enough ordinary bullets in the right places. Keep us underwater long enough, we'll drown. Cutting out our hearts pretty much guarantees it, too. That kind of thing."

Her head spun. She braced herself on the counter to keep focused. "Usual ways. Right."

He was still standing, but outside of putting her coffee table back into place, he hadn't moved away from the couch. She was extremely grateful for the space.

"What else?" she asked.

"What else do you want to know?"

"What else can you do?"

"The speed you saw earlier."

She snorted.

"And our hearing is significantly better than a human's. So is our vision and sense of smell."

"How good are they?"

"We have excellent night vision, and I can pick up a lot more through smell than a human could—like the way I could identify Lin in tiger form. Spike and I are more alike that way than I am with a human."

"Sure." Because of course that all made perfect sense in a world that no longer made sense.

He narrowed his eyes. "Amy, if your father is a tiger, it means you're in danger from my people."

"Why?" She had to believe in tiger shifters now—unless she was dreaming. She pinched her hand just to be sure, and winced at the pain. Nope, not dreaming. But the idea that her biological father had been a mythical being still seemed impossible.

Ethan ran a hand through his hair. "We… We're on the verge of extinction as a species. Females are very rare, our birthrates are low. And until very recently, we thought matings between humans and tigers couldn't happen."

She nodded. "Ah. You think that's why my birth father didn't think I was his." It was an explanation. Not one she'd ever have imagined, but if she believed in tiger shifters, maybe she could believe the rest.

"We know hybrids like you exist now," Ethan continued. "Though not how many of you there are. And we know there are some humans who can have children with tigers. That tingling sensation you feel when Lin is around. Or when I'm around… It turns out hybrids can sense tiger shifters. We can't sense the hybrids, but they can tell when one of my kind is nearby."

"You think that's what I'm doing?"

"I'm almost certain. It explains a lot, doesn't it?"

"Hmm." She wasn't sure what to think anymore. "Why would I be in danger from your people?"

"The presence of hybrids in our community is still

controversial. Some see them as the answer to the extinction issue. Others…”

“Don’t?” she asked.

He grunted and glanced away. She waited him out.

“There are those among my people who think the hybrids will drive us to extinction faster by diluting our bloodlines,” he said quietly. “Those tigers aren’t above violence toward the hybrids. The tigers who see hybrids as saviors…they aren’t above pushing their attentions.”

“Both options sound pretty crappy,” Amy said.

He shrugged. “I can’t argue with that.” After a moment, he frowned and said, “The other hybrids, even the ones who couldn’t shift, they had good night vision and sense of smell, like a full tiger.”

“Are you asking if I have good night vision?”

“Yes.”

“Yes,” she said. “Excellent. I don’t know if my sense of smell is unusual. I am sensitive to smells, but not to the point that the city drives me nuts. I do have really good hearing.”

“How good?”

She gestured toward the back of the apartment. “I can hear Cat talking to herself in the bedroom right now. And Spike just jumped up onto her bed because she’s not paying attention. Spike makes a little grunting sound when she does that.”

“I heard that, too. Wondered what she was grunting about. You never noticed your hearing was…unusual?”

“It’s never come up.” She thought back over her life, seeing things she’d considered normal in a strange new light now. "Not sure I've ever told anyone how good my hearing is actually."

"That's probably best."

"Are you good or evil?"

It was a weird question, and not the next most important one to ask, but she felt the need to know. Especially since it seemed she might be related to these beings by blood. She didn't really believe in her mother's god, in angels and demons or the supernatural of any kind. She was an artist who hadn't believed in real muses until she'd met Ethan. It was one place she and her sister were very much alike. They were both very grounded in reality, especially after their parents' deaths. Facing the "reality" that was a tiger shifter had shaken up that solid world view, and now she was rethinking a lot of the things she'd assumed to be true.

"Tiger shifters are…like humans. Some are good. Some aren't. Some are extremely dangerous." He winced. "Okay, we're all potentially dangerous, but some tigers are more dangerous than others."

"You?"

"Only to bad guys." He tried to smile but the expression fell away.

"You're worried about how I see you now, aren't you?" That wasn't the next most important question either, but she could see by the way he held his shoulders and the tightness in his jaw, he cared about how she felt, how she would deal with all this.

"We can talk about that later. You believe me, though?"

"Ha! How could I not?"

"You believe Lin is dangerous?"

"Since you claim that was him earlier? Yeah, I believe he's dangerous." She frowned. "Did I really chase him away with pepper spray? That seems…less likely now that I know he wasn't just an ordinary tiger." She'd already doubted the power of mace on an ordinary tiger, nonetheless something decidedly *not* ordinary.

"With our sensitive senses, yeah, pepper spray is still a deterrent. Its affects won't last as long on us, but it's a good distraction."

"He let us go," she said. It wasn't a question.

"He did. He could have killed us both."

She shivered and hugged her arms around herself, a trembling of delayed terror tightening in her stomach.

"Do you have more questions?" Ethan asked quietly. "If not, I need to make a call."

"Who?"

"Someone who might be able to tell me who Lin is. That might help us understand what he wants with you."

Amy swallowed hard. "Make your calls. I need to check on Cat and Spike."

She left the kitchen and went back to Cat's bedroom, her limbs shaking as the rush of fear and shock took their toll on her.

Cat barely acknowledged her existence. Her sister's full concentration was on one of her whiteboards and the thick, opened book she held in one hand. Amy glanced at the board and book but couldn't make heads or tails of what Cat was doing so she didn't try. She'd learned a long time ago not to hurt her brain trying to decipher Cat's complex thinking process. When Cat had it figured out, she'd explain in simple terms Amy could understand. Until then, there was no point in disrupting her sister. Cat wouldn't be able to come out of her own thoughts just then anyway.

Amy sat on the bed next to Spike and scratched her behind the ears until her purple puff-ball tail wagged. Cat had added a thick pink ring of color around the dog's shoulders just yesterday, making it look like Spike had a necklace.

"You doing okay, girl?" she murmured. Spike licked her knee in response. Amy sighed. At least one of them was recovering. She glanced at Cat. Okay, two of them. Cat didn't even seem worried about the whole tiger thing.

Amy on the other hand… In a matter of hours, her world had turned upside down. There were tiger shifters in the world. One of them was stalking her. She'd been falling hard for another. And it was just possible her biological father had been one. She heard her mother's no-nonsense voice in her head, reminding her not to let fantasy carry her away, reminding her to stay realistic and practical because it was the only way to get by in this world.

And she wondered what kind of advice her mother would have had for navigating this new *real* world.

CHAPTER TEN

Ethan hung up with Alexis, not as reassured as he'd hoped to be. The former Tracker didn't have any information on John Lin, which meant the name was likely an alias. Ethan had been afraid of that. The way Lin had been following Amy, the way he fought… There was more to him than just an ordinary shifter. Though Ethan didn't like to admit it, he'd been out of his depth in that fight. He'd gotten the distinct impression Lin had been toying with him—which was as humbling as it was scary. Ethan hadn't been formally trained to fight, but he had sparred with his sister frequently, and she *had* been trained to fight —by Alexis herself. While he might not be up to the level of a Tracker, Ethan knew he could hold his own with most shifters, even fighting in human form to their animal form.

Lin had been a very different story. Whoever the hell he was, he was far deadlier than a normal tiger.

Ethan took solace in the fact that Alexis had promised

to do some digging. She had the connections and skills to uncover Lin's real identity, and hopefully his reason for stalking Amy. Alexis' advice for keeping Amy and her sister safe was less comforting. She'd told him to bring them before the elders so they were made an official part of the tiger community and couldn't be hurt.

But he'd heard the hesitance in the former Tracker's voice, like she didn't fully believe what she was saying. Being "official" hadn't kept a crazy tiger from going after the first hybrid brought to their people's attention. It hadn't kept other crazy tigers from going after the little girl that was brought before the elders next. Which didn't make the elders' compound in West Virginia feel like a particularly safe option.

Granted, once the two hybrids had been formally recognized as part of the community, the threats to their lives ended. At least any obvious threats.

But once Amy was accepted as a hybrid by his people, Ethan would be forced to give her up. Or he'd be forced to compete for her with dozens of other males. He didn't think he could face that again, couldn't face what it had done to him. And yet, he didn't want to let Amy go.

He stared down at the cellphone in his hand. He wasn't sure he *could* let her go now.

She stalked past the living room just then, heading right into the kitchen without looking at him, and he sighed. He might not have a choice about whether he gave her up or not. After tonight, he might have already lost her.

She came back out of the kitchen a few minutes later with a steaming cup of tea—chamomile from the scent.

"Do you want some?" she asked, lifting the cup.

"No thank you. Maybe later."

"How did your call go?"

"Not as well as I'd hoped."

She settled on the couch, opposite where he sat, and faced him. The fact that she was comfortable enough to sit so close loosened his tense muscles.

"Okay," she said, "tell me everything."

"My brother-in-law's aunt, Alexis Tarasova—she's a former Tracker."

"Trackers are?"

"Our version of police, military, bounty hunters, occasional executioners all rolled into one. Basically, they're our law enforcement, whatever enforcement is needed."

"Do I want to know what the executioner part entails?"

"Maybe later. When you've gotten used to this world a little more. You should know that killing a human is a crime punishable by death among my people. That'll give Cat some protection."

"And me?"

"Because you're a hybrid...likely hybrid...you fall under a different part of the law."

"One where someone attacking me is punished by death?" she asked.

"I don't think Lin was trying to kill you."

"I'd like to know what he wants from me, though."

"Me too. Alexis is looking into that."

"And in the meantime, your laws will keep him from killing me?"

She sounded as doubtful of that as Ethan felt. "Being a woman also helps."

"Why?"

"Like I said, we don't have very many left. We're close to extinction so every female who might be able to have children with a tiger shifter is valuable. Our laws are in the process of changing to accommodate hybrids. That helps you, too. But Alexis recommended I bring you and Cat before the elders—our governing body—for official recognition. That's protected the other hybrids brought before our people."

Her eyes narrowed and he knew she'd heard his hesitance.

"You're not convinced that will work?" she asked, before sipping her tea.

"It's not that. Alexis sounded…worried. That was not reassuring."

"Are the other hybrids safe now?"

"As far as I know. I haven't heard of any other attempts on their lives."

"There were attempts though?"

He nodded.

"Is that what John Lin is here to do?"

"If he was, he would have killed you already. Weeks ago. Before I realized what you might be."

She made a face and pursed her lips, looking off into the distance.

"I'm not even sure how he found you," Ethan said to fill the silence. "Hybrids are extremely rare—at least we think they are. I don't know a lot about it, just what's filtered through the community."

"Do you suppose the man who fathered me knows I exist? Could that be what Lin wants?"

"There's one way to find out."

Her gaze returned to his, and for a moment Ethan forgot everything else but her. Her scent wrapped around him, stronger here in her home, calling to his tiger. Without thinking, he leaned a little closer, pleased when she didn't move away. More pleased when the scent of her desire filtered into the space between them.

Sliding across the couch, he risked reaching out to tug at one of her curls where it rested against her cheek. Her mouth opened, a small sound he couldn't interpret escaped. But she didn't pull away.

The soft feel of her hair made his heart thump harder. Awareness filled him, of her heat, her scent, her lush body, the delicious taste of her. His gaze dropped to her mouth, and everything else fell away. His attention still on her lips, he took her tea mug and set it aside on the coffee table. Then he kissed her.

Gently at first, testing. She didn't stop him, but for a long moment, she didn't respond either. He brushed his lips over hers in a final caress, intending to pull away. Then she opened to him, leaning in, with a passion that overwhelmed him.

The fear of what could have happened tonight swamped him, ramping up the need to feel her, hold her. He could have lost her to Lin. He might still lose her to his people.

But in that moment, she was his. She was safe. And she was eagerly in his arms.

For that moment, his world was perfect.

He slid the hand he had in her hair down the side of her neck, savoring her slight tremor, her faint moan. She had the most sensitive neck. Taking advantage of that, he moved his hand to the back of her head, tangling his fingers in her hair as he kissed his way across her jaw to the delicate skin under her ear. She tasted fresh and spicy all at once, a little salty, a lot sweet.

He gently nipped and kissed the column of her throat, moved down to the bend where her neck met her shoulder. She groaned and tilted her head to the side, giving over to his exploration. He breathed in her essence, the flavor of her scent, and savored it like the finest wine. Better than wine. Better than anything he'd ever tasted.

When he finally dragged his mouth back to hers, there was no longer any hint of hesitation, from either of them. He drank her in, memorizing her taste, her shape. He slid his hands down her back and eased her closer, until she wrapped her arms around his neck and pressed tightly against him. Everywhere he was hard, she was soft and yielding, the feel of her breasts pressed against his chest like a brand. And even the thin barrier of their clothing felt like too much.

Somewhere in the back of his mind, he was aware of Cat in the other room, aware that he wasn't alone with Amy, and they still had too much to discuss to take this any farther than a kiss. But his body didn't seem to care. Neither did his tiger. He wanted her naked. He wanted to strip off her clothes slowly, revealing her skin, her luscious curves. He wanted to kiss and taste and suck every part of her. His hands tightened reflexively against her back, pressing her closer as his fingers clenched into the soft cotton of her t-shirt. So easy to tear away. So easy to remove that thin barrier…

For a split second, he forgot that they weren't alone, that she wasn't an ordinary human, that there was a real world beyond this little bubble of desire. *Yes*, his tiger growled. *Mine.*

He groaned, holding her tighter for a half a beat more before forcing himself to ease back. He was breathing hard, his heartbeat racing, his body tight and hot, his tiger ready to pounce. It didn't help his equilibrium that she was also panting, a fine tremor shivering over her skin, the scent of her lust strong now, overriding the other confusion of emotions. She wet her lips, and the gesture nearly upended his logic. Why had he pulled back? Why wasn't he carrying her to bed now?

The sound of Cat clearing her throat reminded him of at least one of the answers.

"Sorry to interrupt, but I have questions," Cat said.

He glanced past Amy toward the hallway where Cat was hiding from view in a charming attempt at giving them privacy. Amy's cheeks flashed instantly pink. She rolled her eyes and huffed out a sound somewhere between a laugh and a groan.

He cupped her face between his hands, brushing her lips one last time because he couldn't help himself. Then he called to her sister, "Ask your questions."

Cat started to talk from the hallway. Amy looked back, shook her head, and snapped, "Get in here."

Cat came around the corner grinning, her eyes sparkling with mischief.

Amy gave her sister a *look*. Cat's grin grew. She settled into an overstuffed chair next to the couch, not looking at all repentant as Amy continued to scowl at her. With a sigh, Amy settled against the couch, turning sideways so there was space between her and Ethan, pulled her knees up and wrapped her arms around them, then waved her hand for Cat to start.

The future was still up in the air. But one thing was certain, he wanted Amy, even now, even knowing he'd have to fight his own kind to keep her. Something he'd never thought he'd *want* to do again. The realization left him reeling even as he attempted to explain shapeshifters to a twenty-year-old genius.

A my was a little surprised that Ethan could answer any of Cat's questions about how his physiology worked. Most people didn't understand the physics behind their own biology. And as far as Ethan was concerned, the ability to shift was just part of his biology. Amy kept silent as her sister grilled Ethan, trying to process feelings so mixed and chaotic she wasn't sure a month of processing would help.

One thing was certain, seeing Ethan turn into a tiger hadn't done a thing to kill the lust she felt for him. She was acutely aware him, sitting close enough she could feel his heat even though they were no longer touching. He smelled so damned good, she wanted to plaster herself against him and just breathe him in. Her skin felt hot everywhere, and her pulse throbbed as her imagination filled with remembered sensations—the feel of his mouth, hard against hers, trailing over her neck, over her jaw, demanding and giving at the same time; the way her breasts had rubbed against his chest with every breath, the sensation lighting sparks of fire in her; the way his fingers had clenched in her shirt, like he was on the verge of ripping it off. That thought made her shiver a little.

Ethan glanced at her, frowning slightly in question, but she shook him off as Cat tossed another question at him. Amy wasn't about to explain that shiver in front of her sister.

She felt a little perverse, sitting here fantasizing about Ethan, but she couldn't seem to help herself. What the hell was it about him? He was trying to explain what it felt like to twist himself inside out and become a tiger, and all Amy could focus on was how much she wanted to run her hands over all those lovely muscles of his, how much she wanted to strip him and finally do all those things she hadn't allowed herself to consider while he was modeling for her class. At least she'd tried to ignore those fantasies during the sessions. At home, at night, her dreams had been full of Ethan. And now, she wanted to make those dreams real.

As she watched him talk, she wondered what he'd do if she leaned forward and settled her hand on his thigh, how he'd react if she slid her fingers up his thigh to his cock, what sounds he'd make if she stroked him, if she put her mouth on him. Her imagination once again ran away with the fantasy, drawing it out in exquisite detail that made her hot and achy. She clenched her thighs and hugged her knees tighter, both to elevate some of the building tension and in an attempt to keep her hands to herself.

Ethan adjusted his position a little, moving just a hair's breath closer, a subtle tension rippling through his body, and she heard him take a deep inhale that sounded just a bit shaky. When he answered Cat's next question, his voice was deeper and huskier than it had been just moments before.

Heat pulsed through Amy's skin, and she knew she was blushing. She glanced at Cat, glad to see she was staring at the notebook in her lap and not paying close attention to either Ethan or Amy. If her sister did notice her blush, she hoped Cat would think it was because she'd caught Amy and Ethan making out earlier. It would be more than a little mortifying if her sister even suspected what Amy was thinking about right then. It was already mortifying to realize she couldn't control her imagination or her lust for Ethan.

As the discussion moved from the physical shift to Ethan's heightened tiger senses, a slow creeping realization sank in. He'd said he could detect things by smell that humans couldn't… She glanced at him out of the corner of her eye. Was she sending out pheromones now that she wasn't aware of? Could he tell she was having a lot of inappropriate thoughts?

Good god, had he been able to tell she'd lusted after him when they'd first met, while he was modeling?

She swallowed, keeping her gaze on the coffee table as she blurted out, "You can smell things humans can't. Like…emotions?"

A stillness settled over him. "Yes," he said slowly.

"What emotions?" Cat asked, missing the undercurrent in the conversation.

He nodded at Cat, "I could tell you weren't scared when I shifted." He glanced at Amy. "I could tell you were."

She winced. "Yeah, well." She narrowed her eyes. "So all kinds of emotions?"

He held her gaze, heat burning in their dark depths. "Yes."

"Damn," she muttered.

"What's wrong?" Cat asked, though she was distracted by a note she was making in her book.

"Nothing," Amy said quickly. "Just realized something."

Ethan's nostrils flared, a very slight smile lifting his lips.

He knew what she'd been thinking this whole time! At least, he knew how she felt. Her skin flamed so hot she was afraid she'd combust. She raised a hand to her cheek, her palm cool against the burn of embarrassment. It was one thing for him to know intellectually that she wanted him—she'd practically crawled onto his lap when they were kissing earlier, so it wasn't like she'd been trying to hide her desire. But it was another thing all together that he could tell what she was feeling *all* the time.

"That's not fair," she murmured to him, hoping Cat missed the comment.

His grin flashed quick and lethal. "If it makes you feel better," he whispered, leaning close to her, speaking so low she was sure Cat would never hear, "you've been torturing me for weeks. Knowing what you were feeling."

She wanted to be annoyed, but she was a little pleased to know he'd been tortured as much as she had.

"We'll talk about this more later." She attempted a prim tone that failed miserably.

He didn't respond, but the look in his eyes was enough to set her imagination running riot again.

She forced herself to focus on Cat and the myriad of questions her sister continued to pelt Ethan with, things most people wouldn't even think about. Like what happened to the extra weight when he went from tiger to human—his full-grown Bengal tiger form was more than two and a half times the weight if his human form. Ethan didn't know. And while he was human, was the tiger fur actually still inside his body or did it retract into specialized cells? Ethan could only say that if you dissected the human form of a tiger shifter, you wouldn't see any physical signs of their differences. It would take blood and genetic tests to pinpoint the differences.

"How different is your DNA from a human's?" Cat asked. "More than say the difference between a human and a chimp?"

"It's kind of complicated," Ethan said. "I'm an accountant not a geneticist so you'd have to ask one of our scientists, but as I understand it, our DNA is…unique compared to a human's. There's a mix that's both compatible and very different all at once."

Cat frowned. "That doesn't make sense."

He shrugged. "Like I said, I don't really understand it. The differences are why we always assumed we couldn't have children with humans, though. We're a different species. We just happen to have two forms that look like two other animals on this planet."

"I couldn't really see any difference between your tiger and a real tiger," Cat said.

"There isn't much of one. Just in our eyes mostly. We can blend in well with our animal counterparts. The same way we can blend in with humans without it being noticeable that we're different."

"There are different kinds of shifters?" Amy asked, her own curiosity helping to offset the still-pulsing lust throbbing through her body.

"There are. Some have animal forms that blend in, some are…more obvious."

"Like?" Cat waved her hand in a gesture for him to give an example.

He shrugged. "You'd never confuse a werewolf in its wolf form for a normal wolf. They're bigger, heavier, and shaped slightly differently—bigger shoulders, for instance. As humans, they look like everyone else, but you'd know you were looking at a werewolf if you saw them in their wolf form."

Werewolves? That was terrifying. She glanced at her canister of pepper spray on the kitchen counter, wondering if it would help against werewolves—and if she should get a few more canisters, just in case.

"Do you suppose I could talk to one of your geneticists?" Cat asked.

Still not showing any signs of distress at hearing there were *fucking werewolves* in the world. Amy wasn't sure if she should worry about her sister taking all this so easily or not. There was a reason the saying "curiosity killed the cat" was a cliché.

"I might be able to arrange something," Ethan said. "We need to get you both officially acknowledged by my people first."

"Thanks. I've got some reading to do. Genetics isn't my specialty." She grinned, rolled across the arm of the chair with her notebook still open.

"Wait," Ethan called, stopping Cat before she ran off. He turned a little to face Amy. "We need to talk about getting you to the elders."

Amy pressed her lips together for a moment, considering. "I can probably take some time off next weekend—"

"This needs to happen faster than that if we're going to protect you and Cat from Lin."

"Why is Cat in danger from him?"

"She's the daughter of a human woman who had a baby with a tiger. There's every possibility she could have a baby with a tiger. That means my people will be interested in her."

"Fuck," she muttered. This just got worse. She rubbed a hand over her eyes, suddenly so tired all she could think about was crawling into bed and sleeping until this was over. "When?"

"Tomorrow would be best," he said. "We need to get the information on your biological father first. That will help your case."

"I have work tomorrow. I can probably get to the bank during my lunch break but that'll depend on what's happening at the office."

Ethan straightened and turned to face her fully. "You can't go to work tomorrow. Not with Lin still out there and your status in limbo. You'll need to call in sick or something."

"I've never had to do that before." She rubbed her forehead, massaging her temples. "And there's my class. We're nearing midterm exams. I don't want to miss a lecture now." She was mostly talking to herself at that point. She knew he was right, she just didn't want to accept it. So much had happened in just a few hours, and now she had to risk everything she'd worked hard for over the last seven years because beings she hadn't even known existed before tonight were a threat to her.

Ethan's frown deepened. "This isn't a normal situation, Amy. Going about your usual routine puts a target on your back until we can assure your safety through formal recognition."

She ran a hand up into her hair, loosening the clips that held it back from her face. Sighing, she removed the clips. "How long will this recognition thing take?"

"I have no idea. Not long. A few days. We'll have to go to West Virginia, to the elders' compound."

"Even though your contact was worried? Shouldn't we at least find out more about Lin first?"

"The longer we wait, the more chance he'll have of getting to you. Or Cat."

She cursed under her breath. The man already knew her Achilles heel. "Maybe all this Lin guy wants is to talk. You said he wasn't trying to kill me tonight."

"If all he wanted was to talk, he wouldn't have shown up tonight as a tiger. You willing to take chances where he's concerned?"

"No. I'm just looking for excuses not to toss over my real life, my work, and everything I've been striving for for years just because you tell me I'm related to mythical beings and this puts me and my sister in danger."

His mouth tipped up in an almost smile that didn't reach his eyes.

Cat sat on the edge of the couch next to Amy, looking so young but too wise all at once. "There's nothing we can't replace," she said quietly. "We can retake all our classes if we miss too much. We can find new jobs." Her voice dropped, but her gaze was steady. "I can't replace my sister, though. And she's all I've got left."

"Ah, sweetie. You won't lose me." She hugged Cat close, resting her head against her sister's. "I'll call in sick and skip my class. That goes for you, too," she said to Cat.

Cat nodded, her arms tightening around Amy. "I'm ahead in most of my classes anyway."

"Of course you are."

"Except for English." She stuck out her tongue. "I hate English."

"That's because your teacher sucks." To Ethan, she said, "We'll go to the bank first thing in the morning. Then we'll head to West Virginia."

"I'll check flights—" Ethan started.

"We'd better drive," Amy interrupted, glancing at Cat who cringed at the mention of flying. "Spike hates airplanes. We tried flying with her once and it was…not good."

"Spike?"

"Is coming with us," Amy said firmly. She made a face. "Only problem is we don't have a car."

"We can rent one," he said.

She exchanged a look with Cat. "Neither of us has a driver's license."

Ethan closed his eyes and shook his head. "New Yorkers." When he opened his eyes, he said, "Fine. I'll do all the driving. But we split the gas."

"Deal."

"Road trip!" Cat bounced up off the couch. "Better go pull out Spike's carrier."

Ethan winced. "You don't have anyone you can leave Spike with? We'll be taking her into a den of tiger shifters. You think she freaked out tonight? She's going to be seriously overwhelmed at the compound."

"Spike's part of the family," Amy said. "She comes with us or we don't go."

"We can keep her in the carrier when we're around the other shapeshifters," Cat said. "She'll be okay."

"I can't change your minds?" Ethan said.

"No," Amy and Cat said at the same time—cheerfully.

"Fine. Spike joins the crew. This is going to be an interesting trip."

Cat clapped her hands. "I have to pack. And sleep. And work out some more math. See you in the morning!"

"Will she be doing those three things in that order?" Ethan asked.

"Probably. Cyclically."

He frowned and Amy waved that off, standing. "I'll go get you a pillow and some blankets."

He blinked a few times and she almost laughed. "You're not going to argue about me staying here?" he asked.

"If I kicked you out, what would you do?"

"Hang around outside the building to make sure Lin doesn't come back." He winced. "What I'd been planning to do before he attacked."

She nodded. "You'll do us more good in here." She leveled a look at him. "On the couch."

His expression changed, just a little, a sexy glint filtering into his dark eyes. She swallowed and hurried to her room for the spare blankets. When she returned, he stood, pulling her into his arms after she'd dropped the linens.

"What were you thinking about earlier?" he murmured near her ear.

The feel of his breath hot against her skin made her shiver. "None of your business." She scowled. "As if you didn't already know anyway."

He chuckled, the sound like a caress across her sensitive throat. He followed that torture by kissing her earlobe softly, then moving his lips lower, gliding over the side of her neck in languid delicious nips and licks.

Without meaning to, she moaned and leaned into him. "I'm not inviting you into my bed tonight," she said—as much to herself as to him.

"I know. I wouldn't want to take you to bed while the threat of another attack is hanging over us. When I take you to bed, I want time to savor you."

She was breathing harder now because he brushed his lips against the underside of her jaw, in a spot that pressed all her buttons and made heat pulse through her core. "You sound very sure we'll end up in bed."

"I'm not."

The rueful bitterness in his tone dimmed some of her lust-haze. She leaned back to look up at him, frowning her question.

"But when all this is settled," he murmured against her lips, "we'll revisit this conversation."

He kissed her hard then, with intent and promise, the kind of kiss she felt in her entire body. Everything in her tightened into a hot ball of want, ready to explode at a touch. She leaned into him so her chest was pressed against his, loving the way his hard muscles felt against her breasts, the way she could feel his heart thumping.

She wanted to wrap around him, absorb him into her very pores. But for tonight at least, she couldn't risk it. She eased away from the kiss reluctantly.

"We'll definitely revisit this conversation," she said, her voice shaky and rough. "Goodnight."

She rushed into her room so she wouldn't get lost in

fantasies again. It was entirely too easy doing that with Ethan.

Which was going to make the next few days torturous.

* * *

Zhong watched Amy Donovan's apartment window from a building roof two blocks away, still trying to control the rage of memories wrapping around him. The evening air was cold and biting, a sharp wind lifting his hair. The scents of a nearby bagel shop, already working on tomorrow's stock, reached his sensitive nose, mixing with the faint scent of a nearby grassy park and the closer scents of roof tar and electrical equipment in a small metal shed behind him.

His nostrils flared as his lip lifted in a faint, almost involuntary snarl.

He'd gone to the gallery tonight to test Catalina Donovan's scent. Just in case. Hoping he was wrong. There were other possibilities. There had been other males in New York when Amy had been conceived. The familiarity of her scent could have been because at some point he'd met her mother—even if he couldn't remember it.

But there was nothing familiar in Cat's scent. So he'd taken a chance, coming at Amy in his tiger form—the form that could analyze scent best, that wouldn't complicate that analysis with feelings and memories…

And for a moment, when he'd had his face in Amy's, his blood already pumping from the fight with Gupta, he'd come so close to killing her. A heartbeat from ripping

Roman's child from this world, knowing too well the pain it would inflict on his former mentor.

He blamed her pepper spray for his inaction. And the fact that he still had a job to do, that he was supposed to hand her over to his client alive. He refused to acknowledge there might have been another reason he couldn't bring himself to kill her.

The lights in her window went out. Gupta was still there, guarding her. Zhong smiled a little, a cynical smile. Would Gupta tell her the truth? Would he explain what he was, what she was?

Zhong's client didn't want that.

Sitting on the roof, watching her home for the last few hours, he'd considered the other things he'd learned in the last few weeks, about what his client *did* want from the hybrids. He still needed to learn more. He hadn't been able to find out what experiments the elder was conducting, only that he was using the hybrids in those experiments.

Now that he knew the truth about Amy's parentage, he had to rethink his plans. What would be kinder—killing her or handing her over to his client? Which would hurt Roman more?

A knife sliced through his soul, though he hadn't thought he had much of a soul left after all these years. He snarled at the darkness, his faint hiss barely a sound.

Memories had never been his friends.

Whether Gupta told her the truth about her nature as a hybrid or not, whether Gupta even made the connections and figured out she was a hybrid, Zhong knew he had to make a decision tonight. By tomorrow, Gupta would go to the elders—if he hadn't already—because she'd been attacked by a tiger shifter. Zhong's client would either move up the deadline for acquiring Amy, or he'd call off this particular job and send Zhong on to another hunt. Amy might even go looking for her real father, if she survived the next few days. Tomorrow would be his last chance to act.

His last chance to finally exact real revenge on the man who'd betrayed him.

CHAPTER ELEVEN

Ethan woke surrounded by Amy's scent and a heavy weight settled on the middle of his chest. For half a heartbeat, he thought the weight was Amy, his mind playing tricks with his senses and melding with the dream he'd just been having. Amy naked, in his arms, straddling him, his hands on her breasts…

Then a more pungent canine smell filtered into his brain, bringing him fully awake.

He opened his eyes.

Spike sprawled on his chest, staring at him. She yipped in greeting when he looked at her, her tongue out, her tail pounding his stomach.

"Good morning," he said. "I suppose you think you're the boss now?"

Spike bark-yipped again and licked his face. He half-winced, half-laughed. Not exactly the good morning kiss he'd been hoping for. But at least Spike wasn't afraid of him. After the tiger attack—and the fact that he'd smell like tiger to the Spike—he'd been afraid he'd have an uphill battle getting the poodle to accept him.

A quiet chuckle drew his attention to the kitchen. Amy was leaning against the counter with a mug in her hand, smiling at his predicament. Her curls were piled on top of her head in a loose bun, tendrils falling around her cheeks and down her neck. He could only see the top half of her body, but she had on a soft-looking red robe over a t-shirt.

"I guess she likes you," Amy said, raising her cup to the poodle. "Now you're doomed."

Ethan scratched behind Spike's ears. "I've never been owned by a dog before. It'll be an interesting experience."

"I didn't know dogs could own big cats."

"Only pink, blue, and purple poodles."

She chuckled again. "How did you sleep?"

A loaded question. He'd been restless and half aroused most of the night, surrounded by her scent and aware of her presence only a short distance away. Between lust and worry, he kept waking every few hours to make sure nothing was wrong. Then he'd catch her scent, his imagination would turn to her bed, and getting back to sleep proved difficult at best.

But he didn't think she'd want to hear the real answer so he said, "Fine. You?"

"Fine." She shrugged, a faint blush rising across her cheeks. He caught the deliciously tempting spice of her desire in her scent and had to hide his satisfied smile. Maybe he wasn't the only one who'd had trouble sleeping.

"You want some coffee?" she asked, lifting her mug.

"That'd be great, thanks. I just need to use the bathroom first." He frowned at the poodle on his chest. "If Spike will let me up, that is."

"Just pick her up and put her on the floor. She'll survive."

He considered the dog for a long moment first. Spike looked very settled in her position. Ethan didn't really want to damage their new understanding by upsetting her. When it became obvious Spike had no intentions of getting down on her own, Ethan gave in to the inevitable. Spike wiggled happily as Ethan picked her up—until she realized she was being moved to the floor. As he set her on the rug, Spike twitched her tail and stalked off to the kitchen. Ethan could swear he heard the dog harrumph. Could dogs do that?

By the time he joined Amy, she had a hot mug of dark-roast coffee waiting for him on the counter as well as a sugar bowl and milk.

"I didn't know what you'd want."

"Black is fine. Thanks."

The morning ritual felt awkward and yet...nice. Intimate. He would have preferred the experience after a night of making love to her—and welcomed the exhaustion of staying up for that—but this hint of what it could be like was surprisingly pleasant. Now that he could see her fully, he took in the blue polka dot pajama pants and the flowers on her oversized purple shirt. In combination with the fuzzy red robe, she was definitely not dressed to seduce. He wondered if she'd be surprised to realize she *was* seducing him with that outfit. She looked soft and mussed and kissable. He gripped his mug a little tighter to resist the temptation to see just how much more mussed he could get her.

They had no idea what the future held. He had no idea if he'd be allowed to have a relationship with her after they met with the elders. He had to keep some distance between them until then, until he knew what he'd have to do to claim her. Which meant he really needed to keep his hands to himself. Even if he couldn't seem to keep his imagination tamed.

"Where's Cat?" he asked. A reminder to himself that they weren't alone more than curiosity—he could hear Cat moving around in her bedroom.

"She's assembling Spike's carrier for the trip. We don't use it often so it was buried in a closet under the Halloween decorations."

"I booked a rental car last night at a place not far from here," he said. "Big enough for all of us and Spike. Since I'm the only one driving, it'll take a bit of time to reach the compound. A few days. If it's safe, we'll try to stop at a hotel along the way. If not, we'll drive straight through."

"You'll be too tired to drive that much. We'll need to stop."

"I can go without sleep for a while before it really affects my driving. We have to keep ahead of Lin— whoever he is."

She pursed her lips and stared at her mug, her brow furrowed. "I left a voicemail for my boss, that I'd been throwing up all night and couldn't make it in. And I called the temp agency and let them know they needed to send a replacement for the next few work days." She sighed.

"Hopefully I'll still have that job when I come back. I liked working for Louise."

"With luck, this won't take more than a week. Then you can get back to your regular life. Though you might get more visits from male tigers looking to…interest you."

"Interest me?"

"You and Cat both will probably attract a lot of attention from the males who don't mind having children with hybrids."

She scowled. "How romantic."

Her response made him chuckle, but it didn't loosen the tension in his chest. She'd have so many options soon. The choice of any male she wanted. She'd have the choice to forgo a tiger mate period, too—despite community pressure.

"How do you feel about…hybrids?" she asked.

He blinked. "I never really thought much about them one way or the other. My brother-in-law's brother is engaged to the first hybrid brought before the community. She's a nice woman. A vet who specializes in treating big cats. I like her. I'm not one of the tigers that's adamantly against hybrids in our community. But…"

"But?"

"I never expected to meet you, and…" He sighed. "I accepted a couple of years ago that I wasn't destined for a family. I have a niece I adore and will likely have more nieces and nephews since my sister is so happily married. That was enough for me. I was happy with the idea of eventually having a long-term relationship with a human woman, even if I couldn't have children with her."

"Do you want kids?" She seemed startled by the thought.

He couldn't blame her. She was still young and busy and probably hadn't given marriage and children much thought yet, especially since she'd spent the last seven years taking care of Cat. But among his people, children and procreation were a driving force, a focus from a very early age because of their extinction problem. His family had expected him to be one of the few males to find a mate and have children. They hadn't even questioned that he might not.

Which had made the results of his Mate Runs all the more bitter.

He shook off the memories. "I wouldn't say no to children." He hedged around his real feelings. "But since I'd accepted I wouldn't have any of my own, I'm not focused on that."

Her shoulders slumped a little and relief filtered into her scent. He had trouble deciding if he was more amused or irritated by the reaction.

Amusement won out when she blinked and looked up at him suddenly, her eyes wide, as if she realized he'd noticed her relief.

To give them both a break, he switched subjects. "Where is your safety deposit box?"

"Midtown, Seventh Avenue and 57th Street." She hummed under her breath. "Parking in that part of town is brutal and expensive. I'll take the subway in, get what I need, and meet you and Cat back here. Shouldn't take me longer than two, two and half hours. At the most."

"I don't want you going anywhere without me."

When her eyebrows went up in challenge, he raised a consolatory hand. "Lin, remember? Still a potential threat."

"We don't even know what he wants. Beside he's hardly going to attack me in the middle of a business day in Midtown."

"You don't know that. But even if he's not the real threat, there are other tiger shifters who are dangerous to you because of what you are. Since Lin's found you, others won't be far behind."

"How is it that I'm suddenly in danger from all these tiger shifters, after twenty-six years of being a hybrid and being perfectly safe?" She sounded more annoyed than scared.

"Because tigers didn't know about hybrids for most of those twenty-six years. Because until just recently, none of my people knew about you specifically. But they do now. Or they will soon. It won't remain a secret for long and we need to take advantage of it still being one. Why are you arguing with me?"

"It chafes okay? I just want to live my life. I've been through more than enough in the last few years. I did not need this extra complication. And having to deal with it is annoying. Having to worry about Cat all over again is devastating." The last sentence was quiet, filled with feelings she tried to hide behind a mulish expression.

Ethan's gut tightened in sympathy. What he wouldn't give to make it all go away. For her to be an ordinary human woman who never needed to know about his world. But then, if not for the threat from Lin, Ethan might have walked away from her in the beginning, too afraid of the feeling she invoked in him, too stubborn to risk his heart again. She'd be safe, though, and she wouldn't have to worry about his people.

"I'm sorry," he said. "I truly am. It's a lot to process and accept. And it will change things for you and Cat going forward. More than you'd like." Her obstinate frown called to him. He set his coffee mug down and cupped her face between his palms, urging her to look up at him. "I'll do what I can to make it an easier transition. I'll be here to help."

"For how long?" she asked, her chin jutting out.

He had no idea how to answer that. She seemed to realize she'd broached a topic neither of them was ready to confront because she shook her head and gave one of his wrists a quick squeeze.

"I'm sorry," she said. "That wasn't a fair question. I'm…annoyed. And scared. I really hate being scared, so it brings out the bitch in me."

He smiled a little, and leaned in to kiss her. He meant to offer comfort, but the instant he tasted her, all noble intentions went out the window. He stepped close enough to press into her and realized she was still holding her mug. Without releasing her mouth, he took the cup from her, set it on the counter, then wrapped her in his arms, angling his head to deepen the kiss.

She tasted of coffee and freshness, a slight hint of mint from her toothpaste. The desire that burned between them spiked in her scent. He loved that smell. He could live on that smell. And the taste of her. And the feel of her. God, she felt good. Warm and soft and sweet. The robe bunched under his hands as he tightened his hold, molding her to him. She wasn't wearing a bra under the t-shirt. The feel of her full breasts pressed against his chest, with only a thin layer of material between their bare skin, made his breathing speed.

All the erotic thoughts that had tortured him throughout the long night came roaring forward. He nudged her backward until she was pressed against the counter, then he moved his hands inside her robe to slide up the thin material of her shirt. She had her arms around his neck, her kiss hard and deep, her fingers tight in his hair at the back of his head. When she pressed her hips into his, grinding against his erection, he groaned into her mouth. He moved his hands beneath her shirt, to the heat and silkiness of her skin, no longer able to resist. She scorched his palms with her heat and he loved it.

The thought of lifting her onto the counter, stripping off her pants, sliding into her heat consumed him. She rocked against him and he nearly lost his mind. Slipping her hands under the elastic band of her pajama bottoms, he cupped her ass, only the thin cotton of her underwear separating his hands from her skin. She moaned, grinding harder against his cock, sending fireworks of explosive lust through his blood.

Through the waves of need, Ethan became aware of an incongruous sensation around his ankle. Something cold and wet. It took another few moments for the sensation to penetrate his desire enough to become a distraction. What the hell?

Irritated, he released Amy's mouth to look down. Spike sat on the tiled floor next to them. Staring. When he met the dog's dark eyes, Spike leaned forward and nudged at his trouser leg, licking his ankle.

He groaned, half-laughing as he set his forehead against Amy's. She chuckled, too, cupping his face briefly before leaning back to look at him.

"I need to take her out for a walk. Which means I'd better go get dressed."

He still had his hands on her ass, and he was loath to release her. But if he didn't now, he might not for hours.

He insisted on joining her for the walk, and because Amy was afraid to leave her behind, Cat reluctantly agreed to come with them, though she whined all the way down in the elevator about still having things to do. By silent agreement, he and Amy let the questions and conversation about their relationship go. At least for the time being. Ethan wasn't in a hurry to confront that future yet anyway.

Not when it might mean giving her up.

Though she'd wanted to insist Ethan stay behind, Amy gave in to having both Ethan and Cat come into town with her to get the information about her birth father. Frankly, she was reluctant to leave Cat alone until she could be sure her little sister was safe. And while she'd never admit it to him, she did feel more comfortable having Ethan with them. He knew about this new world they were confronting. That and the fact that he was a badass shifter who'd gone head-to-head with a scary tiger gave her a sense of security that embarrassed her.

She really shouldn't find the fact that he could transform into a tiger so sexy.

She was starting to wonder if there was anything Ethan could do that she wouldn't find sexy. To amuse herself on the train ride into town, she tried imagining things that might distract her from his masculine appeal—him farting in front of her; him chewing with his mouth open and making gross sounds; seeing him on the toilet. She nearly burst into giggles at the thought of confronting Ethan as a real person and not just a scrumptious muse-god.

When he frowned, little crinkles forming at the edges of his gorgeous eyes as he looked questioningly at her, she did laugh. Patting his thigh to reassure him that she wasn't going crazy, she got a funny little feeling in her gut, a tightening and tingling that spread heat through her body.

For reasons she couldn't fathom, even imagining Ethan in the midst of the more disgusting aspects of reality didn't seem to diminish her desire. In fact, all it did was make it softer and fuller—like seeing him as a real person and not a god made him even more attractive.

On the two-block walk from the subway to the bank through Midtown pedestrian traffic, Ethan kept a hand on her lower back, guiding and protective. Amy got that funny little tightening again. In the shadows of the buildings, the wind blowing past was chilly, making her glad of her coat. Ethan was dressed only in his suit—she'd discovered that morning his coat had been shredded in the fight with Lin and it wasn't fit for him to wear without attracting a lot of attention. She wondered if he was cold since it was sharper out than her weather app had indicated it was supposed to be, but as he stood close to her near a stoplight, she could feel his heat even through her coat, the hand on her back spreading warmth through her body.

Or maybe it was just physical contact with Ethan that generated all that heat.

She was so distracted by him, so much of her attention fixed on the feel of his hand on her and his heat seeping into her, memories of how his hands had felt on her ass that morning, she nearly walked past the bank entrance.

It took several minutes to clear all the bells and whistles to get downstairs into the locked safety deposit box section of the bank and then to her box. The subtly patterned green-gray carpets muffled sound and gave the otherwise airy, white-walled room a hushed quality, almost like a library. She found herself speaking quietly for no real reason when she talked with the friendly woman manning the desk.

The woman wore a sleek cream suit, her black hair arranged in an elegantly smooth bob, and her rose colored lipstick a beautiful contrast to her dark skin. The overall look gave the teller that casually professional air Amy was still trying to emulate. One day, she'd have to be able to carry off that kind of confident self-possession. At the moment, she still felt more bohemian artist college student in her dark jeans, black, flower-embroidered peasant top, and boots. Maybe Devine could help her with her style evolution...

For some reason, the mundane considerations felt weirdly out of place, given the situation that had brought her to the bank. She shook off the strange feeling of being in two realities at once and followed the teller back into the rows of deposit boxes.

Midway down the wide aisle between two tall rows of boxes, the teller stopped and motioned for Amy to insert her key into one of the locks while the teller inserted her own key into the other lock. She and the teller turned their keys simultaneously to open the outer brass door, then the teller slipped the silver metal box out and set it on a wooden table in the center of the aisle. With a friendly wave, she left them to open the box in private, reminding Amy to just close the outer door after she'd replaced the box to lock it securely again.

Amy waited until they were alone before she lifted the lid on the long, rectangular box. Her parents hadn't needed anything too large, so it was one of the medium-sized units, big enough to hold some important documents and a couple of the keepsakes their parents had left to her and Cat.

She dug into the box, hunting for the small white envelope. It was the only thing in the box without a label on it to indicate what it was—just a plain, sealed, letter-sized envelope with a single sheet of paper inside. For years, she'd been content to ignore this information. She stared at the blank white face of the envelope, silently apologizing to her parents for what she was about to do.

It still felt a little like a betrayal to go hunting for the biological father who hadn't wanted to claim her, even now, even knowing the truth behind his reasons for doing that. In some ways, the fact that he'd left contact information spoke well of him. He believed completely that Amy couldn't biologically be his offspring, but he'd still been willing to help her mother. That had to make him one of the good guys, didn't it?

Ethan placed a hand over hers. "If you're not ready to open it yet, you don't have to. It can wait."

She smiled up at him, wondering if she should be surprised that he understood her feelings. "It's okay. I just need a minute to…adjust."

She felt Cat's hand on her shoulder, rubbing gently.

"It doesn't change anything," Cat murmured. "Remember that. It doesn't change who your parents were and how much they loved you or you loved them."

"When did you get so wise?" she asked without looking at Cat.

"Birth."

Amy chuckled. She pulled in a deep breath, turned the envelope over, and ran her finger under the sealed flap. It opened in a choppy, ragged edge, and Amy snorted at how mundane that was for such a momentous moment.

Slowly she eased out the plan white sheet of paper, lined in faint blue, the edges ragged like it was pulled out of a notebook, folded in three sections. All so…ordinary. She opened the paper quickly, surprised her hands were actually shaking. Annoyed that discovering the name of her birth father—never important to her before—now brought her such a weird combination of anxiety, excitement, and fear.

The fear had her frowning as she read the short note:

. . .

If you need me, Luciana, I'll be there for you. You can always reach me at the number and address below. Be well and take care. Love, Roman

Amy stared at the short note for a long moment. Beneath the note he'd left his full name, an address in Maine, and a phone number with an area code she presumed was Maine, though she couldn't be certain because she didn't know anyone in Maine.

At least, she hadn't known anyone in Maine.

"Roman Kadnikov," she murmured out loud. "My biological father's name is Roman."

"You okay," Ethan said quietly.

He stood close enough to offer support but was no longer touching her. Cat's hand still rested on her shoulder. Both of their instincts were good in that moment. She could take the contact from her sister, wanted that comfort even. But she'd fall apart if Ethan touched her right now.

And she wasn't even sure why. Why this moment was so significant. Until last night, she'd never even wanted to know who this man was. Not really. Now a fine tremor moved through her muscles, a roll of adrenaline she wasn't sure what to do with. Her nerves jumped with the same sort of anxiety she had during job interviews.

"I don't really understand how I feel right now," she said. "And I'll probably have to figure it out later. We need to get back and collect the rental car and get on the road. I can process all this while we drive."

"If you're sure," Ethan said.

She stuck the letter back into the envelope, folded the whole thing into a smaller square and stuck it into the front pocket of her jeans. She could have put it into her purse, but now that she'd opened the door on this information, she didn't want to risk losing it. After returning the lock box to its place and closing the door, she led Ethan and Cat back to the stairs, waving a friendly farewell to the teller on the way out the steel door and up the stairs to the ground level of the bank.

On the street, she pulled in a deep breath of cool air. It was a bit muggy for March, but still had a welcoming chill blowing down alleyways formed by the towering Midtown buildings. There were hints of rain in the distant roll of gray clouds, but above the shadows of the skyscrapers, the sky was a bright blue.

Somehow that felt appropriate.

She started to turn uptown, heading back to the subway, when that strange sense of awareness shivered down her back, between her shoulders. She grabbed Ethan's hand, out of instinct more than thought.

"I feel that…feeling again," she said.

When Ethan didn't answer, she looked back at him. He was staring at something behind her. She turned to see a man leaning against a building half a block away. He wore a sleek black suit, fitted well to his tall, lean shape, his silver tie the only spot of color in his outfit. His black hair was short and neat, his face cut in sharp, handsome angles. He had his arms crossed over his chest, one ankle crossed over the other, and his head slightly tilted down as he watched people passing. To anyone not paying attention, he looked like an extremely attractive businessman out enjoying the seasonally pleasant weather, maybe waiting for a colleague…

But even from this far away, Amy spotted the tension in him—not obvious in his stance which was relaxed and easy—but in the intensity of his gaze, the set of his jaw, the line of his mouth.

As she stared, the man glanced up and met her gaze, a very slight smile curving his lips. Amy's heartbeat hammered as she recognized the eyes of a predator. Eyes she'd seen in the face of a tiger last night.

"Fuck me," she muttered. "John Lin."

CHAPTER TWELVE

Ethan might have laughed at Amy's curse if he wasn't suddenly on full alert. He edged over to stand in front of Amy as Lin pushed away from the building he'd been leaning against and started toward them, his gaze never wavering from their small group. Ethan was peripherally aware of Cat moving close to Amy and Amy easing her sister behind her, but his full focus was on the approaching male.

Around them New York City continued to bustle past. Cars and taxis whooshed by on 7th Avenue, a constant undercurrent of noise punctuated by sudden bursts of honking or sirens. The pedestrian traffic was heavy and flowed past in waves dictated by changing street lights. The chilly air was flavored with a nearby roasted nuts cart and beyond that a larger kiosk selling coffee and bagels. All very normal for a Friday morning in Midtown Manhattan.

The humans had no idea of the predators in their midst.

John Lin stalked with the grace of a hunter as he closed in on them. More so even than most tiger shifters. In fact, he reminded Ethan of the Trackers in the way he moved, the way he seemed to ignore his surroundings while still remaining completely aware of them. But there was something more to Lin, something deadly that went beyond their shifter natures and the trained-hunter look. Something he'd confronted in their fight last night. Ethan had a feeling he was looking at a stone-cold killer unlike any he'd had to face before.

A killer with a charming smile and an expensive suit.

The veneer of civility only seemed to enhance the impression of danger, and it raised Ethan's hackles. He stepped farther in front of Amy to confront the other man.

Lin glanced past him to Amy and Cat, nodding a friendly greeting that belied the threat he posed.

"It's a pleasure to finally meet you in person, so to speak, Amy Donovan," he said.

He spoke with a faint, almost unnoticeable accent. English was obviously not his native language, but he'd adopted a flat, standard American accent that most humans would confuse for authentic. Ethan tried to catch hints of the man's intentions in his scent, but like the elders, Lin seemed able to hide his emotions, keeping them carefully out of his smell. He couldn't imagine what the man was doing, confronting them on a public street in the middle of the day. Given he'd attacked in his tiger form last night, though, Ethan wouldn't put anything past him.

"That was you last night," Amy said without preamble.

"Why have you been following me? What do you want from me?"

Right to the point. Ethan liked that about her.

Lin glanced past them toward the bank, his eyes narrowing. "Did Gupta tell you what you are?" he asked, his tone pleasant but tight.

Though anyone passing would assume this was a friendly discussion from Lin's expression, Ethan still heard the tension in his voice, the edge.

"He told me what you are," she said.

"You believe him?"

"I do." She was silent a moment. "He…changed for us. I have to believe now."

Lin raised his brows, glancing at Ethan before turning his attention back to Amy. "Do you know who your real father is?"

"My real father died in a train accident seven years ago," she said, her voice hard and tight, as if she were clenching her teeth.

"Your biological father, then," Lin said reasonably. He glanced back at the bank. "Do you know his name?"

Amy's hand flexed against Ethan's arm, and her scent, already thick with fear, spiked with confusion and weariness.

"So," Lin murmured. "You do now." He glanced at the bank again and nodded. "But you haven't known about him before now?"

"What do you want?" Ethan asked.

The other male tilted his head, contemplated them with eyes that were cold and impossible to read, the faint yellow glow in their depths a sign that his tiger was close to the surface.

"I've been hired," Lin finally said. He looked directly at Amy. "To take you." He glanced at Ethan. "And kill anyone who gets in my way."

Ethan's nostrils flared, and a low hiss rose in his throat. His cellphone, stuffed into his jacket pocket, started to vibrate with an incoming call, but he ignored it.

"Why haven't you then?" Amy asked. "You could have last night. You could have killed us both."

A faint half-smile flashed over Lin's face. "He admitted that? Not as prideful as most of our males then."

Ethan didn't rise to the bait. He and Lin both knew that in a fight Lin was the more dangerous male here. That wouldn't stop Ethan from doing his best to kill the man, though, if he attacked Amy again.

Lin glanced back at the bank briefly. "If you meet your father," he said to Amy, "be sure to tell him about last night. And that I *didn't* kill you."

"Why?"

"He'll understand."

"Does that mean…" Amy paused. "Are you leaving me alone now?"

He met Ethan's gaze. "I have until tomorrow night to kill you, making it look like an accident, and take Amy. I never miss a deadline for a client. It's a point of pride. A matter of honor."

"I'll stop you from taking her," Ethan said, so quietly, he wasn't sure Amy would hear him over the noise of

Midtown. But he knew Lin would. "I'll do whatever it takes to keep her safe."

"Die for her?" Lin asked, in the same quiet tone.

"Yes. But I'll kill for her first."

A genuine smile lifted Lin's lips as he nodded. "Good," he said in a normal tone. "She'll need that." He looked at Amy. "I never miss a deadline. But professional honor can be mitigated by…circumstances. You have until tomorrow night to get the elders to formally recognize you."

"What happens then?"

"That breaks the required parameters of my job. You're no longer useful to my client at that stage."

Ethan frowned.

Lin glanced at him. "Don't ask. You know I won't tell you who my client is or what he wants."

"Do you know?" he asked.

There was a faint shift in Lin's expression, some emotion that moved through his dark, faintly glowing eyes before Ethan could catch and interpret it. It wasn't in his scent anywhere, though, and when Ethan blinked, any hint of the strange expression was gone.

Ignoring Ethan's question, he said, "Get the elders to recognize her. Or you'll lose her."

I'll lose her anyway. Ethan didn't say that out loud, but as he and Lin held gazes, he knew the other male understood the subtext.

Lin jerked his chin up in a faint nod. "Better to our community than to my client."

Ethan didn't want to lose Amy at all, but even without

knowing what this mysterious client wanted from her, he was inclined to believe Lin.

"Why are you here now?" Amy asked. "Talking to us. Warning us. After last night…"

She trailed off and from his peripheral vision, Ethan saw her scan their surroundings—and all the people passing.

Lin was silent for a long moment. "Roman will want to meet you. Remember to tell him what I said." To Ethan, "Get this finished by tomorrow night. I don't miss deadlines. That's all the time you've got."

And without another word, he turned and walked away. Strolling down the street as if he hadn't just threatened to kill them, casually checking his wrist watch and tugging his suit jacket back into place—a businessman moving from one meeting to the next.

Ethan gaped after the other tiger. His own tiger was roaring to meet the threat. To attack and kill and rend the danger to pieces. His tiger didn't acknowledge that the other male could kill him. His tiger wanted Amy safe.

Ethan and his animal half were in complete agreement on that.

His phone started vibrating again, even before Lin had disappeared. Without taking his eyes off the other male, Ethan pulled out his phone and answered the call.

"Ethan, this is Alexis. Where are you?"

He frowned. "Midtown. Getting the information about Amy's biological father. What's wrong?"

"Elizaveta and I are on our way to New York now. Get to Elizaveta's *pied-a-tier*." She gave him an Upper East

Side address on Fifth Avenue, not far from the Metropolitan Museum.

"What the hell's happened?" The adrenaline already surging through his blood from the confrontation with Lin spiked again. He watched Lin turn the corner three blocks away.

"That male who came after you, John Lin, I finally found out who he is. His real name is Zhong. He's no ordinary tiger. And you're in a lot of danger."

Something about the name tapped at Ethan's memories, but he couldn't place it.

"Get Amy and her sister to Elizaveta's apartment," Alexis continued. "As soon as you can. The doorman will let you into the building. Elizaveta's assistant is already there, he'll let you into the apartment. You'll be safe there until we arrive."

"I'll want an explanation when you do," he said.

"Just get safe. We'll be there soon."

Alexis disconnected and Ethan stared down at the phone. He realized as he stared at the screen he'd missed eight calls from her and two texts messages. Between the subway and the basement-level part of the bank where the security boxes were, he'd apparently been out of service range most of the morning.

"What?" Amy said, her hand clenching his arm. "Who was that on the phone?"

"Alexis. Warning us about Lin."

Amy glanced in the direction Lin had gone. "We already knew he was dangerous."

"Apparently he's as scary as we thought. Alexis didn't

explain. She told me to take you and Cat to safety. She's coming into New York with Elizaveta Chernikova—one of our most powerful elder. Elizaveta has a *pied-a-tier* in Manhattan. We can wait for them there."

"Is that safe?"

"Of all the elders, Elizaveta is the only one I'd trust to ensure your safety."

"Then why are you still frowning?"

Ethan ran a hand through his hair. "John Lin's real name is Zhong."

"Just…Zhong. Nothing else?"

"I get the feeling I've heard that name before, but I can't place it."

"But obviously he's someone that scares even your friend Alexis?" Amy asked quietly.

"Which means we should be terrified."

"I already was," Cat added, the first thing she'd said since they'd walked out of the bank.

Amy pulled her close and hugged her.

"I thought I was going to pee my pants," Cat said. "Last night, he came across as an ordinary, sexy art patron. Just now… Jesus, I've never been so scared. His eyes looked like they were glowing yellow." She turned to Amy. "He threatened to kidnap you and kill Ethan. We have to do something."

"Don't worry," Amy said, rubbing a hand up and down Cat's back. "We'll take care of it. I'll be okay. We'll be okay."

Her tone was soothing and full of reassurance, none of which made it to her scent. She met Ethan's gaze over her sister's shoulder. Her blue eyes were darker, almost gray in the shadowed morning light, and bright with the fear she wouldn't show Cat. She'd been scared last night, but she'd come after a tiger with pepper spray. She was probably the bravest woman Ethan had ever met. Seeing her terror now, watching her try to hide that from her sister, infuriated him. His mate shouldn't have to be scared for her life, and he intended to do whatever it took to protect her.

Ethan stepped to the edge of the sidewalk to flag a taxi. "Elizaveta's apartment will be safe for now," he said, with as much confidence as he could muster. "We'll get everything worked out soon."

"This has been the most bizarre twenty-four hours..." Amy paused, her mouth twisting into a grimace. "Less than twenty-four hours. How has it been less than a day since all this started?"

"Time warp," Cat suggested, trying for humor but failing.

"Don't worry," Ethan said, holding open the door of the yellow cab that had stopped for them. "Everything will be okay."

He only wished he felt as confident as he sounded.

Elizaveta Chernikova's Manhattan *pied-a-tier* was actually a two-story penthouse in a luxury building on the Upper East Side. Amy had seen apartments like this on television shows and when she skimmed through real estate sites, looking at homes she'd never be able to afford because she liked to see how they were decorated. She never anticipated being shown into a place like this in real life.

The open-plan main room had polished hardwood floors covered with luxuriously thick Turkish rugs, pale yellow walls complimented by collections of subtly sophisticated art, and comfortable-looking couches and chairs scattered around the large space in cozy seating arrangements. Amy assumed the circular stairs to the right went to the second floor, but given the circumstances, she didn't ask for a tour of the place—despite her curiosity. To the left, a small open kitchen with shiny steel appliances and pale wooden cabinets was separated from the main room by a dark granite counter. One entire wall of the main room was made up of floor-to-ceiling windows that looked out over Central Park, a spectacular view of greenery and the pastel shadow-shapes of the equally beautiful buildings lining the opposite side of the park.

A faint, clean, lemony smell underlay the headier scent of freshly brewed coffee.

They were shown into the apartment by a quiet man an inch or two shorter than Ethan, with brown hair cut close to his head and dark brown eyes that seemed a lot older than the face that housed them. He was handsome in an unassuming way, soft spoken, with a faint accent Amy couldn't quite place. He introduced himself as Elizaveta's assistant but didn't give them his name.

Once he'd shown them to a sectional couch and offered coffee—which Amy took gratefully, mostly because she needed to do something with her hands—the man disappeared through a door at the left side of the apartment next to the kitchen, leaving the three of them alone in the echoing quiet.

Cat helped herself to one of the small, individual cakes on a platter next to the coffee.

"Should we be eating anything here?" Amy asked, frowning as her sister stuffed the entire cake into her mouth.

"I'm starving," Cat said, her mouth still half full. "Besides, you're drinking the coffee."

Amy gave in with a shrug. If Elizaveta meant them harm, she could have just left them to Zhong. Ethan trusted this woman, or at least thought she would help them, which meant Amy would give her the benefit of the doubt.

She glanced at Ethan where he was pacing back and forth in front of the large windows. He'd taken off his suit jacket when Elizaveta's assistant had taken their coats, which left him in the simple white button-down shirt he'd been wearing since last night. His clothes were wrinkled from sleeping in them, his hair was mussed from his frequent finger brushes, and yet he still looked unbelievably gorgeous. Perfect even in his unkempt state.

She watched him move, the way his muscles bunched and shifted beneath his shirt, the way his forearms flexed as his hands relaxed and fisted. With the noon sunshine backlighting him, he gave the impression of being a caged animal, trying to pace away frustration. His tiger seemed more on the surface now. Despite having shifted in front of her last night, Amy kept forgetting he was more than human. But it was impossible *not* to see the tiger in that moment.

Gripping the delicate China cup as hard as she dared, she breathed in the rich roast coffee steam and concentrated on slowing her rampaging heartbeat.

They waited like that for what felt like a long time. Sunlight inched across the rugs and finally faded as the sun moved behind the building, casting the room into a cooler afternoon light. Amy tried to resist but she still kept checking the time on her cellphone since there weren't any clocks in the room. Watching the minutes tick past did not help.

There wasn't a television or entertainment center that she could see. And the assistant never came back out to offer them something to do while they waited. So Amy spent most of the time drinking coffee, just to keep her hands busy. None of them spoke much, except to pass a few comments on the time or the deliciousness of one of the treats laid out for them. Cat munched her way through most of the food on the tray, drank two cups of the dark coffee, then started writing in the air—working out a math problem Amy could never hope to understand. Amy hunted for a notebook or something she might doodle in, but with no luck, so she went back to drinking coffee and studying Ethan.

Though, the longer she watched him, the more his expression worried her. As he paced, he spoke less and less frequently. The less he spoke, the more inexplicably nervous she got. She wasn't even sure what she was worried about exactly—beyond the obvious fact of being in mortal jeopardy. Something in Ethan's frown just set off alarm bells, and whenever he looked at her, he seemed to be struggling with something, his gaze dancing away from hers. If not for those brief looks, she might have gone to stand with him, drawn him into conversation just to make the time pass more quickly. But there was a distance in his eyes, a distraction that kept her from moving closer.

When she'd swallowed enough coffee to make a bathroom visit necessary, she knocked on the assistant's door. He showed her to a small half-bath on that floor, the door just off the entryway, which she'd missed when they'd been shown in. By the time she reemerged, giving way for Cat to use the facilities, the assistant was gone again. Ethan hadn't stopped pacing, and he didn't glance in her direction when she came out of the bathroom.

As she returned to the couch—since she didn't know what else to do with herself—she realized she could sense the assistant in his room off the kitchen, the way she'd been able to feel Ethan and Lin…Zhong. She hadn't been paying much attention to that before now, but it was something to focus on besides the dangerous situation she was in or the weird mood that had come over Ethan, so she turned her attention to that sensation, trying to see if she could pinpoint the exact location of the assistant. She turned her attention to Ethan next, keeping her eyes half-closed so she could focus on sensing him rather than getting caught up in studying him. The way she could *feel* him moving, know where he was without having to see him, was distracting enough that she forgot momentarily about being bored and scared, only barely noticing when Cat rejoined her on the couch.

Then Ethan stopped pacing and turned to face a door to the right, just beyond the circular stairs. Amy sat up a little straighter as she realized she could feel more tiger shifters in the apartment. A moment later, the door opened.

The two women who entered the room were an interesting contrast. One was tall, broad shouldered but lean, with shoulder-length brown hair, intelligent blue eyes, and a negligent grace that reminded Amy of the way athletes moved. She wore worn, faded jeans and a blue, long-sleeved t-shift that looked almost too casual for the elegant penthouse setting. There was a slight crease between her brows, and the corners of her eyes crinkled a bit as she took them all in in one sweeping glance. Since she looked to be in her mid-forties, Amy guessed this wasn't the elder. Which meant that unless Elizaveta had a bodyguard or a second assistant, the brunette was likely Alexis Tarasova.

The woman who followed her into the room did look old enough to be called an elder, but only barely. She was also tall, and very slim in that elegant way that Amy associated with rich people. Slim, Amy thought, but not delicate. There was a great deal of contained strength in the older woman's movements. She had beautiful white-silver hair that Amy instantly wanted to recreate in oils, the color more like metallic silver than gray as it caught the afternoon light and fairly sparkled. Her hair hung in loose waves around her shoulders, the style softening the sharp angles of her face and accentuating her long, slim neck.

Beyond a winking pair of diamond studs in her ears,

she wasn't wearing any jewelry that Amy could spot, not even a watch or ring. Her black slacks looked tailored to fit her perfectly and were free of wrinkles, her pale gray silk blouse managed to convey both elegance and a casual air.

This was New York. Amy had encountered and met a lot of wealthy people in her life. Devine's gallery catered to them, and since Devine was determined to help Amy into an art career whether Amy wanted to go there or not, she'd been introduced to many of the wealthy art patrons.

Elizaveta Chernikova was a step beyond anyone Amy had met before. Her wealth seemed to wrap around her like an aura she took for granted, her power emanating from some inner place, the money she obviously wielded just a side-effect of all that power.

So when Elizaveta looked at her and smiled warmly, Amy felt like an awkward teenager confronted by a gracious movie star. For a long moment, words and their meanings fled, leaving her a blinking mute.

Elizaveta glanced at Ethan. "My dear boy, please, sit," she said, her Russian accent rolling the words. "Your sister would be very upset with me if I didn't look after you. Since she's the mother of my great-granddaughter, I want her happy."

There was something in Elizaveta's tone when she said great-granddaughter, a kind of awe and wonder.

Ethan remained standing. "Amy Donovan, Catalina Donovan, this is Elizaveta Chernikova and Alexis Tarasova."

Amy belatedly thought to stand for the introductions, and nodded in greeting at both women.

Elizaveta waved a hand at her. "Sit. I insist. This is a troubling enough meeting. There's no need to stand on ceremony. At least not yet."

She crossed the room to them, her movements as graceful and deadly as a cat. Amy could see the tiger in Elizaveta easily. There would be no forgetting who this woman was.

Elizaveta took Cat's hands and squeezed. "It's a pleasure to meet you. I hear you're a genius. I look forward to discussing some…theories I have."

"Thank you," Cat said. "And maybe I can talk to some of your geneticists?"

"Cat," Amy hissed in warning. This wasn't the time.

Elizaveta smiled, not showing any sign of offense. "I would *love* your brilliant eye turned toward our plight."

"I'm a physicist. I'm not sure I can help with the reproduction thing. I just want to know how the shifting works."

"Every little bit helps," the elder said.

Just behind and to the right of her, Alexis nodded.

"And you are Amy," Elizaveta said. "It is truly a pleasure to meet you."

Elizaveta gripped Amy's hand in a firm shake, and Amy realized that while the older woman might look delicate, her handshake proved she was anything but.

"Pleasure," Amy muttered. "I think."

Elizaveta chuckled, the sound low and throaty. "Precisely. The circumstances are not optimal, but we shall be done with the technicalities soon and I will personally ensure your safety."

"You can do that?" Amy asked.

"Of course. I'm a wealthy, powerful woman. I can do whatever I like."

Alexis rolled her eyes at that.

And though Elizaveta didn't see the gesture, she said, "My daughter teases. In truth, I can do mostly what I like. It's good to be one of the wealthiest people in the world."

That brought a snort from Alexis.

Since Amy had no idea what to say to that, she just smiled—a gesture that felt forced and more a wince than the friendly expression she'd intended.

"Now," Elizaveta said, "you must sit. We have a lot to discuss. First, I would like to hear everything about your interactions with Zhong. In as much detail as you can remember."

After exchanging looks with Ethan and Cat, Amy started from the beginning, explaining everything she could remember from the last month when she'd first noticed the strange awareness of someone watching her.

"You had the same sense with Ethan?" Elizaveta interrupted to ask.

"Yes, but with him I thought it was more…this will sound a little airy fairy…but I thought he was my muse. That I could sense him because he was there to inspire my art."

"Well, he is a very attractive man," Elizaveta said with a half-shrug.

To Amy's amusement, two dark stains of red colored Ethan's cheekbones at the elder's compliment. The man dropped his robe and stood naked for a roomful of people to stare at and sketch him without even thinking about it, but a compliment from Elizaveta made him blush.

That was kind of sweet.

"He is," Amy said, "but I've sketched attractive people before. I'd never come across a person who I could feel even before they came into the room." She shrugged. "A muse for an artist seemed logical. I didn't know such things as tiger shifters existed."

"And Zhong… He felt the same as Ethan to you?"

"No. He scared me. Even before I came face to face with him. I felt…stalked whenever I sensed him."

"That's because you were being stalked," Alexis said, one of the few comments she'd offered to the conversation.

Amy went on to explain the tiger attack last night, the trip to the bank this morning, and the confrontation with Zhong outside the bank.

"He mentioned Roman by name?" Elizaveta asked. She and Alexis exchanged a look that seemed to convey a lot of unspoken information.

"Who is this guy?" Amy asked. "What does he have to do with my birth father?"

Another long look passed between Alexis and Elizaveta.

"You need to tell them everything now," Alexis said.

"I do not," Elizaveta said.

Alexis sighed. "I meant you *should* tell them about Zhong and what we suspect."

Elizaveta sniffed. When she faced Amy again, she said, "I allow her too much leeway because she's my adopted daughter. She thinks she can get away with telling me what I have to do."

"I do get away with it."

"Ha! Only when I let you." Before Alexis could respond to that, she said, "Zhong is… He has a complicated background. Now, he is a finder for lack of a better word. For a great deal of money, he will find and retrieve anything for anyone willing to pay, with very little scruples over doing what is necessary to achieve results. He's amassed a significant fortune because he's so good at this work. But before he specialized in finding…he was a hired assassin. Quite efficient and deadly."

Amy swallowed hard. Hearing the confirmation that Zhong could have killed them easily, at any time made her fingers numb.

"That's where I've heard his name," Ethan said. "A story my older brother told me…twenty years ago of a ghost assassinating a Chinese triad leader and his people. The one person who survived the attack claimed the killer was a demon tiger or something. But Peter was always trying to scare me with spook stories. I never believed it was actually true, and that Zhong was a real person, nonetheless one of *our* people."

"He's real," Elizaveta confirmed. "And quite deadly."

She spoke so casually about it, with the same tone she'd used to say Ethan was attractive. Like being deadly was a compliment or a desired attribute.

Elizaveta must have noticed something in Amy's expression because she said, "Deadly in our world is not unusual. In fact, it is a matter of survival at times. Being dangerous is not in and of itself a bad thing. It is how this skill is used. Zhong is very efficient and mercenary. Under most circumstances, I prefer this brand of deadly." She shrugged. "Mercenaries work for the money, not a cause or a belief. It is the fanatics working for a cause you must really fear."

"Zhong was pretty scary even without a cause," Amy said.

"But you are lucky the hybrids are not a cause to him."

"Are there…" Ethan hesitated. "Are there more hybrids than we know about?"

"There are," Elizaveta said. Again so casually. "They are still very rare. But there are more than the community realizes. And it is safer that way. For the hybrids. At least until we can refine our laws to better protect them." She glanced away. "Or that's what I thought before this incident."

For the first time since she'd entered the room, Elizaveta sounded hesitant and a little tired. That worried Amy more than knowing just how deadly Zhong was.

Elizaveta pulled in a breath, and when she spoke again, there was no further sign of the hesitance. "But that is for a different day."

"You haven't explained what Zhong has to do with my birth father yet," Amy said.

Elizaveta answered after a quiet moment, "Roman was a former Tracker. What is not common knowledge… The man known as Zhong now, he was trained as a Tracker."

"By Roman," Alexis said.

"What happened between them?" Amy leaned forward a little, as if she might catch the details faster that way.

"Zhong was on a path to being one of our best Trackers," Elizaveta said. "Roman was an excellent teacher. Like Alexis."

Alexis smiled a little and gave the elder a strange look, as if she hadn't expected the comment and wasn't entirely sure it was a compliment.

"Zhong had only one brother, a twin who, though very young, had managed to claim a mate and was expecting his first child. The brother and his mate lived in a village in China that was…overseen by member of the Chinese mafia. Neither brother was concerned with this fact. Tiger shifters don't pay much attention to the human world around them except to use it as camouflage. It never occurred to either Zhong or his twin to worry about the humans—Zhong gave his brother enough money to pay the required bribes, so they didn't consider the gang a threat. But Zhong's brother's mate was extremely beautiful and she drew the attention of a dangerous human male."

Amy closed her eyes briefly, afraid she knew where the story was going.

"Once a tiger female is pregnant," Alexis said quietly, "she can't shift. If she does, she'll lose the baby. She's still strong and fast, but without being able to let her tiger out, she is a little more vulnerable."

"The brother and his mate were taken by surprise," Elizaveta said. "While Zhong was away with Roman on a job. I do not know all the details because Roman never talked about them, and of course neither did Zhong. But both his brother and his brother's mate were killed, along with the unborn baby." She let out a long, low sigh. "Apparently, the child would have been a female. A true tragedy for us all."

"What did Zhong do?" Amy asked.

Elizaveta said, "He took revenge against the men who'd killed his family. But they were human. That is against our laws. Roman was sent to bring him in for punishment."

Amy sat back. "Ethan told me that was a crime punishable by death among your people."

Something moved through Elizaveta's expression. "It is. It is seen as even worse if the murder is committed in tiger form." She glanced away. "Thirty years ago, the elders decided there could be no more exceptions to that law, no more extenuating circumstances to allow for leniency. Before that, there had been occasions…" She trailed off.

The woman looked older in that moment, worn and sad, but in a blink, she shook it off as if the moment had never happened.

Amy wanted to ask about that pause, about the sadness she'd seen in the elder's eyes, but she was afraid it would take them off topic and she wanted to hear the rest of Roman and Zhong's story.

"At any rate," Elizaveta said, her tone once more casual and cool. "Roman has never explained what passed between him and Zhong when he went after him. Zhong got away and has been an outcast ever since. Roman quit his job as a Tracker and refused to train any more people."

"He saw the failure with Zhong as his fault," Alexis said.

"You know him?" Amy asked.

"We met a few times, after he moved to the U.S., back when I was still a Tracker."

"So as you can see, there is some history between the two men," Elizaveta said.

"What does that mean for me?" Amy asked.

"At the moment? Nothing. You are here. We will have you confirmed as a hybrid. Zhong will leave you alone."

"If he's killed humans before…"

Elizaveta waved that away. "As I said, he's mercenary now. The hybrids are not his cause. He has no reason to kill you. In fact, it seems from the message he wanted you to pass on to Roman, he specifically wants you alive."

"What about the person who hired him?"

Elizaveta shrugged. "I will take care of that."

"But…"

"It was not an anti-hybrid tiger," Alexis said. "We know that much or you'd be dead. Whoever it was, we'll find him and take care of the situation. You'll be safe as soon as the elders formally recognize you."

"The fact that you have the name of your tiger father is a great advantage," Elizaveta said. "Not all of the hybrids will know this. The two brought before the community to this point had confirmed tiger parents, which made it impossible to deny their heritage. There are some in our community who would attempt to deny a hybrid their place without such information, and this would leave those individuals vulnerable to the anti-hybrid faction among our kind." She shrugged. "It's another reason for keeping the identities of other hybrids secret."

"How many are there?" Ethan asked, his voice quiet.

Amy looked at him, closely this time. He was a little pale, but also very intent. And she couldn't read his expression.

"I am keeping watch over six others at the moment," Elizaveta said quietly. "I trust you will not say this to anyone, Ethan. As a member of my family, I expect you to preserve the secret."

Ethan blinked a few times, seeming startled by his inclusion in Elizaveta's family, as well as her trust in him to keep a secret.

"How many females?" he murmured.

"Five of the six."

"So," he paused and wet his lips. "So of the…nine hybrids you know of, eight of them have been female."

Elizaveta nodded, her brows raised. "Actually, there was a tenth hybrid as well, who was also female."

"Right, right. I almost forgot. Paige Williams' mother."

"Precisely. So you can see why this is valuable information."

Amy frowned a question at Ethan, but he was lost in thought.

"Paige Williams is a human," Alexis said into the quiet. "But her mother was a hybrid. By the time we learned of the mother's nature, she was already dead. However, Paige can sense tiger shifters like you can, and we've confirmed she can have children with a tiger shifter as well. Paige married my husband's best friend," she added with a slight smile.

"They really could help, then, couldn't they?" Ethan said, a touch of awe in his voice.

"It is more possible now than I have ever thought before," Elizaveta said. She faced Amy again. "Your mother was fully human, as are you Cat, but because your mother could mate with a tiger and create a child, there's every possibility that Cat can, too. Amy, if you chose a human mate to have children with, those children could possibly reproduce with a tiger—they would likely be able to sense tigers just as you can, just as Paige can. The number of options grows the more we learn."

"There's something you're not saying, though, isn't there?" Amy asked.

"As smart as your sister, I see," Elizaveta said with a slight smile. "Because of the extinction issue, we have had a tightly controlled process amongst tigers for choosing mates—to protect the females and give the males the illusion of competition. The Mate Run."

Ethan sucked in a breath and his expression closed up, the awe gone, a mask in place. Amy frowned at his reaction, but he didn't acknowledge her unspoken question.

"The laws around the Mate Run govern all reproduction in our community at the moment. However, those laws break down when we introduce hybrids."

"Those like you who can't shift," Alexis said, "can't physically participate in a Mate Run. The humans like Cat and your mother couldn't participate in a Mate Run. If you have children with a human man, they'll be human and not able to participate."

"They can't be controlled by our current laws," Ethan said, his tone flat. "They don't have to mate with a tiger if they don't want to."

His tone alerted Amy to something unspoken. "Are you saying female tigers *have* to mate with another tiger? They have to have kids? What if they don't want kids, or fall in love with someone who's not a tiger shifter?"

"The law is the law. We are on the verge of extinction," Elizaveta said. And left it at that.

Amy wasn't sure how to feel about all this. And from the look on Ethan's face, he had some serious issues with this Mate Run, too. But from the way he'd shut down, she figured that was a better conversation to have in private.

So she got back to the issue at hand. "All this is fascinating, and I'm sure I'll need to learn more, but at the moment, my real concern is staying alive and protecting my sister. How do we accomplish that?"

"I will confirm your connection to Roman Kadnikov. It will help to have a blood sample, if you don't object. My assistant Reginald is also a medic and can take the blood safely. For tonight, you should stay here where we can protect you from whoever hired Zhong to find you. Tomorrow, the other elders will convene to formally acknowledge you as a part of our community. At that point, you should be safe."

"What if it wasn't a tiger shifter who hired Zhong?" Ethan asked. "What if it wasn't someone controlled by our laws?"

"Then I will have him eliminated," the elder said matter-of-factly. "I will not allow threats to my people from an outside force. A threat to the hybrids *is* a threat to the tigers."

Amy swallowed. This talk of "eliminating" people, discussed so casually, was so far beyond her experience it was unreal. This was like being in some demented movie, an over-the-top action film with a paranormal twist where even good guys weren't *good*.

Was this really a world she wanted to be part of? A world she wanted Cat exposed to?

She glanced at Ethan. If she wanted him in her life, she'd always be part of this tiger shifter world, like it or not. She'd be confronted with this reality daily. Was he worth that to her? Was any man worth that?

Ethan finally looked at her then, holding her gaze. She couldn't tell if he knew what she was thinking or not, though based on what he'd told her, he could probably smell something of what she was feeling. How did he feel about all this? Did *he* want to live with this reality, of dating a hybrid, of having to confront parts of his community he could avoid simply by choosing another woman?

They'd known each other for such a short period of time, only a couple of months. They were still in the early stages of a relationship. But Amy had seen it as a potentially serious one. Very serious. Confronting this decision already, when there was still so much potential between them, felt horrible. There was so much still to learn and say to each other.

She tried to think of what her world might be like if she just gave up on a future with Ethan. She could let him go, move on, let him move on. Avoid the complications all together, and they could both go their separate ways.

Her world dimmed a little at the thought, the colors around her growing duller and less vital. And she was afraid if she did give up, she wouldn't just lose a muse. She'd lose her heart.

Cat broke into the growing silence to remind everyone of Spike.

"Spike?" Alexis asked.

"Our dog," Amy said. "We can't leave her alone all night. She'll worry. And she needs to be walked."

Alexis smiled. "A dog named Spike. I like it. What is she? A bulldog or something?"

"She's a miniature poodle," Ethan said. "With fluffy white fur."

"Actually blue, purple, pink, and white fur," Amy said, her chin raised. "She likes color."

Alexis nodded and said with no hint of sarcasm, "Of course. Sounds exactly right."

Amy decided she liked Alexis. "We really can't leave her," she said. "She does have a carrier, though. If your building allows pets, she won't be a problem. She doesn't even shed."

"The building will allow Spike," Elizaveta said. "I own it, so they have to do what I say."

Amy blinked a few times, as the realization sank in that the elder didn't just own this magnificent apartment, but the *entire* Upper East Side building. "Wow, you really are rich."

Elizaveta's smile was wide and genuine. "Yes, I am. It's very handy."

Alexis snorted and shook her head. "Don't encourage her," she said. "About Spike, it's probably not safe for you to return to your apartment. If Zhong's client even suspects you've been warned about his intentions, he may bypass Zhong and send someone else after you."

"Then how do we get Spike?" Cat sounded on the verge of panic. She leaned forward, intent on Alexis.

"My assistant can collect her," Elizaveta said. "He is actually quite good with dogs. For a cat."

"Spike's not going to like a strange man sticking her in her carrier," Amy warned. "Especially one that smells like a tiger shifter." She glanced at Cat. "Maybe I can go with your assistant?"

"No," Elizaveta said firmly. "We can't risk it." The elder glanced at Ethan, her eyes narrowed. "However, since Spike knows Ethan already, perhaps he would accompany

Reginald. Between the two of them, they should be able to avoid any threats and retrieve Spike safely."

"I'd be happy to," Ethan said, with no hesitance at all.

Amy smiled at him, grateful, relieved, and worried all at once. "Just be careful, okay. Zhong is supposed to kill you for his client."

"He'll wait until closer to the deadline," Ethan said sardonically. "I have till tomorrow before I need to worry."

She made a face but reached out and gripped his hand, for once glad he'd be able to read her emotions because she wanted him to know how she felt just then.

Since Amy and Cat had already packed for a trip, and Ethan knew the general layout of the apartment, making arrangements to have their travel packs, the carrier, and Spike collected was easy enough. Amy spent most of the arrangement time trying to talk Cat out of going with the two shifters. The only thing that convinced Cat to stay at the elder's apartment was Elizaveta promising to discuss tiger shifter DNA and everything her genetics labs had learned in their years of research. Cat was too intrigued to say no.

Amy tried to relax while Ethan was gone, attempting a little stilted small-talk with Alexis, but in the end she couldn't focus enough for conversation. She ended up pacing in front of the large wall of windows, just as Ethan had before they'd met Elizaveta.

"Bored, or worried?" Alexis asked quietly, joining her at the windows.

"I'm sorry. I don't mean to be rude. I'm worried. And restless. I don't know what to do with my hands."

"You're an artist? Just a minute. I think we have something around here that might help."

She disappeared through the door to the left, to the room where Reginald had gone after letting them into the apartment. When she came back out again, she had a notebook and a sharpened pencil.

"It's a blank notebook," Alexis said. "Not exactly artist quality pencil and paper, but you can at least keep your hands busy."

Amy smiled, taking the proffered notebook and pencil gratefully. "Thanks."

Alexis waved away the thanks and rejoined Elizaveta and Cat on the couch. Amy settled into a cushioned chair by the window and looked out over Central Park, taking in the views, looking for a perspective, then letting the pencil scratch over a page. The familiar movements, the concentration and distraction of bringing the skyline to life, pushed aside all other thoughts and worries. Time blurred as she flipped pages, sketching different angles, small details, studying the interplay of early evening light on one of the trees across the street at the edge of the park. Her work so consumed her focus, she blinked up in surprise when she heard Spike barking wildly.

She dropped the notebook and pencil and hurried to the carrier Ethan held. "Spike! You're okay." To Ethan she said, "Did she give you any trouble?"

"She gave Reginald some problems, but after I took her out for a short walk, I was a hero so she cuddled up to me."

Amy chuckled. "That's a good dog," she said through

the holes in the wired door, sticking her fingers through an open square so Spike could lick them.

Cat joined her as she took Spike's carrier and set it down on the ground. She looked at Elizaveta. "I'd like to let her out, but…she will claim your apartment as her own."

"Let her," Elizaveta said with a hand wave. "That's what I have a cleaning staff for."

Amy opened the carrier door. Spike hovered inside for a long moment, staring out at her strange surroundings. A low growl rose from the carrier's interior. "Come on Spike. It's okay. I know there are a lot of cats in the room, but they'll be nice to you. Just like Ethan."

Spike nudged her head just outside the opening. Ethan had left her spiked collar on, which meant that as she eased out of the carrier, her true badass nature was on full display.

"That's my girl," Amy said.

Cat didn't wait for Spike to fully emerge before she swept the dog up into her arms and gave her a scratch behind the ears. "See, baby, no problems at all."

Spike still growled faintly, her lip lifting to reveal pink gums and sharp teeth. But she leaned into Cat's scratching and her little doggy expression turned happy. Her puffball tail wagged even as she continued the low growl.

Amy shook her head.

"Now, we are all set," Elizaveta said. "Come with me and I'll show you to your rooms."

The elder led the way up the spiraling staircase. Amy gripped the intricate copper railing and focused on not looking between her feet through the open stairs. She wasn't exactly afraid of heights, but she didn't like being able to see open space beneath her. Which was why she preferred roller coasters to Ferris wheels.

The second floor was as simply luxurious as the first. The corridor was lined with more classic art, most of it nature focused. Doors to several rooms opened off the hallway, though most of them were closed.

Elizaveta stopped at a door and gestured to the one across the hall. "For Cat and Amy." She moved a few yards away and gestured at another door. "Ethan, you can stay here." She waved a hand farther up the hallway. "There is a main bathroom that way, but there are small half-baths in your rooms. When you're through settling in, please come back downstairs. We have a few more things to discuss."

Amy pushed into her room and stopped on the threshold for a long moment, taking in the space. As was typical even in luxury apartment buildings in Manhattan, the room wasn't particularly large, but it was beautifully perfect in its simplicity—glossy hardwood floors, soft green walls, a bed so tall there was a step to get up to it, a few *arts de object* on asymmetrically arranged floating shelves, huge windows that looked toward the park, a door to the left into a small, neat bathroom, and a walk-in closet at the other end of the room. There was a cushioned bench at the base of the bed and a mixture of wildflowers in two crystal vases on the chrome and glass bedside tables.

It was such a nice room, Amy thought it a shame she'd only be here to enjoy it for one night.

She glanced back to see Cat had disappeared into her

own room. Amy could hear her opening and closing things as she explored, talking to Spike the whole time.

Tossing her backpack onto the bench at the foot of the bed, Amy sat down and took a deep breath, pulling in the soft, floral scent from the wildflowers. The tension of the day washed over her, the adrenaline that had kept her moving finally abandoning her. Exhaustion washed over her and for a long moment, all she could do was sit and stare at the floor.

"Now what?" she murmured to the quiet room.

From below, the sounds of Fifth Avenue traffic just reached her, a few horns and the noise of a passing firetruck the only real sounds in the room beyond her own breathing.

"Get a grip, Amy. You're almost done with this. Then..." She glanced back at the open door. Then she'd have some decisions to make. She'd been working in survival mode since last night, focusing on the immediate future. But by tomorrow this should be settled, and she'd have to decide where she went from there.

"Back to college and work," she murmured, shaking her head. Back to real life.

But back to real life alone?

That was the question.

CHAPTER FOURTEEN

Amy was still awake, lying in the huge bed, staring at the ceiling well past when everyone else had gone to bed. She glanced at her phone, charging on the bedside table. Three in the morning. She sighed and pressed her hand to her forehead. Considering how tired she was, she was more than a little annoyed she couldn't actually fall asleep.

The luxurious 1,500-threadcount Egyptian cotton sheets were wasted on her tonight. After flopping around a few more times, she gave in to the inevitable. She'd face the elders tomorrow with bags under her eyes and a grumpy, sleep-deprived attitude.

From what Alexis and Ethan had hinted about the rest of the elders, Amy had a feeling that attitude would probably work better for her anyway.

Throwing the thick, snuggly blankets back, she swung out of the huge bed, almost collapsing to the floor because she'd forgotten how high the mattress was and hadn't used the step. Scowling back at the bed, like it was the bed's fault she'd almost fallen, she pulled on the sweater she had tossed across the bench at the foot of the bed, slipping it over her pajamas. Then she padded to the closed door and paused to listen.

Silence.

The door opened without making noise, but she took the time to click it closed quietly behind her. She didn't want to wake anyone else. She paused in the hall. With that weird sense she could now blame on being a hybrid, she could feel Ethan in his bedroom, as well as Alexis and Elizaveta in their individual rooms at the opposite end of the corridor. If she focused really hard, she could sense Reginald in a room on the first floor—the room by the kitchen she'd assumed was an office but must be a bedroom.

She hesitated. Given their sensitive hearing, she didn't want to wake Reginald by going downstairs for water. He probably needed all the sleep he could get, working for Elizaveta. But thirst and restlessness won out. She tiptoed down the long rug running the length of the hallway to the spiral stairs. The wooden steps creaked a little as she went down, but she moved slowly in an attempt to minimize the noise.

In the open kitchen, Amy hunted the cabinets until she found a glass. The water from the faucet was cold and crisp. Cradling the glass, she wandered to the wall of windows and looked out over the park. The skyline was dotted with spots of light in building windows, so many she could almost forget it was three in the morning. She sipped her water. The city that never sleeps, indeed. She smiled, her gaze drawn to the street below. Traffic was a lot lighter now, with just a few taxis and some delivery trucks quietly sliding past. A few blocks south, the grand white edifice of the Metropolitan Museum of Art fairly glowed in the street lights. Was it really just three weeks ago that she'd been there with Ethan on their first date? A first date that had hinted at so much…possibility.

Distracted by the view, she didn't notice the awareness along her spine until the scent of soap and male reached her. She didn't turn to look at him when she said, "I didn't wake you, did I?"

"No." Ethan's voice was quiet. "I couldn't sleep. I keep waking up every time I hear the slightest noise. My tiger is on watch tonight and won't settle."

She did face him then. "On watch?"

"Making sure you're safe."

She pulled in a breath, swamped with a tenderness that seemed at odds with the length of time they'd known each other. "You're worried about that here?"

"I've been worried about you since I saw Zhong at the gallery Thursday night."

"Was that really just Thursday night? Seems like weeks have passed."

He smiled a little. He was standing near enough for her to reach out and touch. In the room's darkness, lit only by streetlights and the ambient city glow, the shadows cut into his features, emphasizing the curve of his jaw, the darkness of his eyes. He was wearing a pair of loose sweats and a t-shirt—curtesy of Reginald since Ethan hadn't been home to pack clothes yet. The t-shirt was too small so it fit his muscled physique like a second skin, and all she could think about was stripping it off and running her hands over all those muscles.

Would his skin taste as delicious as his kisses?

In the dark, it felt like another world, another reality. A place where she could touch him, kiss him, and not worry about what happened tomorrow.

A nagging part of her insisted the changes weren't a big deal. It didn't matter what she was, or what he was, they were still the same people. But she got the distinct impression from him that he felt a change between them as much as she did, something that had gotten progressively more obvious through the evening.

"Can we talk without waking Reginald?" she asked.

"He'll ignore us and go back to sleep if he does hear us."

She glanced toward the closed door to Reginald's room, then back at Ethan. He seemed closer now, but that might be because she was so aware of him. "Let's sit."

He swept his hand out for her to lead the way. The gesture made her smile. They settled on the large couch close enough to speak quietly.

But as she stared at him, she couldn't decide where to start. She wasn't even sure how to put her thoughts into words. The intimacy of the darkness helped, though. Like she had permission to say things now that she couldn't say aloud in daylight.

"Why does me being a hybrid change things for you?"

she finally said. "Don't say it doesn't. It has changed something between us. I've noticed it since the fight with Zhong. It got more obvious tonight over dinner. I'd like to understand why that is, from your perspective."

"Has it changed things for you? Now that you've seen me shift. Now that you understand a little more about my world?"

"I thought it would much more than it has, frankly." She laid her cards on the table, because prevaricating now seemed pointless. "I still want you, which I know you've realized. I still like you. A lot. Maybe more than just like—or at least it could be more than that at some point. But… something is different for you."

He sighed and glanced toward the windows, his expression shadowed and impossible to read.

"It has to do with the Mate Run," he said finally, quietly. "The…the way our people have to find mates that can give them children. The expectations and disappointments."

"You're not being very clear."

He shook his head, half-smiling when he looked back at her. "It was always assumed by my family that I'd be one of the rare males to get a tiger shifter mate. I've never been sure why me above my older brother. Maybe because he's never shown much interest in children and family—much to my mother's chagrin. But as far back as I can remember, I've wanted a wife, children of my own, the kind of love and family my parents had together. The kind my sister has now."

"But?"

He shrugged. "It didn't work out that way."

"You did these Mate Runs?"

"Most males who want children do. It's almost more biological than a conscious choice. Because the chances of having kids are so slim, most tiger males really really want them."

"If nothing else, that would prove just how different your species is to humans," she said with a little snort.

"Maybe outwardly. When push comes to shove, though, most men want to…pass on their genes. Most species do. And when the chances are as low as they are with my people, that drive increases."

"So what happens with your Mate Runs?"

"During Runs, the female makes the choice of which male she'll pick. When she comes into estrous, she runs, we chase, she picks a male—or males—to spend her estrous with, let's them catch her, and the couple spends the three days of her cycle…fucking in the hopes of getting her pregnant."

Amy blinked a few times, the thought of the whole thing so…alien. "And you all do this voluntarily, right?"

"Yes." He shrugged. "Well, technically. It's the law— the only way to earn a mate and get a tiger shifter female is through the Mate Run. She has the choice of which male she selects, but females are required to participate and have children."

"What if they don't want children?" Elizaveta had brushed that question aside. Did any of these people consider that? Amy had a number of friends who never intended to have kids. They'd be pissed if someone tried to force children on them.

"Most do," Ethan said. "As far as I know, no female has refused the duty to our people. Well, Alexis got around the Runs, but even then she still had kids. It's as much a biological call for the females as it is for the males."

"How did your sister feel about all this?"

"She wanted kids. So she ran." He lifted his brows, his head tilted to one side. "Actually, she ran for a long time before she met her husband. There's more there than she'll admit to." He smiled faintly. "During her Runs, before Nick joined, Tiana just keep running, never actually picking a male. A lot of people thought she didn't want kids."

"But she did?"

"And once Nick finally entered her Run, they got pregnant immediately."

"So it worked out for your sister."

"In the end. And after three years of worrying her family."

Amy chuckled softly. "But she wanted children. What if a woman really doesn't want them—are they forced to have them because of the law?"

He frowned, his forehead crinkling. "They're…encouraged."

"Sounds barbaric."

"From your perspective, I guess it might. It's so much a part of our society, a lot of us only see the good the Run has done us. The Mate Run was put into place to prevent deaths and chaos. More than two hundred years ago, when the low number of females really became obvious, we descended into anarchy—males killing males, kidnappings, gang rapes which often resulted in killing the tigress, a lot of violence and bloodshed that pushed us to the very brink. The Mate Run stopped that, gave us a structure that we've been clinging to ever since. When the alternative is that kind of violence, I guess the current laws look much more civilized."

"Why don't your males just control themselves? You're grown-ups, right?"

He snorted. "There's the question. As it happens, a question a lot of our people are asking right now. Things have changed in the last few years. The hybrids coming to our attention, some other stuff happening… Some say it's the death knell for the Mate Run. But we don't have an alternative yet, so we keep running."

Amy wasn't sure how to feel about all this. The whole thing sounded very restrictive and…forced, to her. If she didn't want kids, she wouldn't have them. The fact that tiger shifter women didn't seem to have that choice grated against her feminist principles.

She wanted to argue the point more, but that wouldn't get her the answers she'd wanted when she'd started this conversation. "Okay, politics aside, you wanted kids, so you took part in the Mate Runs."

"Yes."

A strange thought occurred to her, one she hadn't even thought to ask before now. "Do you have kids?"

"No."

"What happened?" She sensed it was something significant—even if his dark expression hadn't already given his mood away.

"There was a tigress… Siya. She picked me. Three Runs in a row, we were together. She said she loved me. I thought I loved her. When that happens, a couple will just keep coming together during the Run until they get pregnant. They aren't allowed to see each other outside the Run—"

"Why?"

"There can't be any blatant signs of a male trying to curry favor with a female outside the Run territory. To prevent fights. It's very illegal for us to interact with females between their Runs and can get us banned from participating."

"Did you go to her between Runs? Is that what happened?" She was trying not to let the stab of jealousy at hearing he'd been in love with another woman dig too deeply. She hadn't even known him then. But her chest squeezed tight with the sensation anyway. She leaned over to set her water glass on the coffee table so he wouldn't see her expression.

"No, I followed the rules," he said quietly. "I wanted a family, remember. If I'd broken the law, we couldn't have been together, ever. I thought I was in love. I thought she was the one, my future wife, the future mother of my children. As far as I was concerned, it was just a matter of time. We'd run until she was pregnant, and then we'd live happily ever after."

Amy could practically taste the bitterness in his voice, sharp and angry, full of sadness. Lost in dark thoughts, he fell silent, and she waited him out, not wanting to break into that inner turmoil with her questions.

Finally, he said, "On the fourth Run, she picked someone else."

"I thought you said…"

"She wanted children more than she wanted me. When we weren't pregnant after three tries, she decided to try a new male."

"If she was in love with you…" Amy frowned. Why would any woman in her right mind give up Ethan? "Does it usually only take a time or two to get pregnant?"

"It can take years, and has for some couples. If they're in love, they stick together."

"What did you do?"

"Got very angry and left the territory like a wounded animal, nursing my hurt feelings. But I came back for her next Run, thinking she'd have gotten this out of her system and come back to me." He made a face. "I was an idiot."

Amy wanted to reach out and comfort him but was afraid he'd reject the offer.

"That Run, she picked yet another male. I started to think she was torturing me on purpose, pushing to see how much I really wanted her. Trying to get me to fight for her."

"Did you?"

"We're not supposed to fight during the Run. That's the point of it, to prevent death matches."

"Death matches?"

"When tiger males challenge one another over a female, those fights can end in the death of one or both males."

"Jesus," Amy muttered. "But you thought this tigress wanted you to fight anyway?"

"After the second Run, when she chose another male, I did. I'm not proud of what happened in those months. I turned into someone I don't recognize now. I went crazy, with a consuming sort of desperation—" He cut himself off and ran a hand through his hair. "By the time I came back for her next Run, I'd convinced myself she was testing me and I had to prove myself by beating the crap out of any male that got near her." He grimaced. "I wasn't thinking clearly at that stage. The jealousy was…warping my logic."

"You fought?"

"I did. And I'm ashamed of it now. So much for being a grown up, right?"

Amy didn't respond, and Ethan didn't wait for an answer.

"Siya let the male she'd picked right after me catch her on that Run," he continued. "I challenged him, we fought, and we almost killed each other. Then she left us bleeding to go off with yet another male."

Amy couldn't resist the need to comfort anymore. She reached out and gripped his wrist. "Ethan," she breathed, not sure what she wanted to say. Outside of wanting to call this other woman a bitch. And worse.

He didn't react to her touch, but he didn't pull away. The pain in his expression was palpable, stark and difficult to witness.

"I never told my family what happened," he said. "I didn't want them to worry, although they did anyway when they realized I'd stopped running. I never wanted them to know what I'd done, what I'd become in my jealousy." He turned his hand over and gripped hers, staring at their linked fingers. "I swore I'd never put myself into that situation again. Never risk my heart on those hopes of family and love with a tigress. I turned my back on my people, intending to live in the human world and to hell with the tigers outside of my own family." He kept his gaze averted. "I've only dated human women since."

She was starting to get an inkling of why things were different now between them, but she didn't want to guess. She waited for him to say the words.

"When I met you," he said. He blew out a breath. "I had the same sort of…overwhelming draw toward you that I'd had with Siya. I fully intended to run away from those emotions."

She blinked. "Why didn't you?"

He shook his head, huffing out a quiet, derisive snort. "I couldn't. I made excuses. I sensed a male following you and convinced myself I needed to protect you."

"So…" She swallowed. Something inside Amy started to curl in on itself, protective and sad and hurt for reasons she was still working out. "So when you asked for my phone number, our first date? It was all just a…a lie?" The pain of that cut a lot deeper than she wanted to admit. She'd known he was out of her league. She'd known risking her heart on someone like him was a mistake. She let her fingers slip out of his, staring at her closed fist so she wouldn't have to meet his gaze.

"I never meant to hurt you," he said quietly. "I thought we could have a nice afternoon at the museum and say goodbye without either of us getting hurt. I was lying to myself."

"Meaning?"

"I wanted you so much I ached with it. So much, it terrified me. I might have fooled myself into thinking I was trying to protect you, but that wasn't why I asked you out. I just couldn't let you go."

She jerked her chin in a slight nod, a confusion of feelings clogging her throat.

"What happened with Siya," he said, "I never wanted to turn into that man again. And I thought, with you, I'd go down that same road."

"You still think that?"

"I was just starting to believe things were different. That because you were human, we'd never have to deal with the pressure and competition that consumes my people and their relationships. That I could stay myself and still love you."

Her chest tightened. "But now that's all changed." It wasn't a question.

"You'll have your choice of any tiger male you want. You can even choose to forgo this world and stick to the human world, find a human man…"

He cleared his throat and she finally looked up at him.

"The elders will encourage you to let males compete for you, and for you to select a tiger male. They'll encourage you to have children."

"Where does that leave you?"

"I swore I'd never compete for a female again. That I'd never lose myself that way again."

She nodded, understanding his reasons even as pain exploded in her chest. "So…" She stood, her throat thick, trying to force down the prickling sensation in her eyes. "Okay then."

"Amy…"

"Don't. It's okay. I understand. I can't blame you." She blinked back the moisture in her eyes and swallowed hard around the lump in her throat. "For the record, I would never pit you against another man just for shits and giggles. I wouldn't hurt you that way. I like who you are and wouldn't want you to do anything that made you feel… regret. And so you know, you were my choice. But we've only just started to… It's still early enough that we can end things now and walk away without getting too hurt."

He reached out and took hold of her wrist in a gentle hold, tugging her closer when she tried to pull away.

"That's the thing, though," he murmured. "I can't walk away from you now. Even if I wanted to. It turns out, in a painful twist of fate, it actually is too late for me to avoid getting hurt if you disappear from my life. It was too late for me the moment I first saw you."

CHAPTER FIFTEEN

Ethan held her gaze, making an effort to breathe as he waited for her reaction. He could see the hurt in her eyes, and the confusion. And he cursed himself for ever lying to her. Especially since it had all been in service of a lie to himself—one he'd never even believed. He could never have really walked away from her. It would wreck him now to do it. He realized with a shock that he would fight for her if he had to—he'd fight his people; he'd defy the laws…whatever it took.

But ultimately, the choice was hers.

As the silence stretched out painfully, he started to think he'd ruined what they'd been building toward, no matter what choices she might have made before this. He'd hurt her and he didn't know how to fix that.

Ethan let her wrist slide out of his grip, reluctant to let her go but not wanting to push her any further.

She caught him just before he released her, turning her palm into his so she was holding his hand, their fingers intertwined. With a gentle tug, she pulled him to his feet. He went, frowning, unsure of her and unable to read her. There was a lot there, all tangled together—in her scent, her expression, her body language—and none of it gave him the first clue what she was thinking.

Then she reached up and kissed him. At first just a soft brush of lips, a gentle pressure, a sip. He'd barely registered the impact when she flowed against him, her body pressed to the length of his, her curves all warm and soft, and all his hesitance dissolved into nothingness.

He wrapped his arms around her, deepening the kiss because a taste wasn't enough. He wanted to drink her in, absorb her, take her into his very soul and hold her there. Their tongues tangled, danced, explored in a kiss that was both languid and passionate, building to more. And the more he took, the more she gave, the more he wanted.

He worked his hands down her spine in a long caress that made her arch against him like a cat. The comparison made him smile against her lips. She moaned quietly when he slid his hands up under her sweater and shirt to stroke the skin along her back. She was so warm, so smooth, he lost himself for a moment just exploring her textures, the flex of her muscles, the way she trembled when he ran a finger along the delicate indent of her spine, her groan when he caressed her waist, smoothing up to her ribs and just beneath her breasts. She was a glorious combination of strength and delicacy, a complex blend of pure femininity that made him dizzy.

The call to explore her further, to follow the brush of fingers with the caress of lips had him tugging her toward the stairs. Though he was reluctant to release her even a little, he lifted his head to look down at her. She was flushed and breathing faster, her lips deliciously plump and glistening with moisture. Her eyes a little unfocused, like she was as dazed as he felt. Caught in the sleepy sexiness of her eyes, he almost forgot what he'd been doing.

"Upstairs," she murmured, her voice husky.

The reminder was all he needed. He picked her up, which made her squeal against his shoulder to muffle the sound.

"Ethan, what are you doing?"

"Being impatient," he said. "And wanting to show off a little."

Before she could respond, he moved, reaching the second floor and the door of his room in two short seconds. He set her down and she wobbled. Catching her, he lifted her chin with one hand. "You okay?"

"Wow," she murmured.

Then she was kissing him again, making him forget to preen under her compliment, too caught up in her to wonder if she *had* complimented him.

He scrambled to open the door, pushing inside while still trying to keep his hands on her. Though tempted to just kick the door closed, a small part of his conscious recognized that waking the rest of the apartment just then would be a bad idea—and a disruption he didn't want to deal with.

But once the door clicked into place, his world became the woman in his arms.

Without releasing her, he backed to the ridiculously high bed—he had no idea what Elizaveta saw in beds like this—until he bumped into the mattress. He helped Amy up onto the bed and crawled up after her, returning to her mouth like his next breath depended on it. They stripped quickly—her sweater and cozy pajamas that shouldn't have been sexy but were hit the ground in a rush. His sweatpants and t-shirt followed. In the back of his mind, he wondered if he should have moved slower, taking his time to remove her clothes, but he didn't have the patience and she didn't seem to mind.

Once he had her naked, stretched out next to him, some of the underlying desperation eased. He wanted to savor every inch of her, worship her the way he'd been dreaming about for weeks. Kissing his way to the side of her neck, he bit gently and reveled in her moan. Her scent called to him, and he nuzzled against her hot skin, soaking up the essence of her even as his hands worked down her sides to her stomach. Her muscles bunched and quivered under his touch. For a moment, he just held his hand against her lower abdomen, caressing her in gentle strokes, listening to her breathing turn ragged.

So damned sensitive. He kissed the delicate skin beneath her ear, and she gripped his hair, holding him there as he explored the side of her neck. By soft, circular sweeps, he moved his palm up her ribs, letting his fingers brush the skin under her breast. She rolled a little, pulling him closer, wrapping her leg up over his hip. The feel of her heat so close to his erection nearly overwhelmed his desire to move slower and savor.

As if she knew she'd tipped the balance, she reached for his cock, gripping him with hot, silky strength. He closed his eyes, groaning.

"I can't tell you how hard it was not to think about you doing just this during those art sessions," he said. "Your scent was like a drug."

"I've spent two months now imagining you while I'm in the shower, your hands on me, my hands on you like this." She squeezed a little harder, then stroked the length of him.

"Fuck." The curse came out from between clenched teeth. Sparks swam in his vision behind his closed eyelids.

"My mouth on you," she whispered.

She broke him with that. Restraint and savoring went out the window. He captured her mouth, devouring her. He cupped her breasts, kneading the soft flesh, pinching her nipples. She arched and groaned and panted, and each sound, each movement drove him crazier. He had to taste more. Dropping his mouth to her breast, he sucked her until she was as wild as he was, her hands tugging and pulling at him as if she didn't know where she wanted him most. When he bit gently, testing her, she pressed a hand to her mouth to hold in a near scream.

"I love how sensitive your skin is," he growled and moved farther down her body, tasting her like the finest ambrosia.

"Ethan," she whimpered. "If you put your mouth on me now I'm going to come."

"How could I resist that?" He settled between her thighs and licked into her, breathing in her heat and flavor.

He'd never get enough. He knew in that moment, he'd never be able to get enough of her. She was his, and there was no going back. He didn't even regret his fall. He went so willingly it was like she'd always been a part of his life, a part of him.

He licked and sucked until she was panting, her hands clenched in the pillow over her head. The position lifted her breasts, and they bounced as she panted. She was probably the sexiest thing he'd ever seen. He reached one hand up to pinch her nipple, his other under her ass to lift her closer to his mouth, and he focused all his attentions on her swollen clitoris until she shook and writhed. Then she tightened, stiffened, and came with a shuttering, muffled cry that seared his soul.

She was still shuttering when he slipped into her, and he felt her every tremor along his cock, pulling him into her wet heat, making him dizzy with the sensations. He pressed his forehead to hers, breathing shallowly, trying to control the flood of need. She cupped his face in her hands, angling his chin up until she could kiss him. Sweet and sexy, her taste swept him beyond thinking. He moved with her as they found a rhythm, rocking together in a hard, steady beat. Every pulse of his body met hers, driving faster, rougher, until nothing but Amy remained. His orgasm ripped through him like a lightning storm, leaving him stunned, electrified, shattered.

And whole.

* * *

Amy dozed for what felt like a very short time before she woke to Ethan kissing across her shoulder, his hand low on her stomach. She had her back to his front, snuggled close, surrounded by his heat. At some point, he'd pulled the blanket up over them, but he produced so much warmth she didn't really need it.

She remained still as his fingers caressed closer to her curls and he nuzzled the back of her neck. Warmth spread across her skin, down her stomach, pooling between her legs. She could get used to waking up this way. She didn't want to open her eyes, didn't want to know what time it was. She just wanted to enjoy this state of half-awake sensation that was so heady and drugging.

His hand continued lower, his fingers sliding across her heat to cup her. Her breath sped as he stroked gently, hitting her clitoris with teasing swipes that weren't nearly enough. He had to know she was awake by now, but she kept her eyes closed and ground back against him. His hard cock pressed into her ass and made her moan. Wordlessly, she reached back and gripped him, holding his hard length tightly. He increased the teasing play of his fingers, focusing more directly on her clit, circling and flicking the delicate bud. Her thighs clenched, tightening on his hand and for a moment he stilled. Frustration made her groan.

She almost protested when he slipped his hand from between her legs and gently removed her hand from his cock. Until he rolled her onto her back and his mouth started down her body. He paused at her breasts, sucking each nipple into a hard peek, kneading her breasts until she was about to pop off the bed with all the tension gathering in her core. And then he moved lower. Her nerves, sensitive from sleep and their earlier lovemaking, jumped under the wet brush of his mouth, almost too overwhelmed by the delicious slide of his rough tongue.

If her stomach was this sensitive, she worried she wouldn't be able to take his mouth on her again, but she was too desperate now to stop him. When he moved between her thighs, settled his mouth over her heat, she trembled and gripped the sheets like she might fly off the bed if she didn't hold on. His mouth was hot and wet, his tongue dancing with the perfect amount of pressure against her most sensitive places. She panted, trying to hold back an orgasm so she could relish all the sensations battering her system. But her efforts didn't…couldn't last long. Her body came apart in a powerful explosion that left her shaking and breathless—and now way too sensitive for his mouth.

She sat up and gripped his face, pulling him up for a kiss, taking him with her as she lay back down. He pressed her into the bed, kissing her deeply, then moved and rolled her onto her side again, with her back once more to his front. He lifted her top leg over his thighs, angling to settle his cock against her entrance, then slid up into her in a slow, deliberate stretch that made her gasp. The friction was delicious from this position.

She moaned and rocked back against him, everything lighting and sparking and drawing tight again. He held her hip in one hand, keeping her still as he thrust into her in slow, hard strokes. She was panting, shivering, on the very edge when he moved his fingers from her hip to her curls, then lower to her clit. She came so hard it was almost painful, and she bit the pillow to hold back her scream. As she settled, her body still pulsing, she wallowed in pure female satisfaction hearing him groan her name with his release.

She dropped her leg from over his, and he slid out of her, but he didn't let her move away. He wrapped his arm around her waist, the one beneath her neck angling across her breasts to her arm. The full body hug made her feel cossetted and cozy. She hugged his arms back, snuggling against him, trying to get even closer than they already were, breathing in his scent while her mind drifted back toward sleep.

The sound of a passing firetruck down on Fifth Avenue disrupted that slow fall and she opened her eyes. Faint light was just starting to brighten the sky, filling the room with a warm sort of darkness that was unique to the dawn. She watched the change, caught up in the interplay of light and shadow, the way the colors in the room changed as the golden sun washed over the bed. She stroked Ethan's arm in a gentle caress, the texture of his firm muscles and arm hair, the feel of his warmth surrounding her, his crisp chest hair against her back all intertwined with her experience of the new morning.

"I could stay like this all day," he murmured.

She smiled. "I thought you'd fallen back to sleep."

"I might yet. It's still early."

"What woke you up?"

"Your scent."

"Feel free to wake me up that way as often as you like," she said and hugged him closer when he chuckled.

Letting out a little huff that teased her temple, he murmured, "I forgot about birth control. I don't normally have to think about it."

"I'm on the pill, so we're good. It's too soon for *that* aspect of this new world."

"Agreed." He pressed a tender kiss to her shoulder. "It's going to be a long day. Sleep. We have time. Elizaveta is the only one up."

"How can you tell?"

"I can sense her downstairs."

Amy concentrated and realized she could feel a second tiger downstairs, too. "I can't tell who it is, but I can feel someone there. How do you know it's Elizaveta?"

"Hard to describe. A little bit of it is scent—the apartment is self-contained enough that I can catch everyone's scent signatures if I focus. Some of it is sound—Elizaveta has a different way of walking than either Alexis or Reginald. And some of it is just the awareness of her tiger. When I concentrate, that awareness conveys a sense of the other shifter's essence, who they are. And with Elizaveta's strong presence, it's impossible to confuse her for anyone else."

Amy laughed at that. "Do you think, if I practice, I'll be able to do that, too? Tell who the tiger is when I sense them?"

"Maybe. Nila's been practicing and said she's better at it now."

"Will I be able to meet the other hybrids?"

"I'm sure it can be arranged."

Something in his voice made her half-roll over so she could look at him. "What?"

He cupped her cheek, his gaze on her lips instead of meeting her eyes. "If we stay together, if this works out between us, you'll definitely meet Nila. Her fiancé is my brother-in-law. She's part of the family."

Because he seemed uncertain about their future, she rolled fully to face him, then nudged his chin up so he'd have to meet her gaze. "Are you worried about us... working out?"

"Not my feelings for you. But I am concerned that once the reality of my world sinks in, you'll regret this."

"Does Nila regret being with your brother-in-law?"

"Not that I know of. I've never asked her. Frankly, I didn't expect to be in a similar situation."

"Now that you are?"

"When I think about my future," he said quietly, "you're there. I start planning a trip to see my family, and I find myself considering your schedule and when we could go. If I'm thinking of accepting an invitation to something, I want to talk to you about it and see if you're free to go with me. I want to talk with you about the next modeling job I'm taking, and what you think about this particular open-session group." He shrugged. "I woke up to your scent and for a sleepy instant, it felt so...natural to have you beside me I forgot that this was our first night together." He both frowned and smiled at once. "That was disorienting."

"If it helps, I'm a little disoriented, too. It doesn't seem like we've been together long, but at the same time, I keep forgetting that you *haven't* been in my life for years. I keep trying to insert you into memories where you couldn't be. Thinking 'where was Ethan when that was happening,' and realizing that whatever *that* was happened well before we'd ever met. That's weird, isn't it?"

He pushed his fingers into her hair, the curls tangling around his hand like they had a mind of their own. "I understand. I keep getting the same feeling."

"I don't believe in fate any more than I believe real muses exist," she said quietly. "But I feel like…" She shrugged. "I feel like we have a good chance"

"I hope we do. Does this mean you've forgiven me for lying to you in the beginning?"

"If you told me the truth last night, you never did lie to me, only yourself."

He snorted. "I was telling the truth about that."

"Have you forgiven yourself?"

He shifted back just a little, frowning, his gaze turned inward. "I'm not sure yet." He made a face. "I was an ass."

"Only a little." She touched his cheek, a gentle caress. "You can, you know. Forgive yourself."

"I'll do better going forward."

"I think you're doing just fine," she said. Then she kissed him. Long and hard, and drugging.

When they finally came up for air, she snuggled under his chin so she could hold him. Today would be a difficult but necessary step to settling things. Then they could see to this strange new relationship without threats from the tiger shifter world.

At least, she hoped it would be that simple. She had a lot riding on this. Not just her future, but her heart.

my pushed into her apartment, Spike scrambling through her feet to reclaim her territory.

Cat followed her inside, dropped her bag in a corner of the entryway, and said, "I need coffee. Lots and lots of coffee. And like a whole cake. And a pizza."

Ethan frowned a question at Amy as he closed the door, locking the bolt.

Amy smiled because he'd thought to lock her door behind him. "Cat gets very hungry when someone has required her to sit in one place for too long. It goes against her nature. It's like when someone is tired and they crave carbs. Cat starts craving food when people make her sit still. She says it makes her brain itchy and she can't think."

"What happens when she's free to move and think?"

"If she's not careful, she starts to lose weight. She forgets about food all together, and never notices being hungry. I've seen her lose like five pounds in two days, because she was thinking so hard. I have the exact opposite experience. If I'm thinking too hard, I eat. Which means now, I need pizza and cake, too."

He pulled her into a hug. "Thank god. I could eat a house right now. My metabolism churned through breakfast hours ago."

"Cat," she called toward the front of the apartment, "you'd better order three pizzas." To Ethan, she asked, "What do you want on them?"

"Doesn't matter. It's pizza. Except no pineapple, please. Fruit does not belong on a pizza."

She grinned. "I knew there was a reason I liked you. No pineapple," she shouted to Cat. "Everything else is good."

"Pineapple is gross on pizza," Cat called back. "I knew I liked Ethan."

He chuckled. "Guess I've passed muster, then?"

"Spike likes you, Cat likes you, and you think fruit on pizza is criminal. In this house, you're good."

"Would you be surprised to know I'm really relieved to hear that?"

"Yes. And also flattered. Come on in. My head is still spinning from that meeting."

She really was a little dizzy. The elders had kept them in a conference room on the ground floor of Elizaveta's building for hours. Five elders—including Elizaveta—were there in person. Three were out of the country so had to video conference. Although Elizaveta had introduced them, Amy had only managed to retain two or three names, but she had memorized all their faces.

During the interminable time they'd been stuck in the

too-cold room, the elders had mostly just talked at each other and argued over topics that didn't seem to have much to do with why they were there. Occasionally, they spoke directly to Amy. They paid little to no attention to Cat, which only aggravated Cat's difficulties with sitting still. And Ethan was treated with cool irritation at best. Two of the elders were openly hostile to him for reasons Amy could never manage to decipher from all the arguing, but she'd gotten the feeling it had to do with what he'd told her last night about their mating laws. Though it was never brought up directly, the fact that she and Ethan were obviously a couple seemed to piss several elders off.

It didn't make much sense to her. Ethan had said they'd want her to pick a tiger mate. She had, so she wasn't entirely sure why they were mad. But at this stage she no longer cared. After all those hours of debate and argument and *talking*, in the end the vote to accept her status as a hybrid and cover her under tiger law—making hurting or killing her a crime punishable by death—had happened in a matter of minutes and was unanimous.

The vote to ensure Cat was covered under those same tiger laws had, at Elizaveta's insistence, taken place immediately after. Only one elder voted against protecting Cat under their laws. Pavel Ivankin. A name Amy intended to remember for future reference as an asshole of the highest order, and a potential threat to her sister.

She tossed her overnight bag back into her bedroom and then made her way to the kitchen. She could already smell the coffee Cat had put on and heard Cat ordering enough food to feed at least a dozen people, including salads and pasta with the three large pizzas. At least they wouldn't have to go grocery shopping for a week with all the leftovers.

Amy stopped just inside the living room, soaking in the familiar feel of her home. Ethan stopped behind her and wrapped his arms around her waist.

She leaned into him. "It is so weird to think all this started less than forty-eight hours ago. And it's done now. It is done, right? Zhong has officially missed his deadline and because he's a tiger, he can't actually hurt me now. Right?"

"According to our laws." He kissed the top of her head. "Honestly, I thought something nefarious would happen during the meeting."

"Zhong attacking?" She looked back at him. "I kept thinking the same thing. Like his warning us about his deadline was all a trick or something. I know there was all that security. And more tigers there than I saw?"

"A dozen or so Trackers guarding and monitoring the area."

"With so many, I couldn't pinpoint them all anymore. I just had this sort of general awareness of them being everywhere."

"Probably because you've never had to try before. We can practice."

She rubbed his arms, knowing she could relax now and yet not feeling entirely settled. Zhong was out there somewhere, with a complicated history that involved her birth father, and she still didn't understand why he'd let her get away. She got the impression tiger law didn't mean enough to him for that to be a real deterrent. So something else was driving him, and not knowing what it was left her edgy.

Then there was a strange sense that she wasn't done with the elders yet either. She couldn't say why, just this niggling impression that they were waiting in the wings to screw up her life. It was like waiting for the other shoe to drop.

Or maybe she was just crashing from the adrenaline high of the last two days.

"You want some coffee?" she asked Ethan.

"This late in the afternoon?"

She glanced up at him again, smiling just a little. "I thought we might be staying up late tonight," she whispered so Cat wouldn't hear.

"Coffee. Yes. Black."

She chuckled at his rush to accept the dose of caffeine. Her knees nearly gave out when he caressed her ass through her jeans. She turned into his kiss, hungry for more than just pizza now. She wasn't entirely sure she'd be able to wait until later. Then her stomach grumbled, and she accepted the inevitable with a grin. Food first.

Then she could whisk Ethan off to bed.

The troublesome sense that things weren't entirely settled would just have to wait until tomorrow.

* * *

Amy buzzed into Ethan's apartment building in Brooklyn, savoring a quiet feeling of contentment. She'd passed a major test this week, had a good day at work, enjoyed her evening lecture, and had just had a lovely chat with Reese over coffee, where he only nagged a little bit about her pursuing an art career. And every night for the last two weeks, she'd spent with Ethan.

Her life had mostly gotten back to normal after the meeting with the elders. She'd seen no sign of Zhong in all that time, and there was no second shoe dropping from the elders. The only real thing that had changed in Amy's life was having Ethan in it. A change that had made the last two weeks glorious.

They spent as much time together now as their schedules allowed, moving back and forth between each other's apartments. They had more privacy at his, but she was still hesitant to leave Cat alone for long periods of time, so she used the excuse of having to help with Spike for staying at her own apartment every other night. Ethan never argued. While they didn't talk about it directly, she knew he understood her need to keep Cat safe, and she adored him all the more for it.

With no sign of any other tiger shifters over the last few weeks, though, she was finally starting to believe that all the hybrid business wouldn't have much of an impact on her life or Cat's. They could live normally, just with the knowledge that life was more...complex than they'd always believed.

Ethan met her at his apartment door when she stepped out of the elevator. He was smiling, but there was a crease between his brows. A punch of apprehension tightened her gut, poking a hole in her mood, but she tried to push it aside as a kneejerk reaction to the anxiety of the last few months.

She kissed him softly, then brushed her fingers over the lines on his brow. "What's wrong?"

"How was coffee with Reese?" He opened his door wider, letting her inside.

His studio apartment was open and airy, with a twelve-foot ceiling, brick walls, and hardwood floors that spoke strongly of New York. The single room was separated into a small "kitchen" to the right of the room—since it consisted of a single counter with a sink, a microwave, and a snack-sized refrigerator, she had trouble thinking of it as a real kitchen. There was a very large and comfortable bed under the windows across from the door, and a tiny bathroom to the left. A section in the center of the room was set up to simulate a living room space, with a huge purple and green rug under a cushioned couch. Across from the couch, a TV stood on a sturdy wooden stand. A low bookshelf behind the couch was stuffed with books, and the coffee table in front of the couch was cluttered with magazines. Ethan's scent filled the space, wrapping around Amy the minute she stepped inside.

"You're avoiding my question," she said as she set her backpack and purse down by the front door and let Ethan help her out of her coat. "Why?"

"Tell me about coffee with Reese first, then I'll talk."

She growled a little, which made him grin. The expression lightened the worry lines on his brow. "Coffee was great. He's taken up Devine's cause and is trying to get me to consider a show."

"You should. You're too good to keep producing in obscurity. And you've built up a substantial enough collection. It would be a crime not to exhibit it."

She jerked her hands up in a gesture of surrender. "How can I argue with all three of you? If it makes you feel better, I'm actually thinking about doing it." For the first time in her life, the practical voice of her mother was dimmer than the encouraging voices of her friends. It felt really good to consider the option of being more than a hobbyist with her art. And she wasn't sure she'd ever have opened herself up to that possibility before Ethan. In a world where tiger shifters were a part of reality, having an art career didn't seem so airy fairy and impractical anymore.

"I'm glad to hear it." He gestured her inside after hanging her coat in the small closet next to the door. "Would you like something to drink? I opened a bottle of wine earlier. Dinner should be delivered soon."

"I've been looking forward to Thai food all day. Wine would be good. And then you're going to spill why you look worried."

He grunted a noncommittal reply and went to his little kitchenette to pour her a glass of Cabernet Sauvignon.

He handed the glass to her, but didn't immediately sit next to her on the couch. "I'm not even sure how to start this."

"You're really worrying me now," she said. "Is this about us?"

"Sort of."

She braced herself. She didn't think this was a break-up

conversation, but she wasn't feeling as content and happy as she had when she'd arrived.

"The other two males living in the city want to meet you," Ethan said through clenched teeth.

"Why?"

"They…they want to give you a chance to know them in case things don't work out with me."

She nearly choked on her sip of wine. "What the hell does that mean?"

Scowling, he sat on the couch next to her. "Normally, with a tigress, they'd have the Mate Run to convince you to pick them. Because you can't participate in a Mate Run—"

"And wouldn't even if I could," she put in.

"Because that's not an option, they want another way of…courting you."

"They know we're a couple, right? I made my choice already."

"Yes, but because you're not pregnant, and we're not engaged, in my world that means you're still free to choose someone else."

She blinked at him for several long moments. "This is weird. What do they think, I'll just throw you over because they show up and say *hi*?"

"They feel they have the right to an introduction. That I've…taken advantage of the situation, and it's not fair, and they should be given a chance to prove they're better males."

"That's really stupid."

He snorted but didn't look any happier.

"Not to mention you didn't take advantage of the situation since you thought I was human. The whole idea is just…stupid," she repeated, at a loss for a better word.

He shrugged. "Maybe in your world. In ours, females who could give us children are so rare that their attentions and choices are taken very seriously."

"Again, I made my choice. I know we talked about this stuff before the meeting with the elders, but I assumed afterward everyone knew where I stood."

"The illusion of giving males a fair chance to be selected by a female is what keeps us from descending into chaos again," he said. "The others are arguing that they never got that fair chance with you."

"Life isn't fair. And how I choose who I date isn't subject to 'fairness' for men."

"Tell that to desperate males who might never have the chance to have children."

"Your world makes my head hurt." It also made her feel sorry for tiger shifter women. That they had to deal with all this male bullshit all the time, and even follow laws designed to appease males who couldn't control themselves. The thought pissed her off for the sake of all the tigresses. "What if I say no to meeting these other men?"

Ethan looked away, still scowling. "This is the part I really didn't want to tell you."

"Say it." Her tone was flat.

"The elders want you to allow the meetings."

"Want?"

He snarled. "They voted. Five of the eight agree that you need to allow other tiger males to introduce themselves. To give them at least a chance."

"No."

He finally met her gaze. "The elders are threatening to take away protections for you and Cat if you don't."

And there was the other shoe. She stood, so angry she couldn't stay seated, cursing under her breath in a steady stream just to release some of the outrage.

She set her wine on the coffee table so she didn't break the glass. "Are you serious? They want to force me into a… series of blind dates with other men? No. Absolutely not. I'm already dating someone."

His mouth lifted a little at that declaration. "I'm glad to hear you hate the idea as much as I do. I did get the concession that I be allowed to accompany you to any meetings with other males. But they are insistent you at least allow introductions."

"'Introductions'?"

"That's it. Nothing more. Just an introduction to the males who want to meet you. And you and Cat will continue to have protections under our laws."

She started to pace the apartment. "What did Elizaveta have to say about all this?"

"She was one of the three who voted against it. She agrees you've already made your choice."

"Damn straight I have. What the ever-loving fuck?"

"But we're not engaged. And you're not pregnant."

She stopped to scowl at him. "First, I'm not planning on getting pregnant for some time, thank you very much. I have things to do before I start considering a family."

"Fair enough."

"Second, how the hell do the other hybrids deal with this?"

"Nila is engaged. To a tiger shifter. They got engaged at the same time as she was being accepted into the society, so it was never a question with her. The other acknowledged hybrid is a child, just four years old, so she's years away from having to deal with all this. The woman who's the daughter of a hybrid, she's married now, too—to a tiger shifter. So until you, the males haven't had this option with an acknowledged hybrid."

"They don't have the option now," she said defiantly but distractedly as she ran through the realities and her choices. "What about Cat? Will they expect her to…meet tiger males, too?"

"They'd like her to. But she's fully human and still quite young. They will encourage her, but frankly, they know they have more leverage with you."

"Why?"

"Because of Cat. You made no secret of the fact that you wanted her protected. They know you'll be more *encouraged* to do what they want if they use Cat's protections as a bargaining chip."

"Sonofabitch. Those old bastards."

"That they are."

"How do you feel about all this?"

"I hate it. I hate it to the marrow of my bones."

"Because it's stupid."

"Because I'm afraid you'll find someone better than me."

She stopped pacing to stare at him, not quite believing

she'd just heard that. He was a mythical god made flesh, exquisite beyond all sense, the sort of man women tripped over themselves to get closer to. He was also as smart, kind, and fun as he was stunning to look at. Yet *he* was worried *she'd* want someone else?

The story of the tigress who'd broken his heart and nearly gotten him killed came back to her, and she realized having her as part of his world this way would no doubt bring up all that old resentment. And all the fears of repeating the mistake he'd made with the tigress.

She settled on the couch next to him and took his face in her hands, making him look her in the eyes. "There is no one else for me, Ethan. I promise I won't do to you what that other woman did. And I will not push you into doing anything you'd regret later."

He pulled her into a hug, holding her so tight she had trouble breathing. Recognizing why he'd been so upset settled her own anger somewhat. She kissed him, letting him know with her actions what she found so hard to put into words. The kiss was deep, and lush, and full of all the feelings that had been growing between them, all the promise their future held. She savored, then she devoured, then she melted. By the time she surfaced for a breath, she was panting and could barely remember what they'd been talking about. She just wanted to strip him and take him to bed.

It was an annoyance, what the elders were asking of her. And she sure as hell didn't like being blackmailed. But they just wanted her to meet other tigers. If Ethan was allowed to be with her when she met them, she could probably tolerate it.

She blinked and leaned back so she could see his expression. "Wait, how many males are we talking about here? Just the two in the city, right?"

He snarled. "They're asking you to meet all the males who want to meet you."

"How many is that?"

"There are about twenty-eight hundred male tigers in the US."

She stared at him. "They want me to meet almost three thousand men?"

"No, no. Some of them are too old or too young. Some are…"

"Are?"

"Some are anti-hybrid, so they aren't interested in you."

"Gee, isn't that nice," she deadpanned, heavy on the sarcasm.

Ethan shrugged. "In reality, you're probably only looking at around a thousand, and I'm sure we can argue that number down to just the east coast males since this is your territory."

Amy shook her head. "I do not have time for that kind of thing. It would take me years. Plus, it's pointless because…you."

He smiled at that, the expression making her stomach dance. "I'm glad to hear it's pointless."

"Listen, for the sake of peace—even though I'm majorly pissed off about being blackmailed this way—I will agree to meet with *some* males as a formality of your people's process. *But* I will not have my life taken over by this useless exercise." She ran a finger over his jaw. "I'd rather spend my free time with you, not talking with men I have no interest in meeting."

That comment earned her a kiss, a long, deliciously thorough kiss. She felt like purring by the time he lifted his head. Which, given what he was, made her smile.

"Maybe we can organize an…event?" he said. "A party or something where the interested males can show up, make their introductions, and the whole thing can be done in a night."

"That would be perfect. I could make time for that. Barely. When and where?"

"I'll talk to Alexis, have her run it past Elizaveta. If anyone can organize a party of that scale, it's Elizaveta. The big question is, do you want them coming to you here in New York, or do you want to go to neutral ground and ensure this city is kept as your territory?"

"Does it make a difference?"

"For my people, it does. The males will respect your territorial boundaries if you insist. They'll stay away from you while you're in your territory." He winced. "Given this is New York City, the territory will have to be pretty specific, probably to the Forest Hills area. But at least you'll be able to go home without having to worry about uninvited tiger visitors."

"Ugh. This is much more complicated than it's supposed to be." But as complicated as she'd first feared. She pulled in a deep breath and let it out in a whoosh. "Fine. In that case, I want to… Claim?"

He nodded.

"Claim Forest Hills as my territory. And if this party idea works, I'd prefer neutral territory. The less these strangers know about me and my schedule, the better."

"I'm good with that, too." He frowned as he ran a hand up through her hair, tangling his fingers in the curls that had worked free of her ponytail. "I feel like I should thank you for agreeing to this. But I hate it. To the depths of my soul, I hate that I have to…"

"To?"

"To risk it. To risk you."

"We'll survive, I promise. It's just a party. And I'll keep you close the whole time. You won't have to worry about becoming someone you're not or fighting an actual fight for me. This isn't a competition, even if the others want to pretend it is."

He leaned in to kiss her again just as the buzzer for the main door sounded. "That's the Thai food. Be right back." But he did take the time to give her a quick, hard kiss before going to get the door.

She savored the kiss as much as she intended to savor her Thai food. And then him.

She'd worry about the other tigers later.

CHAPTER SEVENTEEN

"This is the most uncomfortable party I've ever been to," Amy murmured under her breath to Ethan.

"They're all tiger shifters," he whispered back. "They can hear you."

She rolled her eyes.

The ballroom at the elders' West Virginia compound was a huge, beautiful room full of light and air, white walls, fresh greenery, polished marble floors, and the ceiling painted to look like a spring sky. There were a few elaborate decorations in sparkling gold, but mostly the space's elegance came from its simplicity.

The open room was packed with men. Outside of maybe three women that she'd spotted so far, the room was entirely men. And all of them kept…looking at her.

The moment she'd entered the room with Ethan and Elizaveta, she'd been surrounded by people pushing to introduce themselves. She'd felt like a deer in the headlights, or like a rock star surrounded by rabid fans. She'd actually ducked back against Ethan, worried all those strangers would start tearing at her. Since she'd never in her entire life been the center of attention to quite that degree, it was beyond overwhelming. And she'd very nearly bolted—elders' blackmail or not.

But with a few curt orders from Elizaveta, a group of five Trackers, acting almost like bodyguards, pushed the crowd back and imposed order on the chaos. Since then, the group of about two hundred men had come up to her in ones or twos to introduce themselves, making an attempt at civility.

It was absolutely the weirdest thing she'd ever lived through, and uncomfortable was really an understatement for how she felt right now.

She gripped her glass of wine—wishing it was something stronger—holding it in front of her like a shield, and forced herself to smile at the young man who introduced himself to her. All of their names and faces had started to blend together at this stage. They all looked either like earnest young men, or overly eager older men, and all of them gave her the creeps.

That probably wasn't fair to them. When she could separate herself from the bizarreness of the party, she recognized that a few of the men who spoke with her seemed very nice. Perfectly ordinary guys just chatting as if this wasn't the most awkward mass blind date in the history of dating. Those occasional men even engaged Ethan in casual conversation, instead of attempting to elbow him aside or ignoring him. Or worse, growling at him in challenge.

The challengers were the ones Amy moved on from quickly, making sure they knew where she stood. She didn't have any tolerance for that show—especially since it was obvious she was here with Ethan.

As yet another earnest young man moved on, casting a hopeful glance over his shoulder, Amy leaned into Ethan and whispered, "Can I go now?"

"Almost. I promise."

"This is never happening again, by the way."

"Agreed."

The slight growl in his tone, the way his hand rested protectively at the small of her back, made her stomach dance with happy little tingles. It felt like they were facing this together, like they were a team and they had each other's backs. That kind of relationship reminded her of her own parents, the way they'd supported each other through everything. It was the kind of relationship she'd always wanted.

The awkward party was almost worth it to realize she and Ethan could have that together.

Alexis and her husband Victor ambled up, Alexis with a sympathetic expression, Victor—who Amy had met earlier that afternoon—with an annoyed frown.

"You doing okay?" Alexis asked her.

"Peachy."

Victor grinned at that and signed something. Alexis translated it as, "Sarcasm is a lost art."

Amy smiled.

"I think you've met almost everyone now," Alexis said, glancing over the room. "There are maybe four more males who haven't braved Ethan's glare."

"Can I go then?" Amy heard the whine in her voice and grimaced. She sounded like a pouty teenager. But if anything could push her to revert to childish behavior, this party was it.

"Hopefully. Let me go talk with Elizaveta and Elder Qiang. That reminds me, though, you haven't met Elder Kamal in person yet. He's just arrived at the compound and will want to meet you officially."

"Which one was Kamal again?" Amy rubbed her forehead. So many names and faces. She was usually good with faces, but at this stage they had all run together like a Salvador Dali painting.

"He's the only other pro-hybrid elder," Alexis said.

"He was one of the ones on video at the meeting, right?"

"He was."

"My brain feels like it's going to explode with all these new names and faces." She sighed and leaned back into Ethan's arm, letting his unwavering strength support her.

Alexis gave her arm a quick, reassuring squeeze, then wandered off to find the elders who could end Amy's torture.

At least Cat didn't have to suffer through this yet. Thanks to her age, she'd been allowed to stay in the guest wing of the compound, in the suite of rooms they'd been assigned. She was so busy talking with one of the geneticists who worked for Elizaveta, she'd barely noticed when

Amy had left for the party. Now that Cat had turned her spectacular brain to the puzzle that was a shapeshifter, Amy had a feeling she'd be hearing a lot about tiger genetics for the next few months.

Amy felt Ethan's muscles tighten behind her, and she braced herself to meet yet another male. She looked up with a forced smile plastered to her face, then almost dropped her glass of wine as Zhong stopped in front of them and dipped his head in greeting.

"What are you doing here?" Amy asked, as a spike of fear surged through her.

Zhong smiled. "It's good to see you again, too."

Amy scowled. "Why are you here? I thought..." She looked around, remembering what Ethan had said about the room full of shifters being able to hear her.

"I have a residence on this coast," Zhong said. "I was invited."

"You've already met me. You didn't have to come."

"I had some business here."

She narrowed her eyes at the very faint hint of something in his tone. Like tension but so well disguised it could have been amusement. She took in his look—as immaculate as the last time she'd seen him. He wore a dark gray suit over a crisp white shirt that was open at the collar, giving him a casual, classy appearance. He stood with his hands in his pants' pockets, looking relaxed and friendly. But she watched his shoulders tighten ever so slightly whenever someone passed too close behind him.

"Do the elders know you're here?" Ethan asked. "Does Elizaveta?"

Amy realized, given his past, Zhong was probably still wanted as a criminal by the tigers. Under a death sentence. Elizaveta had never said his crimes had been forgiven. Why the hell would he risk this?

Zhong's cocky grin widened. "They know one of my aliases is here. It'll be fun to see how long it takes them to figure out it was me. If they ever do. They never have before." He focused the full intensity of his dark gaze on Amy. "Have you met your father…your biological father yet?"

"No."

"You should consider saying hello. Don't forget to give him my message when you do."

"He's here?"

He ignored her question and said to Ethan, "You need to watch your back. You inadvertently put yourself in the way of someone's plans. Someone powerful. They aren't happy about it."

"Are you threatening me?" Ethan asked quietly.

"Me?" Zhong put a hand on his chest. "I only do that when someone is paying me to." Quieter, he said, "I've moved on from my previous client. I have another job to take care of. But I'm not the only dangerous person in this room."

"You keep giving us warnings," Amy said, so quietly she wasn't sure if he'd be able to hear her. "Why?"

He glanced at her, his faint smile both charming and patronizing all at once. "It's entertaining." Then more seriously. "And a poignant revenge."

Without another word, he turned and faded into the crowd, so thoroughly he might as well have vanished.

"He scares the shit out of me," she said under her breath.

"You have very good instincts," Ethan said.

He nudged her around to face him. "Roman is here. Do you want to meet him?"

She pursed her lips, letting her gaze travel over the room, wondering which of all those men was the tiger who'd fathered her. "I'm not sure," she said honestly. "I hadn't even thought about it yet. Once things were settled with the elders, I put him out of my head. Now..." She swallowed and met Ethan's gaze. "I'm not sure I'm ready."

"He's here and hasn't approached you yet. He's waiting for you. You don't have to deal with that introduction now." Ethan waved at the crowd. "This is enough for one day."

She snorted at that. "I just need to think about it a bit longer. Maybe we can arrange something for tomorrow when I'm not so worn out..." She was about to say more but Ethan's expression changed from open and concerned to closed and angry in the space of a heartbeat. The change was so fast she swung around, looking for Zhong again.

Instead, there was a curvy, beautiful brunette standing behind her, smiling past Amy at Ethan.

"What a wonderful surprise," the woman said. "I hoped you'd be here."

Ethan's faint growl made the hairs on Amy's neck prickle. She frowned up at him, but he was focused completely on the other woman.

"Can we talk?" the woman asked him, speaking past

Amy as if she wasn't standing there.

"You've already said enough to me," Ethan answered, his voice low.

"Please."

He grunted and moved around Amy to follow the woman to the side of the room. Amy's eyes widened. He hadn't even excused himself or said anything to her before leaving. Just abandoned her. A combination of shock and hurt mingled with suspicion in her gut. From his reaction, there was only one woman this could be. The tigress that had broken his heart. Siya. The woman he'd been in love with.

Amy hadn't known what to expect of Siya. She hadn't actually thought she'd ever have to see her. She shouldn't have really been surprised that the tigress was stunning, her dark hair thick and straight, her eyes a deep rich blue, her body both slim and lush. The tigress was so beautiful it was almost unreal, like she'd stepped off the pages of a fashion magazine or out of a movie. She was as stunning as Ethan. And to Amy's horror, Ethan and the woman looked good together, like they belonged with each other—two gorgeous beings too magnificent for the ordinary world; two demi-gods beyond the touch of mere mortals.

Her chest tightened, and pain stabbed into her gut. She pressed a hand to her stomach, trying to settle the churning. She probably shouldn't watch their conversation. She couldn't hear them at this distance, but it still felt like eavesdropping to stare at them.

She reminded herself that this woman had devastated Ethan, driven him to do things he still felt guilty and ashamed of. There was no way Ethan would want anything more to do with her. She wasn't a threat. Whatever Siya might want from him, Ethan was hardly going to want her back in his life. He didn't like the person he was with Siya. That had to count for something, right.

Right?

She tried to look away, tried to move, to give them a semblance of privacy, but felt frozen in place. The tigress sidled closer to Ethan, stroking a hand over his shoulder. He didn't move away from the contact. Siya looked up at him with an expression that was too personal for people at odds, and Ethan held her gaze, his frown softening. The tension left his body the longer he spoke to her, the anger and aggression draining away before Amy's eyes.

When Siya touched Ethan's cheek, Amy had to turn away. She couldn't watch anymore of this, just staring like an idiot as a goddess made moves on Ethan. Amy didn't know what they were talking about, she had no reason to believe Ethan would take the woman back, or if that was even part of their conversation. She couldn't even be sure the goddess tiger was the same one who'd broken Ethan's heart. But she did know she couldn't continue watching that stunning woman attempt to seduce the man Amy was pretty sure she was in love with.

She needed air. Just a bit of space. She wasn't going to panic and assume the worst. But she needed some room to breathe. Hunting for an escape, her cheeks flushed and hot, she pushed through the throngs of men to the exit, ignoring the ones who tried to stop her. She hit the door and hurried into the outer corridor, sucking in deep gulps of air.

. . .

Ethan stared down at Siya, his emotions in so much turmoil he could barely think. He hadn't come face to face with her since that last Run, when she'd urged him to fight and almost die for her, then rejected him. He still had trouble recognizing himself in the man he'd been at that Run, and he resented confronting the reality that he'd sunk that low, all for a false promise. After all this time, he did not want to face the woman who'd driven him to that state.

"Why are you here?" he asked, the words hard to force out past his clenched teeth.

"It's been a while," she said, her voice low and husky. "I've missed you."

"Bullshit."

"I really have, Ethan. Really. I expected you to come back to my Run. Why didn't you?"

He almost couldn't believe she was asking. He blinked at her a few times, wondering if he'd heard her wrong. "Have you forgotten the last Run I did participate in?"

"Of course not. You were magnificent in that fight."

"I nearly died. I nearly killed someone. And you ran off with another male."

She shrugged and moved in closer. Her scent surrounded him, a combination of honey and ginger spice with her feminine essence, a combination he'd once found the most delicious scent in the world. In the back of his mind, he noticed how different Siya's scent was from Amy's softly floral honeysuckle flavor.

"I just wanted proof," Siya murmured. "I wanted proof that you really, truly wanted me. Forever."

"Then you wouldn't have kept choosing other males. You wanted children. Not me."

"No." She set a hand on his chest, so close now he could feel her heat. "No, it was always supposed to be you. You're right, I did want children. Desperately. But I wanted them to be yours."

He took in her earnest expression. She wasn't lying to him. He'd have picked that up in her scent. In this moment, she was sincere.

Some of his anger eased. A little. "You chose the wrong way to ensure that," he said quietly.

"I know. And that's why I'm here. To apologize. I hurt you. I didn't mean to."

More of his anger drained away. He let out a breath.

And he realized as it left that he wasn't nearly as hurt as he'd once been. His thoughts turned to Amy again, how he'd almost sacrificed his relationship with her because of how he felt about Siya's betrayal, about himself in the wake of his relationship with her. Yet with Amy, he'd never felt like a different man. In fact, with Amy he felt like a better man than he'd ever been with Siya. The kind of man he wanted to be.

With that realization, the last of his anger dissolved. He still harbored some shame, some guilt over his own behavior, but he couldn't keep up his anger with Siya anymore.

"We were never right together," he said quietly. "It's better this way."

"I'm still sorry."

"What's done is done," he said. "It was a long time ago. And you landed on your feet. Congratulations on the second baby." All newborns were well known to the community. He'd heard about each of her pregnancies, even though he hadn't wanted to know.

Her smile widened. "Thank you. He's beautiful."

"With you as a mother, I'm sure he is. Have you married?" He nodded behind him to the room full of eligible males, belatedly remembering that if she was still running for a new mate, she wouldn't have been allowed here.

"Just before our second was born." She reached up and touched his cheek, her fingers gentle. "I'll always regret what we could have been, Ethan. I love my children. My mate is good to me. But I'm sorry I ruined us."

He took the hand she had on his cheek and held it, squeezing in understanding. "You're forgiven." And maybe he could finally forgive himself, too.

He released her and she dropped her hand back to her side. "Now," he said, "I need to get back to…" He glanced over to where he'd left Amy, the sense that something was wrong disrupting his thoughts. He saw her just as she disappeared into the throng of males, pushing toward the ballroom's exit.

"I have to go," he said to Siya without looking at her.

He rushed through the crowd, shoving people out of the way as he hurried to reach Amy, following her scent through the room when he could no longer see her, worry and a growing fear biting at his heels.

CHAPTER EIGHTEEN

After a few cleansing breaths, Amy stalked toward the bathroom. The open space of the corridor, without all the oppressive attention, eased the building panic. She kept reminding herself she had nothing to panic about. But an image of Siya and Ethan staring at each other kept taunting her, poking at insecurities she'd thought she'd laid to rest.

Irritated by her own behavior, she cursed quietly. If she wasn't so stressed and overwhelmed by the situation, she'd have probably handled that better. Now that she was outside, the cool air and clean, earthy scent of the place wrapping around her, she recognized that she'd likely made more of that scene than she should have. She'd splash some cold water on her face, get herself together, then go back into the room and talk to him like a reasonable adult.

She was just outside the bathroom door when someone quietly cleared their throat, drawing her attention. An innocuous looking young man stood not ten feet away. She frowned. He hadn't been there a moment ago. She might be distracted, but she would have noticed someone standing so close to her.

"Can I help you?" she asked, glancing around to see if anyone else had come into the corridor.

He was probably one of the men from the ballroom, maybe one she'd met already though she couldn't say for sure. She didn't want to be rude. But she wasn't happy about being stopped just outside the women's room.

"Are you okay?" he asked. "You looked upset."

"Fine." She forced a smile. "Just got a little overheated and needed some fresh air."

"It was pretty oppressive in there." The man smiled and stepped closer.

Amy frowned. Whether he meant to or not, he was crowding her now.

She took an involuntary step backward. "Yes, well…" She nodded toward the bathroom. "I just need a minute. Excuse me."

The man grabbed her arm, and panic surged through her again for a completely different reason this time.

"I thought we might talk," he said. "It's quieter out here." He nodded to the ballroom. "It's semi-soundproofed and so noisy in there no one will notice. You can spare me a few minutes."

"Not unless you want me to piss on the floor," she said, trying to control the growing fear making her heart thump. She tugged at her arm but the man's grip tightened.

"I'm not going to hurt you," he said, but his fingers

bit into her biceps, belying his statement. "I just wanted a minute alone with you. You and I, we had a moment inside. I know we did. I thought, without that other male hovering over you, you'd be able to see that."

"I'm not sure what you're talking about. I do need to go now. If you don't let me go, we're going to have a problem."

"No. We won't."

Amy blinked and suddenly there were two more males behind him.

The man's pleasant expression remained as he took another step closer. "The Trackers are distracted with a fight inside," he said. "We have time."

Fear overwhelmed her then. Not just anger, not just worry, but actual terror. Shit. Shit. They could smell her fear. Shit!

"We just want a chance," the first man said. "And it's only fair you give us a chance."

"No. You don't get a chance just because you think you deserve one. I have a boyfriend. I'm doing this…farce of a party for reasons that have nothing to do with the rest of you. Now let me go. There's a room full of people just behind us that don't want to see me hurt. The room is only semi-soundproof according to you. They'll hear me scream."

The two newcomers glanced toward the ballroom, then exchanged a look. But they didn't leave or argue with the original man.

That man put his face in hers. "You won't scream. I

could break your neck in a heartbeat, before you get your mouth open."

She held his gaze. "You suck at flirting."

Her comment made him blink, his hold loosened fractionally.

And in the next moment she was standing behind a large, very familiar back.

"Back off, Bill," Ethan growled. "She said to leave her alone."

Bill snarled. "You think you're allowed to just have whatever woman you want, Gupta? It doesn't work that way."

"Assaulting me isn't how it works either," Amy snapped from behind Ethan's back. She felt a little silly pretending at bravado while hiding behind Ethan, but these were shapeshifters that turned into deadly animals and moved at lightning speeds. She was too pragmatic *not* to hide behind Ethan.

Bill ignored her. "Because of you, I lost a good chance at a mate. Because of you, Siya ended up with someone else. She should have been mine. And now, you think you can just have another chance, just walk away with another woman without a challenge?"

"You asshole. Siya did the same thing to me that she did to you. You want to be pissed, be pissed at her. But Amy is not an option for you. She's taken."

She was glad to hear him say that—at least she thought she was—but they had some talking to do about *Siya* when Amy was no longer in danger of getting killed by a bunch of strangers.

"That's not how it works," Bill said, his voice dropping into a growl. "You want her, you'll have to fight for her."

"No." Amy shouted to be heard above the growing growls and hisses. "No fights. No challenge matches. That's the point of this fucking party. No fights!"

She couldn't believe this was happening. Ethan had been hurt once already, nearly killed, by a woman who forced him into a fight like this. She did not want to do the same thing to him, even accidentally. She'd promised him she'd never make him do something like this.

"No fights," she said again even as Ethan took several steps back, moving her away from the other three men.

"Stay back," he said over his shoulder, not looking away from Bill.

"This is the guy you fought before? You both almost died. No fights. I'll just get someone…Alexis and Victor. They can stop this. Or Elizaveta."

Even as she turned toward the ballroom entrance, the two tigers behind Bill rushed into new positions, circling her and Ethan, cutting off her path to help so fast it was like they'd materialized there. Damn it, the sonsabitches could move.

"I'll keep you safe," Ethan said. He glanced back very briefly making eye contact before returning his full concentration to the other males. "I can take him this time."

"But I don't want you to have to. I'm not that other woman, and I won't have you getting hurt because of me." She lowered her voice. "I don't want you to do something you'll regret."

"I'm not fighting to earn you, I'm fighting to protect

you. There's a difference. This is more important."

He sounded so deadly serious she blinked at the hard lines of his back, and shivered a little at the protective tone —a shiver of excitement. Geez, what had happened to her?

She pushed off questioning her sensibilities until later, because before she could argue further, Bill launched himself at Ethan. He moved so fast, Amy didn't even see what happened, just blurs of motion and Ethan was ripped away from her. When she spotted him again, he and Bill were crouched low, circling each other. Flashes of Ethan's fight with Zhong in tiger form came back to her, spiking her fear, and she cursed that Elizaveta had made her leave her pepper spray up in the room.

She glanced toward the ballroom. Where was everyone? Someone should have noticed she was missing by now. Someone had to hear the fight with all their super shifter hearing.

Keeping her back pressed against a wall so no one could sneak up on her, she started edging back toward the ballroom's door. If she could just reach the door, she could get help.

Ethan and Bill flew together again, blurring into motion, the whirling of colors so disorienting it made Amy dizzy to watch. She kept her gaze generally toward the two men, but couldn't look directly at them. From her peripheral vision, she knew the other two tigers were watching the fight, paying attention to it and not her, which was good. They probably figured they'd reach her before she got far anyway. So she kept her movements measured and unobtrusive.

Suddenly, one of the two fighting men went flying through the air, slamming into a wall not far from Amy. She gasped, almost screaming, until she realized it was Bill and not Ethan. Ethan launched himself at the downed tiger, but the other two men moved into motion then, jumping Ethan while Bill got back to his feet and shook himself. Then he rejoined the fight.

Amy bit back another warning shout. Could Ethan fight off three of them? Damn it, she was never going anywhere without her mace again. Ignoring caution, she sprinted toward the ballroom door. And came up hard against a large, solid chest. She looked up to see yet another strange man grinning down at her.

"Going somewhere?" he asked, his pleasant tone doing nothing to disguise the glimmer of malice in his eyes. "Hybrid bitch."

She opened her mouth to scream, but barely made a strangled grunt before the new male was ripped away from her. She blinked. Zhong stood there, adjusting the cuffs of his suit, a small smile curving his lips.

"Need some help?" he asked.

"I—" Before she could say more, Zhong flowed away from her, moving at that speed she couldn't follow, taking the newest attacker with him.

She squinted at the two groups fighting as they came together. Then she sprinted to the ballroom door, threw it open, and searched the immediate area. Everyone in the room turned to look at her. Then almost in one motion, they looked past her to the corridor.

She pressed back against the ballroom wall, getting out

of the doorway as people she thought were Trackers pushed through crowd and charged into the corridor.

By the time she got back into the hallway, the fight was over. Ethan was standing over Bill, who was laid out on the carpet like he'd been knocked out. Trackers were holding the three males who'd been with Bill. And another one was talking to Ethan, pointing angrily down at the man on the carpet.

Oh, they better not blame Ethan for this. She started toward the group, but stopped when someone caught her shoulder. She spun to yell at whoever it was because she really really needed to yell at someone. Zhong, his hand gentle on her, stared at Ethan and the group of Trackers.

"You're okay?" he asked without looking down at her.

"Fine. Thank you." She snapped out the words so they didn't sound very gracious, but she wasn't in the mood to be gracious.

His mouth ticked up in that small smile again. And then he was gone.

She stood there blinking, her mouth half open, raising her hands in an irritated surrender. "Argh!" she shouted at the empty air, then swung around to protect Ethan from the Trackers.

She heard him defending himself as she approached. Without hesitating, she stepped between him and a Tracker, looked the Tracker in the eyes, and said, "These other assholes were harassing me and Ethan saved me. That jerk —" she pointed to Bill who was still laid out on the ground, "—challenged Ethan. And if you even think of punishing

Ethan for protecting me, I will make so much trouble for you, you won't remember your own name."

The Tracker, a tall man with sandy brown hair and blue eyes, raised his brows at her. He glanced at Ethan, then back at her. "Fair enough," he said. He hauled Bill to his feet and said, "You and your buddies need some time in confinement." Bill started to protest but the Tracker shook his head. "You know the rules. Argue with me and I'll make sure you stay in confinement longer."

Amy grinned at that. "Go on," she urged. "Argue with him. For me. Please."

Bill snarled at her. "Bitch."

She put her face close to his. "Remember that next time you threaten me. Next time, I'll have my pepper spray."

The Tracker pulled Bill away, all four men protesting and cursing as they were dragged down the corridor in a direction Amy had never been.

Ethan gripped her shoulders, turning her to face him. "Are you okay?"

"I'm fine. You're bleeding." She set her fingers gently against the side of his mouth, near where a trickle of blood came from his lip. "Damn it."

"It'll be healed up in the next few minutes. Don't worry."

She still frowned, searching him for other injuries.

"Where did Zhong go?" he asked quietly, so quietly she wasn't sure anyone other than her could have heard him.

"I have no idea. He made sure I was okay, then took off."

Ethan lifted her face, halting her continued hunt for other injuries. "I'm so sorry they scared you."

"Yeah, well, about that…" She glanced past him to the crowd standing just outside the ballroom, her scowl deepening. The men that had gathered in the corridor and at the ballroom door were all talking over each other, the noise loud now, everyone pointing and shouting and arguing. She heard the words "fair" and "our rights" from more than one man and her head just about exploded.

She narrowed her eyes, a new pump of adrenaline washing through her. All the frustration, irritation, annoyance, fear, adrenaline, and terror rushed out of her in one, long, piercing, banshee scream that would have made her Irish father proud. She shouted so loud, and with so much outrage, the entire area fell silent. When she let her screech die out, the room practically rang with the silence.

"Enough," she shouted in the wake of that silence. "Enough with all of this…nonsense! All of you. You do not have any *rights* here—to me, to other women. You aren't *allowed* to press yourselves on me. You can't *insist* I pay attention to you. You don't get a *fair* chance with me. Just. Because. You. Have. Dicks."

She sucked in a breath, panting with her anger. "I am not your prize. You do not get to insist on *anything* from me, just because I'm a woman." She held her hand up and glared when a man near her had the temerity to open his mouth. "No. Life is not fair. It's not meant to be. And you don't get things just because. That's the way a child thinks. Grow up!"

She pointed at all of them. "*This* is no way for grown

people to behave. I don't care if you do turn into tigers. This shit is unacceptable." She stalked closer to the crowd, and to her amusement, some of the men actually took a step backward. "I will not have it, do you understand me? I will not spend my life feeling threatened or scared just because you all think it's your right to reproduce. No one promised you kids. No one promises any of us anything."

She lowered her voice, knowing they'd hear her even at the back of the ballroom because of their super-shifter hearing. "But I will promise you this, if any of you bastards think you can coerce me again, I will not hesitate to tear your fucking nuts off."

She heard a choking sound from behind her that sounded suspiciously like Ethan trying not to laugh, but she ignored it. She was beyond angry, nearly nonsensical with it at this stage. "I don't know about your own women, or why they put up with this crap, but I do know I won't and neither will other women like me. You people need to learn to control yourselves and take responsibility for your actions. Because if you can't, you're done as a species. And it'll be your own fucking faults."

An older man stepped away from the crowd. "Now see here, young lady."

Pavel, the elder she was already angry with, one of the elders who'd insisted on this stupid party.

She glowered at him and got in his face. "Don't you dare condescend to me, you old fart." She waved at the crowd. "This will not happen again. Ever. I'm done with appeasing you." She lowered her voice further, knowing everyone around them would still hear her. "Remember, this is the internet age, and you don't want humans to know about you."

He turned nearly purple in his outrage. "Are you threatening me?"

"Turnabout is fair play," she hissed. "You're not the only ones capable of blackmail."

She held his angry gaze, not flinching because she was too mad to remember she should probably be afraid of him. She'd hated feeling helpless and scared. Being scared always pissed her off. And she had no intentions of feeling this way again—not at the hands of these people.

From the midst of the crowd, a single person started clapping. She blinked and looked past Pavel to see Victor standing next to Alexis, grinning and bringing his hands together in a steady rhythm that sounded loud in the now-silent ballroom and corridor. Alexis had her lips pressed together, as if she was trying not to smile. Just behind her, Elizaveta looked on with raised brows and her mouth pursed in a thoughtful expression, though it was hard to tell if the elder was amused or angry.

Amy raised her chin and nodded at Victor, glared at Pavel, then turned her back on the lot of them and stalked away, heading toward the elevator that would take her back to her and Cat's room.

"Ethan Gupta," Pavel boomed. "You would abandon your people for this…creature?"

Amy spun to glare daggers at Pavel.

Ethan put a hand on his chest, as if confirming Pavel was actually talking to him. "Oh, I'm with her," he said, his expression light and amused.

CHAPTER NINETEEN

E than joined Amy, putting a hand protectively on her lower back, and together they walked away from the gawking crowd. Amy was shaking from all the adrenaline but too damned grateful to finally be putting this stupid party behind her to care.

Under his breath, Ethan said, "That's probably going to come back to haunt us. But it was worth it to watch Pavel turn puce."

She snorted. "I liked the hints of crimson under the puce. It added a satisfying…tone to the asshole's outrage."

"I love you, Amy Donovan," Ethan said.

She almost tripped over the elevator threshold. Looking up at him as the doors closed, eyes narrowed, she said, "What about…Siya? And…" She waved her hand vaguely in the air to indicate the earlier scene in the ballroom.

"She was apologizing."

"She looked like she was hitting on you."

Ethan pulled Amy into his arms. "I was afraid that's what you saw. She wasn't. Not really. She's married now and has two children with the same male."

"Doesn't mean she wasn't hitting on you," Amy said.

"She regretted what happened between us and apologized. That was all."

"Did you forgive her?"

"I did." He shrugged. "People do stupid things and make mistakes."

"Does that mean you've forgiven yourself for what happened?"

He brushed his fingers over her cheek, the caress gentle. "I think so. I'm getting there. Thanks to you."

"What did I do?"

"Showed me what love really is. It isn't losing myself to jealousy. It's being better because I have someone to be better for." He frowned a little. "Though after that exposure to my people…do you think you still want to… Do we still have a future?"

"You notice I haven't pulled out of your arms, yet, right?" she said, going up on her toes to press her lips to his. "We will not be hanging around with most tiger shifters after this."

"I'm good with that. Outside of my family."

She acquiesced with another kiss. "Family is fine. They won't try to kill me or anything, right?"

"Of course not."

"Then they'll be acceptable."

The elevator doors opened and Ethan tugged her out into the hallway.

Then he pulled her close and kissed her again, this time much more seriously, with a lot of heat. Against her mouth, he said, "I'm very glad you aren't mad at me over Siya."

"Since I'm the one you're kissing, I have no reason to be."

He grinned and kissed her again, until she was feeling better than she'd felt most of the night.

"I should check on Cat," she said as his lips trailed across her jaw. "But since she's not expecting us for a few hours, maybe we could sneak away to your room?"

"Yes." He picked her up and ran the rest of the way.

She laughed as he pushed into the small room he'd been given several doors away from her and Cat's suite. She found herself on the bed in the next instant and her shirt already open. She glanced down. "When did you do that?"

He nudged the collar aside, kissing across her collarbone. "I really need you naked."

"Naked is a very very good idea." She pushed him up and pulled his shirt over his head, tossing it aside as he unsnapped her bra and shoved it and her shirt down her arms. For a frustrating and silly moment, she was tangled in her own clothes. She giggled as he growled and ripped everything away.

"I owe you a shirt," he said.

Then he was kissing her again and she didn't think to tease him about the shirt. She was too busy pushing at his slacks, getting through the remaining clothes to his skin. He felt hot and hard and perfect.

And hers.

For the first time, that really sank in. He was hers. All hers. He loved her.

She leaned back and held his face in her hands, her gaze locking on his. "I love you," she said. "I was too…kerfuffle to say it earlier. But I do love you."

"Kerfuffle?"

She shrugged. "Perfect word for it, don't you think?"

"I liked the 'I love you' words the best."

She smiled and kissed him and stopped thinking for the time being so she could savor the man in her arms. He trailed his mouth down to her breasts, sucking on her nipple hard enough to make her tremble. All the earlier adrenaline had morphed into a desperate sort of passion. She couldn't get enough of him, the feel, his taste. Wildly, she pushed him over onto his back so she had better access. Without any attempt at seduction, she took his cock in her hand, stroked once, then took him into her mouth, eager for the taste of him. His hips came off the bed, his hands tangled in her hair. The sounds of his pleasure heightened hers and she sucked harder, lapping the tip of him with her tongue, before pulling him deep into her mouth again.

His muscles bunched and shook under her, a warning she wanted to ignore. He had other plans. He sat up and pulled her head up to his for a kiss, ignoring her pout of protest. Tugging her to the end of the bed, he stood and brought her to her feet.

"My knees are too shaky to stand," she warned.

"I'll hold you."

He turned her to face the bedpost at the foot of the bed, a rounded block of wood tall enough that it reached her mid-chest and gave her something to grip. His hands moved down her waist to her hips then lower as he lifted one of her legs so she could set a foot on the side of the bedframe. From behind, he reached between her legs with one hand, running his fingers through her slick folds, spreading moisture around. She moaned, dropping her head back to his shoulder as he played with her. She arched and pressed her ass to his cock, urging him for more.

Gripping her hip in one hand and guiding his cock with the other, he slid into her heat slowly, filling her. His strokes were steady, even, and so so slow. One hand kneading her breast, the other still on her hip, he rocked against her, taking her up to her toes. The bedpost and Ethan's hands were the only thing keeping her upright. Everything in her was tight and hot, the tension ratcheting up with each stroke. She trembled, and begged him to move faster. But he just kept the steady, hard, slow rhythm.

And when she couldn't stand it anymore, she set her own finger to her clit, just a little pressure that broke all the tension into an explosive, shuddering release that took Ethan with her.

Sweat trickled down her temples as she set her forehead against the bedpost, panting and shaking, her heart pounding fast with the effects of her orgasm. She felt Ethan's lips against her shoulder, his own breath coming in harsh gulps, and smiled.

"I love you," she whispered, surprised at how freeing it was to say that out loud.

"I love you," he said against her temple.

When he slipped out of her, she turned in his arms and

clung to him, her legs so wobbly now she couldn't have supported her own weight if she'd wanted to. He picked her up, though she felt his own muscles trembling, and laid down on the bed with her, hugging her close. They stayed that way for a time, Amy content just to have this peaceful moment. Grateful to be in the arms of the man she loved.

* * *

After a shower that turned into another round of lovemaking, Amy put on one of Ethan's shirts and together they went to check on Cat. Being wrapped in his scent filled Amy with a sense of peace, making her feel both cozy and sexy at once. She wasn't even embarrassed —at least not too much—when he caught her sniffing the shirt. His satisfied, cocky smile and protective arm around her waist were worth it.

They found Cat with her face in her laptop, the geneticist she'd been talking to still in the room. The scientist— Dr. Sarah Chu—glanced up at them and smiled. "Heard there were some problems at the party."

Amy raised her brows. "You heard about that already?" Though, she realized, all the time she'd just spent making love with Ethan, at least an hour or so must have passed since the fight.

Sarah's smile widened. "My husband was one of the Trackers who took the miscreants to holding. He texted to let me know you were okay, in case Cat worried."

"I knew you were fine," Cat said without looking away

from her screen. Her brow furrowed, and she was frowning at something.

"She's studying the gene sequences of tiger shifter DNA," Sarah said, adding in a slightly awed tone, "She learns really fast."

"Yeah, she does." Amy chuckled. She was about to say more but a knock on the door interrupted her. She glanced at Ethan, who was frowning.

"I'll get it," he said.

She went with him, standing next to him as he opened the door. A tall man waited in the hall. He was wearing a suit, as if he'd been at the party, but he looked older than most of the other males she'd met downstairs. He was a little taller than Ethan, had dark hair run through with a few streaks of gray, and blue eyes that were bracketed by faint creases. He looked at her and Ethan, his shoulders stiff, his expression hesitant.

"Hello," he said. His voice was quiet and deep. "I wasn't sure if I should disturb you. But I wanted to make sure you were okay."

Amy frowned. "And you are?"

Ethan's hand on her waist tightened.

The man cleared his throat. "I'm Roman. Roman Kadnikov."

Amy's mouth dropped open. She blinked at the man a few times. Part of her was aware of Ethan moving closer, of Cat coming up behind them, but most of her was focused on the man in the hallway.

Her biological father.

She shook herself when she realized she'd been staring

silently for too long. "Please, come in."

Sarah stood as Roman walked into the suite's living room. "I'll leave you for now." She glanced at Cat. "Keep in touch. We have more to talk about."

Cat closed the door behind Sarah, which was good because Amy wouldn't have remembered the door was even open. She was still processing the fact that the man in front of her was her…her father.

Roman stood awkwardly his gaze moving between her and Ethan. "I don't want to intrude. I wasn't sure you'd want to speak with me." He shrugged. "I just wanted to check you're not… Well, I figured given how things went down there, this might be the last time you'd allow strange tiger shifters around." He smiled a little, the look self-deprecating.

"You're not a strange tiger shifter," she said. "I mean… you are. Wait that sounded wrong. I mean… I would have agreed to meet you. If you'd wanted to meet me, that is." She rolled her eyes. "You know what I mean."

"I get it. It's…awkward."

"Yeah, it is."

He hesitated another moment, then said quietly, "I'm sorry I didn't believe your mom when she said you were mine. It wasn't supposed to be possible."

"Since you found out it was possible, have you thought about getting in touch?" Amy wasn't sure if she'd have agreed to meet with him before, but learning about this new tiger shifter world had changed a lot of how she felt about…a lot of things.

"I have. Then I learned about your parents… I'm very

sorry for your loss. And I thought you might not want to see me after losing them. I'd hoped your mother gave you my information, that you'd maybe come looking for me one day. But I didn't want you to think I was trying to replace your father."

She smiled a little. "I didn't contact you sooner for the same reason. I didn't want you to think I was looking to replace my father."

"He was good to you?"

"The best."

"You were happy? Are happy?"

"Yes. And yes."

His shoulders relaxed. "Good. Good." He glanced around, as if not sure what else to say.

Amy shook her head and gestured to Cat. "This is my sister, Catalina Donovan."

Cat reached around her to shake Roman's extended hand. "Nice to meet you," Cat said.

Roman looked between them. "You both look a lot like Luciana. Different, but I see a lot of her in you."

"You know, you're the only one who uses her full name," Amy said.

He grinned. "She told me the same thing. I always liked the way it rolled off my tongue." He cleared his throat and shoved his hands into his pockets. "I won't keep you. I'm sure you're tired after this evening. But I'm very glad you're okay. And happy."

He started toward the door. Amy rushed to stop him. "Wait... I have a message for you. From Zhong."

He swung around to stare at her. "He was here

tonight?" He glanced away, frowning. "I thought… It's been so long, and he's always been damned good at hiding his scent." He blinked and looked at her again. "What did he say?"

"It wasn't tonight… I mean he was here, but…" She explained, as briefly as she could, the last few months, the weeks of Zhong stalking her, and then helping her. "He said to tell you he didn't kill me. Emphasis on the *didn't*. He said you'd understand."

Roman ran a hand over his face, the creases around his eyes deepening.

"When I asked tonight why he kept helping me, he told me it was a poignant kind of revenge."

Roman let out a half-snort, half-laugh. "Yes." He met her gaze. "Did anyone tell you about my history with Zhong?"

"Elizaveta told me you'd trained Zhong as a Tracker. Then were sent to arrest him when he killed humans."

"The humans deserved to die. But as Trackers we were supposed to uphold tiger law, not break it."

"Why is not killing me Zhong's revenge against you?" she asked. "That doesn't make much sense."

"It's a long story. But basically, he's giving me a sense of what he went through, when his loved ones were killed, letting me know how it would feel to lose a child." He swallowed visibly. "If I'd lost you, even before meeting you… That's what Zhong went through. He's punishing me with the knowledge of what it feels like, would feel like."

"But…" She frowned and glanced at Ethan. "Elizaveta said the baby was his twin brother's."

"A myth we perpetuated to protect his mate, Hualing, and their baby. Zhong was young but very good at being a Tracker. And he'd already made enemies—both tiger and human. Some of them quite dangerous. He wanted his mate and baby protected while he was working—he was away from them a lot—so the four of us put out the story that Hualing was his brother's mate. We thought that would keep her safe…" Roman closed his eyes briefly. "Anyway, Zhong and I are the only ones left alive who know the truth. It's better that way."

"Is he still wanted by the Trackers?" Ethan asked, the first he'd spoken since Roman had come in.

Roman nodded. "They won't ever catch him. But the death sentence hasn't been lifted."

"Why didn't you bring him in…before?" Amy asked.

"Guilt," he said simply. "He lost his baby because of me." When Amy frowned, he waved a hand. "It's too long and complicated a story for tonight. If you'd like to…to meet again at some stage, and you want to hear the whole tale, I'll tell you."

"I'd like that. To meet up I mean. If you'd like to. We don't even have to talk about Zhong. You could tell me embarrassing stories about my mom when she was young and wild. Maybe tell me a little about yourself."

"I get to New York a couple of times a year for business. I'll call next time I'm there."

"Do," she said. She hurriedly scribbled her numbers on a piece of paper from one of Cat's notebooks and handed it to him. "I mean it. Do call."

"I will." He smiled as he folded the piece of paper and

put it in his pocket. "Elizaveta tells me you're an artist?"

She nodded.

"I'm an art history teacher now, and a collector. We have some common ground at least. For…a friendship?"

"Yes. We do."

He gave Ethan and Cat a slight nod. Then to Amy, "Goodnight. I'll see you soon."

Ethan closed the door behind Roman, and then turned to face her. Cat was also staring at her.

"How are you?" Ethan asked.

She thought about that for a long moment. And realized… "I'm good. He seems nice. I hope he'll be in touch."

"I've got a good feeling about him," Cat said.

"Me, too," Amy said, smiling at her sister. "Me, too."

Ethan came up behind her and wrapped her in a hug. She cradled his arms, leaning into him as her life, this new reality settled around her.

Cat frowned at her. "That's not the shirt you left in."

Amy felt her cheeks heating. "You're just noticing?"

Cat grinned and shrugged. "Are we done with this party nonsense so we can go home now? Spike will hardly come out of her carrier with all these big cats around."

"We're done," Amy confirmed. "And yes, we can go home."

Cat glanced at Amy and Ethan, her expression turning sly. "Before we left, I heard there was a studio for rent in our building. Maybe I'll take it. You know, so you two can have the bigger apartment."

Amy narrowed her eyes at Cat. "A studio, huh?"

"For Spike's sake. We'd all still be in the same building, so she wouldn't miss you."

"Oh, you think you'll get to have Spike in your apartment?"

"Well, you'll have Ethan. It's only fair."

Ethan's arms tightened around Amy, hugging her even closer. "She's right. You will have me."

Amy pretended at a dramatic sigh while inside she was floating in happiness. "Fine. But it means you get the bulk of walking duty."

"We'll see," Cat said and sauntered toward her bedroom. "I'm going to sleep. You two have a nice night." At the door, she glanced back. "Let's leave early, okay?"

"Deal."

When they were alone, Ethan turned her to face him. "Are you okay with Cat moving out?"

"She's a grown woman. Mostly. And she'll be in the same building."

"And us?"

"We'll turn her room into an art studio."

"We?"

She leaned into him. "If you're good with moving in?"

"Are you going to marry me eventually?"

"Eventually."

He smiled. "Cat's room does get good light. It'll make a great studio."

Amy chuckled. "I love you."

Ethan kissed her deeply and for some time. She surfaced long enough to pull him to her room, and to the start of their new future, one full of family, and color...and love.

Kamal sat at the long table in the Meeting Hall, listening to the other elders arguing, occasionally adding to the argument just to keep it going. He was surprised at how well all this had worked out, given what a disaster it could have been.

Things hadn't gone to plan, which was irritating. He'd lost a perfectly good hybrid for his experiments. That was a setback given the stage they were at in those experiments. Losing Zhong's services was also annoying. Kamal might have to have him taken care of soon—he did still have a death sentence hanging over him. But the finder could still be useful, so Kamal didn't want to rush things. One never knew when Zhong's particular brand of expertise might come in handy, and Kamal had more than enough money to entice the mercenary back if he needed him again. Still the need to hunt for more hybrids now, without the help of a good finder, was an unexpected and ill-timed frustration.

But Amy Donovan had created a crisis among his fellow elders, and that was enough to make up for the rest.

"You heard her," Pavel snarled at Elizaveta. "She threatened to expose us! The hybrids are a danger to us. Not just genetically. They aren't loyal to our people. They could destroy us."

"You sound like one of the fanatics, Pavel," Elizaveta said, her Russian accent stronger, her expression hiding her feelings. "The poor girl had just been attacked and her mate had to fight. She was upset."

"She's a menace. They all are."

"She meant her threat," Chen added. "She's right. In the internet age, we're working against time before someone reveals our nature to the world. Then the humans will declare war on us."

"And we don't have the numbers to survive," Adarsh added. "If we keep risking our secrecy by accepting and protecting these…half-breeds, we'll destroy ourselves well before extinction takes us."

Elizaveta waved a hand. "If we do not protect them, who will? The ones that can't shift are vulnerable to our males, who have *still* not learned how to control themselves, as Amy pointed out tonight. Would you have us discovered because our males killed hybrids that the human world sees as human?"

"It is the human hybrids that are the risk, the ones who might expose us," Elder Qiang said. "The hybrids who shift have just as much to hide as we do."

If Kamal didn't hate Qiang so much, he might have kissed him for that opening. He hid his satisfaction behind a thoughtful expression and said, as if just considering it, "If all hybrids could shift, there would be less risk of exposure from them."

Pavel snorted. "Yes, but we can't *make* them into shifters, can we?"

Kamal didn't smile. He carefully kept his expression thoughtful and his scent neutral. But inside, his tiger growled in growing triumph. The groundwork had been set.

And soon he would make his move.

Very soon.

Thank you for reading Taming Her Tiger! I hope you enjoyed the story. As you can tell, there is a lot happening in the Tiger Shifters' world, and very soon things will come to a head. Keep watching for more.

In the meantime, I'm also working on a new urban fantasy romance series. All of my paranormal worlds take place in the same general "universe," but this is a new series with new characters and a bigger "world" of paranormal creatures. To keep up to date on the release of this new series as well as more Tiger Shifters books, visit my website or join my newsletter. And if you're interested in finding out more about this new upcoming series, please keep reading for an excerpt from the first book.

THE TROUBLE WITH BLACK CATS AND DEMONS

EXCERPT CARY REDMOND BOOK 1

CHAPTER ONE

"Not again." Cary Redmond ducked as another fireball clipped over her head. "You don't think fireballs are a bit over the top," she shouted up at the ceiling then had to duck again as a dagger whispered past her ear.

Close. Her heart pounded. Way too close.

She needed to find the damned cat and get out of here. She scanned the apartment from her dubious cover behind a table piled high with unopened mail. Fireballs, daggers, gusts of preternatural wind, freezing hail, and the occasional lightning bolt dropped around her, roaring through the living room in a bright cacophony of magical mayhem.

The lightning bolts flashing in the small confines were pretty spectacular. If they hadn't been trying to fry her, she might have enjoyed the show.

"Jaxer, I'm going to kill you for this."

Normally, this kind of thing was just a part of her job. She was a Protector and literally got paid to run around keeping people safe, mostly from magical bad guys. Not that she'd asked for the job, but that was another story. It *was* her job, so she faced off against dangerous stuff because the Nags—her bosses—told her to.

Tonight, however, was not an official assignment. Tonight, she was just doing a favor for her demented faery mentor. The bastard knew exactly how to get to her. All he had to do was mention a defenseless little black kitty cat and she was done for. How could she refuse to help a kitty? People did rotten things to black cats on Halloween.

Except Jaxer had forgotten to warn her about the fireballs.

She screeched through her teeth and dove behind the couch as one of the aforementioned fireballs barreled toward her. She cursed Jaxer as she took a quick look under the couch for the cat. Where the hell was it?

She'd called out to it when she'd first entered the apartment but hadn't gotten any irate kitty responses. After her lurching hunt of the living room and kitchen, the only place left was the bedroom.

She pulled in a deep breath as she contemplated the long space of unprotected ground between her hiding spot behind the couch and the bedroom door. Once she found the cat, this would be easier. When she was actively protecting something, very little of the magical dangers could get to her, and nothing deadly would touch her. She just had to *find* the cat first. And quickly. They had to be out of this cursed apartment before midnight. Before the wizard got home and all hell broke loose.

Again.

She ducked flying objects and ran to the bedroom, squealing when a lightning bolt hit the ground right behind her. Crossing her fingers that there were no nasty spells waiting for her, she lunged through the half-open door and cringed in anticipation of magical repercussions as she fell onto a red-carpeted floor. She held perfectly still, waiting. Nothing. She let out a breath and pushed herself up onto her hands and knees, shaking her head. All this for a cat. That bastard Jaxer had a lot to answer for.

She rose to a crouch, trying to calm her racing pulse, and froze.

In front of her sat a huge bed, which she barely noticed because the naked man lying in the middle of the enormous mattress stopped her heart.

Holy shit.

He was absolutely magnificent. Tanned skin, well-defined muscles, thick, black hair hanging down over his forehead. He was lying against a giant headboard with his head hanging forward so she couldn't get a good look at his face, but his golden eyes seemed to glow up at her from under his brows. Piercing and stunning and breath-stealing.

Cary swallowed. Hard. Because even the captivating gold of his eyes wasn't enough to keep her gaze from wandering over the breadth of his naked chest, the corded muscles of his shoulders and arms, the flat expanse of his stomach. It took a great deal of will power not to follow the line of dark hair arrowing down his abdomen...lower.

The man straightened and Cary heard the clink of chains at the same time as she got a look at his neck—and the thick collar covering most of it.

What the hell had Jaxer gotten her into?

"Who're you?" she asked, breathless and embarrassed.

"Who are you?"

His voice carried a deep reverberation that made her spine tingle. Oh boy.

"I'm looking for a black cat," she said, knowing the explanation sounded inane. Jaxer had told her about Sheldon the Wizard, but this? This was something else all together. What was this guy doing here? He wasn't Sheldon, she was sure of it. But then who was he? And where was the cat?

She blinked and a black leopard lay on the bed where the man had been. She sucked in a sharp breath, blinked again. And the man was back.

"Whoa." Cary swallowed. "*You're* the black cat I came to rescue?"

Oh, she really was going to kill Jaxer now. He hadn't said anything about a fully grown man who happened to be a leopard shifter. He'd made sure she thought she was after a little, harmless kitty cat, not a deadly, dangerous big cat who shifted into a beautiful, naked, very large man.

The faery was dead. Not that she knew how to kill him, but that was beside the point.

"Jaxer sent you?" The man's eyes narrowed and his features took on a dangerous edge. He hissed a curse under his breath and shook his head. "Stupid."

"Hey!" She stood, the better to face his gorgeous

disgust. No one should look that good while insulting you. "You could have done worse, buddy."

She took a step toward the bed, wiping damp palms on her jeans. The chains she'd heard earlier linked the collar on his neck to the headboard, which was brass and made-up of a scrawl of symbols she didn't recognize but looked like they might mean something if she stared at them long enough. He wasn't bound anywhere else that she dared peek, and the chains appeared flimsy enough. So obviously the power keeping him confined was in the collar.

"What is that?" She gestured with her head toward the thick band of metal.

"A binding ring," he said slowly, as if speaking to a child.

She frowned, both at his tone and the news. "But you just shifted."

"It's been designed to contain both my forms. Any other questions before you get me out of here?"

"Yeah, what crawled up your butt and put you in such a pissy mood?"

"Being held captive for sacrifice by a wizard and having a child sent to rescue me has dampened my day a bit," he said.

She grinned and enjoyed watching his eyes narrow suspiciously. "Child, huh? You know, at my age that's a compliment."

"How old could you be? Twenty?"

She shook her head. She'd actually turned thirty-one last April. But when she got tricked into becoming a Protector at twenty-five, she'd stopped aging at a normal rate. One of the few things about the job that didn't irritate her.

She took a quick moment to glance around the rest of the room. The red carpet wasn't the only gaudy element. Lots of black leather covered the walls and an animal skinned rug, which she was afraid to think about too closely given the captive on the overlarge bed, was tossed across the floor in front of what she thought might be a closet. A wood and metal trunk sat against one wall, red silk drapes covered the single window, and the overhead light was covered by thick, dark metal chains which gave the room strange shadows.

Fortunately, there were no nasty attack spells in here, which meant Sheldon the Wizard didn't want his captive accidentally hurt by a stray lightning bolt. That worked in her favor, giving her time to solve the binding ring problem without being pelted by hail.

Though even if there had been spells in here, now that she was officially protecting someone, she could keep them both safe.

She did wonder why Sheldon would care if his shape shifting captive got hurt before the midnight sacrifice. Obviously, he didn't want him dead. You couldn't sacrifice something that was already dead. But an additional warning spell in here probably wouldn't have killed his prisoner. Maybe. If Sheldon had enough control.

If he didn't, and was as powerful as Jaxer claimed, they really needed to get out of here. Fast.

She eased up to the bedside, still leery of traps, and leaned in close to the leopard man, trying to ignore the yummy, stomach-fluttering male scent of him as she studied the binding ring. It was a thick band of silver and copper intertwined in a complex pattern of twists and turns. Over the silver, tiny runic symbols danced and shimmered so they were nearly impossible to read.

"Oh good," she said, "a hard one."

The prisoner shivered, a low growl rising from his throat. The sound made Cary's heartbeat jump.

Speaking of hard ones.

She could feel his glare on the side of her face, but she resisted looking. She had other things to worry about at the moment.

Like how the hell she was going to get this damned magical containment brace off his neck without alerting the entire mystical neighborhood.

"You did that on purpose," the man snarled.

"Huh?" She glanced at him. "What are you talking about?"

"Don't breathe on me again," he said.

She scowled. "What am I supposed to do? Hold my breath until I get your collar off? Just relax, big guy. You'll be out of here in a minute." To herself, she mumbled, "Wouldn't have gotten this much grief from a proper black cat."

"You some kind of witch?"

"No." After a moment, she sighed and shook her head. "Well, there's no help for it. I'm gonna have to use brute force. It'll take too long to get this off subtly."

"We don't have much time. It's nearly midnight now."

"Gee, really?"

He ignored her sarcasm. "Brute force?"

"Hold onto your valuable body parts," she said and tried not to think about his exposed valuable parts. Then she wrapped her hands around the collar, easing her fingers gently under so the backs pressed against his neck. His skin was warm and another shiver danced down her spine.

"Wait."

She met his gaze.

"What the hell are you doing? If I can't break that with my bare hands, you can't—"

He stopped short when she tugged and the collar came away with a quiet click.

"I'm not without some talent," she murmured.

"Who *are* you?"

"Come on. We have to get you out of here. I just made a lot of magical noise with that little stunt."

"Hold on."

He grabbed her hand. The feel of his warm palm wrapped around her fingers sent tiny sparks of electricity dancing over her skin. He dropped his hold, but she saw his eyes widen with the same shock she felt. He inhaled deeply, and against her will, she watched the strong muscles of his chest rise and fall.

"What's your name?" he asked.

"Cary."

"Cary. I'm Deacon."

"Nice to meet you." Did that sounded as stupid to him as it did to her given the circumstances?

He smiled, a slow, deadly grin that made her pulse race. "Nice to meet you, too."

She blinked and shook her head. "Come on, Deacon. We need to move."

As he slid to the edge of the mattress, Cary turned her back to avoid embarrassing them both—despite the temptation to look over every inch of him. The sound of material moving over skin behind her didn't help curb her less polite impulses, though, so she hurried to the door to see how the lightning bolts and fireballs were doing.

Slipping into his jeans, Deacon watched the woman as she peeked around the edge of the doorframe at the living room and the still popping spells Sheldon had set to keep help from reaching him.

She wasn't the rescue he'd been expecting. He'd expected the damned faery to come himself.

Jaxer had convinced him to let the wizard "capture" him, so they could find out *why* Sheldon was kidnapping shifters. They'd only found a few of Sheldon's victims— their bodies anyway. And they'd been little more than desiccated husks. The rest of the missing shifters... Even their bodies had vanished.

Wizards didn't typically go after shapeshifters for sacrifice. They were too hard to contain, and most of them didn't have the kind of magical energy an average human wizard could absorb through ceremonial magic. Shape shifting wasn't typically magic. It was just a species trait.

Deacon knew none of the shifters killed so far had had any actual magic. He was a different case, but he was pretty sure Sheldon didn't know that. Jaxer did, which was why he'd come to Deacon in the first place, and Deacon had felt obliged to help even though none of the shifters taken had been leopards.

He suppressed an irritated growl. This was the last time he'd let the faery use him for bait. He'd been chained to that fucking bed all day with no sign of help. Then Jaxer went and made things worse by sending in this…woman to rescue him instead of coming himself. How dare he endanger someone else when this crusade against Sheldon was his own personal business? Bad enough he dragged Deacon into it.

But as Deacon watched the woman straighten away from the doorframe when a lightning bolt flashed, he realized there *was* something about her. He couldn't deny the power she must have to break through the binding ring. Yet she looked and smelled like a normal, human woman.

Her light brown hair hung in long ponytail her back over a battered brown leather jacket. She wore jeans, hiking boots, and a purple t-shirt with a glittery Happy Halloween emblazoned over a maniacally grinning jack-o-lantern. Her blue eyes had sparkled when he'd called her a child, then flashed with irritation when he'd insulted her. And for reasons he couldn't quite understand, he'd found it hard to look away from her, especially when she'd knelt next to him on the bed.

Something about her…something about her scent tugged at his instincts.

Who the hell was she? *What* was she? She had to be more than human, but none of his sense picked up anything particularly preternatural about her. So where did all that power come from?

Jaxer had some serious explaining to do.

Deacon shook off his preoccupation and walked up behind her to stare at the living room over her head. Black scorch marks marred the hardwood floors, and a layer of frost covered one side table. The air was heavy with electricity and the smell of burning ozone.

Despite the multiple magical eruptions, the apartment was in remarkably good shape. As he watched, a dagger flew toward the bedroom, dropped harmlessly a foot from the doorway, and disappeared as if it hadn't existed.

Clever. Less clean up. And a testament to Sheldon's power.

He couldn't blame Jaxer for being worried about the little shit. But given a choice, Deacon would have taken a more…active approach to getting rid of the wizard.

Unfortunately, and he was reluctant to admit this even to himself, his approach probably would have gotten him killed. The bastard wizard was powerful. How Sheldon managed to be so powerful at his age was a mystery. But maybe that was the reason Jaxer was so obsessed with finding out the *whys* behind Sheldon's actions.

If Deacon got out of this apartment alive, he'd ask the faery. In the meantime, he and this very human woman in front of him had to navigate the bespelled living room and get away before Sheldon got back.

Deacon drew in a slow breath and was hit again by Cary's scent. Vanilla and cinnamon. And something else. Something that shot jolts of lust and need through his gut, making him lean closer to her just so he could feel the heat of her skin. He felt a possessive growl rising in his throat and swallowed it back, fisting his hands by his side to keep from reaching for her.

What the hell? He had more control that this. A lot more. He had to or people got killed. Resisting a woman, even one that smelled like heaven, had never been a problem before. With Cary, it took an effort to resist pulling her close and burying his face in her neck to soak up her essence.

If he didn't know better, he'd think she was a witch, casting a lust spell on him.

His nostrils flared. That scent of hers…

It reached down inside him, calling to a deep instinct. As he breathed her in, his leopard whispered, *Mine*.

Out in the living room, wind-lashed hail whipped toward the bedroom without actually coming through the doorway. And behind that, a lightning bolt sizzled the floor.

"Sheldon didn't make this easy," he said, quirking a brow when she jumped at the sound of his voice.

"Are you dressed?" she asked without turning around.

He couldn't help smiling at the slight panic in her voice. "Yes."

"Okay. Stick close. Stay behind me and don't try to dodge around me. Got it? That's how we'll get out of here alive."

He frowned down at the top of her head. She must have some pretty powerful shields to get through that mess. But she wasn't a witch?

He grunted a noncommittal response, and she swung around to face him. The flash of heat in her eyes made his pulse kick.

"Listen, buddy," she said, her chin tucked back as she glared at him, "if you don't let me protect you, we're both dead. Okay? Don't go trying to be a hero. Just stay close and let me do what I came here to do."

She mumbled something unflattering under her breath as she turned back to the living room, and he had to fight a completely irrational urge to kiss her.

Over the course of the long day, with no sign of help from Jaxer, he'd had to face the possibility of his own death. His reaction to Cary might be a result of that, a need to reaffirm he was alive.

But as he breathed in the heady scent of her again, he wondered…

The Trouble With Black Cats and Demons,
Book 1 in the Cary Redmond series
Coming soon in 2019!

BOOKS BY KAT SIMONS

TIGER SHIFTERS SERIES

1 - Once Upon a Tiger

2 - Along Came a Tiger

3 - Here There Be Tigers

4 - Her Tiger To Take

5 - To Tempt a Tiger

6 - Down Will Come Tiger

7 - To Catch a Tiger

8 - What a Tiger Wants

9 - Taming Her Tiger

Tiger Shifters Series Vol 1 (Books 1 - 3)

Tiger Shifters Series Vol 2 (Books 4 - 6)

ABOUT THE AUTHOR

Kat Simons earned her Ph.D in animal behavior, working with animals as diverse as dolphins and deer. She brought her experience and knowledge of biology to her paranormal romance fiction, where she delights in taking nature and turning it on its ear. After traveling the world, she now lives in New York City with her family. Kat is a stay-at-home mom and a full time writer.

For more on Kat and her future books:

Website: http://www.katsimons.com
Newsletter: http://eepurl.com/OxQQL

www.ingramcontent.com/pod-product-compliance
Lightning Source LLC
Chambersburg PA
CBHW032100180726

48284CB00002B/375